Free of Malice

Liz Lazarus

Published in the United States by Mitchell Cove Publishing

Reprint of the poem, *Desiderata*, public domain verified by DePauw University

Though the event that inspired this novel was real, this book
is fiction. All characters appearing in this work are fictitious—
any resemblance to real persons is purely coincidental.

ISBN 978-0-9909374-0-1

Editing by Jan Risher at The Risher Group, Patricia Coe at
Adsum 365 and Chelsea Apple at JKS Communications
Cover design by Tracy Duhamel at Get Designed
Interior layout by Jill Dible at JillDibleDesign

Cover song, *Let Me Breathe*, by Thomas Barnette

Website: www.freeofmalice.com

ADVANCE READER'S COPY

Dear Reader,

Though this is Liz Lazarus' debut novel, the book doesn't have the feel of a first-time author. Liz knows the tricks of the trade—pulling me in quickly and keeping me hooked because I wanted to know the ending so desperately. In fact, I couldn't put it down and couldn't sleep well that first night because it felt so real.

Without giving too much away, I'll share that I loved that the book went in a direction I didn't expect without veering so far off I was left confused or frustrated. As the story begins, I felt I had a grasp of where this could all lead—that it would be a kind of study of a woman healing, but it turned out to be so much more. I enjoyed the escalation of what began to feel like a real but scary obsession for Laura, the main character.

This book is not a traditional whodunit. The author pulled off a tough balance of having me both suspect yet somehow root for the lead male character. I also liked that I was able to read the therapist's notes, giving me an inside glimpse into her private thoughts and concerns about the main character.

As an added bonus, the song that is described in the book is a real song, written and produced by one of the author's best friends. We invite you to listen to *Let Me Breathe* by Thomas Barnette at www. freeofmalice.com.

I hope you enjoy this psychological legal thriller as much as I did, and join me in championing this incredible novel. Plus, working with Liz was a real joy. I've never known an author to be as dedicated to telling her story.

All my best,
Jan Risher

PS – for our book club members, you will also find discussion questions on the website, but we suggest you only read them once you have read the book—to avoid any spoilers.

 # Thursday, July 6

Run. Run faster. As much as I strained my legs to move, they were immobile, like I was waist deep in quicksand.

Why can't I move?

I tried to scream for help but my mouth was full, like it was stuffed with cotton—no sound would escape.

I felt something clutching my shoulder. No, it was someone. He was pushing me forward and then yanking me back. I tried to jerk away but he had a vice-like grip.

I have to break free.

The tugging got harder, more forceful. He was calling my name—over and over. He knew my name.

"Laura, Laura."

I jolted awake—my husband's hand still on my shoulder.

"Honey, wake up. You're having another bad dream."

Slowly, I turned over in bed and looked at him—his dark brown eyes were fixated on me. I could see them clearly as the light from the bathroom brightened our bedroom.

For a month now, we had slept with this light on.

I could see the small wrinkle on his forehead. I loved that wrinkle though wished he didn't have good reason to be so concerned. I was enduring the nightmares, but he had to deal with my tossing and mumbling in terror.

I remember when we first met—ten years ago in chemistry lab at Georgia Tech. He had walked up to me with those warm eyes and a charming, confident smile and asked, "Want to be partners?"

Two years later he took me to Stone Mountain Park, rented a small rowboat and, in the moonlight, he pulled out a diamond ring and asked me again, "Want to be partners?"

Life had seemed just about perfect.

Until now.

We looked at each other for a moment. Then he propped himself up on his elbow and said softly, "Laura, I feel so helpless. I know it's only been a month, but..."

He hesitated.

"What?" I asked.

"It's just as bad as that first night. After it happened. Look, I want to make you feel safe again, but I don't know how."

He rubbed his eyes and looked away. I waited, staring at him.

What isn't he saying?

"I know you don't want to see a therapist, but seeing someone doesn't mean you're crazy. Therapists don't treat just crazy people. They help people who have been through traumas and you have. Hell, no one even has to know."

He paused for a second.

"Don't be mad at me, but yesterday I made an appointment for you. I was going to talk to you about it in the morning if you had another bad dream. I found a woman who is downtown by my office. She's been practicing for about twenty years, got her doctorate from Emory and comes with really good patient reviews."

He looked for my reaction and continued. "I made the appointment for you at 4:00 so we can go to dinner afterward. You know what you always say. You'll try anything once, right?"

"I told you I don't want to see a psychiatrist," I pushed back. "I just need more time. I'll bounce back. You know I almost came in the house on my own today. Besides, if I see a psychiatrist, on every job application I complete in the future, I'll have to check the 'Yes' box when they ask if I've had mental health treatment."

"Jesus. No you don't. You're too innocent sometimes."

He gently tapped me on the nose.

"You can check the box 'No.' Besides, if that's the only thing stopping you, I think you should give it a try. Her name is Barbara Cole. I'll take you to Houston's afterward," he added.

I ignored the bribe. "But what can she do that you can't? All she'll do is listen and you do that for me already. Psychiatrists are for people who don't have friends or husbands to talk to."

Chris shook his head.

"Please? Do it for me."

The tone in his voice was different—more helpless than normal. Chris had been so understanding, so comforting this past month, especially considering I had been waking him every night. How could I refuse his request?

I sighed. "Okay," I relented. "I'll go."

"One visit. That's all I'm asking. If you don't like it, you don't have to go back. She's a psychologist, by the way, not a psychiatrist. She does therapy, not drugs."

He glanced at the clock. It was 3:30 a.m.

Chris grabbed Konk, my stuffed animal gorilla that I won at the state fair by outshooting him at the basketball game. He had sworn the scum running the game couldn't take his eyes off my butt and let me win.

"Here's Konk," he said. "I'm going to finish my presentation since I'm up. I'll just be in the office. Want the door open?"

"Yes," I said as I wrapped my arms tightly around Konk.

"Hey, we'll celebrate your first therapy visit and my signed contract, I hope, this evening."

"You mean you *hope* my first visit?" I said with a playful smile.

He gave me a look—he was in no mood for jokes.

"Fine. Fine. I'll go," I assured.

"If you're asleep when I leave, just come by my office after the appointment and we'll head to dinner. Try to get some sleep. I love you."

"I love you, too."

 # Friday, July 7 morning

I awoke to a ray of sunlight beaming in my eyes. It streamed through the tiny spaces between the blinds and window trim, brightening the bedroom. Konk was still snuggled between my breasts.

I thought about Chris and felt a pang of guilt that he had to get up early while I could sleep in. I hadn't even heard him leave. I checked the time. He was probably standing at the head of a plush conference room right now, presenting the advantages of his company's medical equipment to a bunch of radiologists and hospital administrators. He would be impressive—tall, handsome, impeccably dressed, an articulate salesman with an engineer's technical background. He was great on stage.

Then again, maybe they would see how tired he was. Maybe he'd be off his game and lose the sale because he wasn't getting any rest.

I tried to brush the thought away as I climbed out of bed. I walked to the kitchen to get some orange juice, impulsively glancing at the red light on the alarm system.

We had installed the system a month ago. Chris had insisted on using the money he was saving for his new wide screen TV to get the best system available. We could have afforded both, but then he refused to buy the TV. I suspected it was because he felt guilty for being out of town that night. He was punishing himself.

When I turned the corner to the kitchen, I saw a post-it note, in Chris' handwriting, on the refrigerator.

DR. BARBARA COLE
1155 PEACHTREE ST., STE. 1015
THE GEORGIA BLDG.

I DIDN'T LEAVE THE PHONE NUMBER SO YOU CAN'T CALL AND CANCEL. HAVE A GOOD DAY. SEE YOU LATER FOR HOUSTON'S!
xoxo

I drank some orange juice, put on my workout clothes and then turned on my exercise DVD. I hadn't really felt much like working out lately. Today was no different. About halfway through the DVD, I turned it off.

I walked to the bathroom, locking the door behind me and looked at the frameless glass shower. I didn't like being naked and vulnerable. I undressed and stepped under the hot beads of water, keeping my eyes on the bathroom door the entire time. I barely shut them to wash my hair. Maybe I should cut my long, brunette hair so it wouldn't take so long to wash. Though I knew the alarm was on, I could still envision him bursting through the bathroom door and grabbing my wet, naked body.

"Be rational," I said out loud to myself. "That's not going to happen. Stop scaring yourself."

When would I ever feel normal again? When would I ever be able to take my long, steamy showers, shut my eyes and not watch the damn door?

I turned off the water, toweled off quickly and put on navy pants with an ocean-blue top. I liked that top—it brought out the blue in my eyes.

Feeling better dressed, I sat down at my desk to work. Admittedly, I had been procrastinating finishing my story for *The Atlanta Magazine*. My deadline was next week and I had already asked for an extension—an embarrassing first for me.

Maybe I should cut back on assignments after this one?

I thought back to that morning, a month ago. The police had arrived, dusted for prints, and questioned me extensively. In the chaos, I had almost forgotten that I had scheduled an interview for my article that day.

Troy, our next door neighbor, had come over and offered to cancel the interview. Instead of cancelling, I finished with the police and had Troy stay with me in the house while I got ready. Then I drove to the meeting and conducted the interview as if nothing had happened, even though my voice was hoarse from the screaming. It wasn't until Chris came home—he had cut his Raleigh trip short—that I even cried.

After aimlessly pecking at my article, I walked back to the kitchen, glancing at the red alarm light. I picked up Chris' note.

"Like I couldn't find the good doctor's number if I wanted to," I said out loud.

I walked back to the office, checking for the red light, and typed *Barbara Cole, Atlanta, Georgia*, into my Google toolbar. I found a link to her office with the address, phone number and a short biography indicating that Dr. Cole had done her undergrad at the University of Virginia and her master's and doctorate at Emory. From the graduation dates, I guessed that Dr. Cole was in her early fifties, but there was no picture to confirm. Her specialties were in anxiety, depression, grief and trauma, including Post-Traumatic Stress Disorder. I wasn't sure how Chris had chosen her, but there was nothing that could be used as an excuse for canceling the appointment.

When 3:00 p.m. drew near, I left the house, reactivated the alarm and got into my car to head downtown. I gave myself some extra time to find the office—the old me would have dashed out of the house to be just in time.

Dr. Cole's building was easy to spot with its pink marble exterior and blue glass windows. As I entered the building, I noticed the immaculate lobby's huge ceilings and ornate chandeliers. The pink marble floors matched the outside décor and there was a small coffee shop with tables in the corner. The lobby was empty except for a few people sipping their drinks and chatting. A chubby security guard manned the front entrance in a blue uniform.

I walked to the elevators and pushed the button for the tenth floor, riding in solitude except for the Muzak playing. I turned to the right as the sign indicated for Dr. Cole's office. As I passed each office, there were doorplates for lawyers, financial planners and a few doctors.

On door 1015 was gold lettering, *Barbara M. Cole, PhD*.

I slowly entered and was relieved to see that the waiting room was empty except for a pretty blonde receptionist.

"I'm Laura Holland. I have an appointment at four."

"Yes, Mrs. Holland. Dr. Cole is expecting you. Could I get your insurance card and photo ID please? Also, would you mind filling out this new patient form and the informed consent form for us?" the young receptionist said in a high-pitched, perky voice.

I took the clipboard and completed the usual questionnaire for a new patient. I checked the box 'No' for past mental illnesses and wondered if I would ever be able to do that again.

After returning the clipboard to the receptionist, I sat down on a maroon leather chair and looked around the waiting room. There was an old issue of *Jezebel* magazine on the end table. I could tell by the cover that it was the one with my article on Atlanta's most outstanding young professionals.

The lobby décor was quite masculine; the dark bookcases and heavy framed pictures of waterfowl reminded me of a men's lodge. It was entirely different from what I had envisioned, but it was surprisingly peaceful.

After a few minutes, the door next to the receptionist opened. There stood a woman with silver wire-rimmed glasses seated on a sharp nose, graying hair pulled back in a bun, and soft grayish-blue eyes. She was stout, but hid it well with a jacket and long, flowing skirt.

"Mrs. Holland," she said, as I stood and shook her hand, "I'm Barbara Cole. Please come in."

I followed Dr. Cole into her office. A desk and chair sat apart from a pastel living room suite, the soft, feminine colors contrasting with the dark waiting room.

"Please have a seat," she said, indicating the couch.

I sat down on the couch to prove it didn't bother me to 'sit on a therapist's couch,' and Dr. Cole sat in the peach floral chair next to me.

"How are you today?" she asked pleasantly.

"Fine, thank you," I said, automatically. Obviously, I wasn't fine.

We chatted briefly about the weather and if I had trouble finding the office. The couch was deep; I adjusted a pillow behind my lower back to get more comfortable.

"Mrs. Holland—may I call you Laura?"

I nodded.

"Could you tell me how I may be of help to you?"

"You don't know?" I asked, surprised that Chris had not given her any background on this visit.

"No. Right now all that I know is that you are a new client and, hopefully, our time together will be a positive experience for you."

I paused for a moment.

Where do I start?

"Well, my husband made this appointment for me. To be honest, I'm here more to appease him than anything else."

Dr. Cole's eyes squinted briefly, like she was troubled, but the expression was gone as quickly as it had appeared.

"Is there a particular reason your husband wanted you to see me?" she asked.

"Yes," I replied.

We sat in silence for a moment.

"Well, Laura, you're here, which tells me that at least a part of you wants to tell me why your husband—and maybe a little of you too—wants you to be here."

I looked down. "I suppose so."

More silence. I took a deep breath. I hadn't realized it would be this hard to get started. Finally, I looked up at her, eye to eye.

"About a month ago, I was attacked in my home."

She nodded. "Are you comfortable telling me what happened?"

"I guess," I replied. "I've told so many other people already—my husband, my mom, my sister, my brother-in-law."

For an instant, I thought of my father. He had died of a heart attack seven years ago. I never liked leaving him out when I talked about my family, but I wasn't sure if I was supposed to qualify that he was dead in the first five minutes of meeting someone—especially a shrink.

Dr. Cole was watching me. Slowly, I began recounting the events of that night. I told her how the intruder had kicked open my locked bedroom door and attacked me when Chris was out of town. I recalled how I tried to fight him off, how much I had screamed, and then, much to my surprise, how he had fled, leaving me physically unharmed except for bite marks on my left hand. Telling her felt different, not like telling my family. My voice was shaking. Today, in this office, I didn't have to be strong.

"Thank you for sharing that with me. I'm sure it is not easy to relive even if you have told the story repeatedly," said Dr. Cole. "And what happened after he ran away?"

"Well, I ran to the porch after him. I tried screaming so someone would wake up and catch him but he got away. Then, I ran back into the house and called my neighbor, Troy. I was pretty frantic, I guess, because he was over in seconds with his shotgun in hand.

"Troy is like a brother to me—and to Chris, too. I don't think I could endure Chris traveling as much as he does if Troy weren't around. Well, anyway, Troy came over and I told him what happened. He called the police right away and two officers showed up about ten minutes later. I repeated to them what happened and they asked to see the bedroom."

I paused for a moment, picturing my bedroom the morning the police arrived—tangled sheets, broken lamp and the dish towel.

"And then what happened?" asked Dr. Cole.

My voice began to quiver again, betraying the composed façade I had hoped to maintain.

"That's when I saw one of our kitchen steak knives wrapped in a dish towel by the bed. I didn't even know he had a knife until then. I'm glad I didn't know or I might have thought twice about fighting back."

For a brief moment, I pictured him slitting my throat—a pencil thin line of red blood seeping from the cut down my neck.

Dr. Cole interrupted the image. "Did the police find anything?"

"The police dusted the knife but couldn't find any prints. Then, they looked around the house to try to figure out how he got in. We didn't have an alarm system then. We just dead bolted the door at night. After all, our neighborhood has always been very safe. While we were trying to find out how he got in, I noticed our white wedding album in the den. We usually leave it under the coffee table. It was open with all of the pages torn out. Some of the pages were sliced into shreds. And the photos of me and Chris were cut, surgically sliced to remove my picture."

"That's disturbing," said Dr. Cole.

I nodded.

"It creeps me out to know that he was sitting on my couch in my house while I was asleep in the next room and I didn't even know it. And now he can look at my photos whenever he wants, and probably do disgusting things while staring at them."

"Surely the police found prints on the album?"

"They didn't. The police didn't find any signs of a forced entry into the house so they started asking me if I was sure that I had locked the door. I was so infuriated. I knew I had locked the door. I always do, especially when Chris is gone, and especially after the weird feeling I had before going to bed that night. I mean, for them to think I was the cause of my own attack! Troy and I began to search the house. He actually found where the kitchen window had been pried open."

"Your window was pried open?" interjected Dr. Cole.

"It was. Even worse was that the police couldn't find any finger-prints there, either. Well, except Troy's from when he discovered it, but that doesn't count. Then, they asked me to describe my attacker, but I never got a good look at him. I knew he was black, around six feet tall, maybe taller, wide shoulders, but that was it."

"Is there anything else you can remember?" the doctor asked.

I shook my head. "When we were in college, my sister, Lucy, taught me a few self-defense moves. She said to always try to find a distinguishing feature on an attacker so he could be identified later. I guess that was one piece of her advice that I forgot. That is the part that is most unnerving. He got away and I don't even know who he is. He could pass me on the street tomorrow and I wouldn't recognize him."

Dr. Cole replied, "What an ordeal. You were very brave."

After a short silence, she asked, "Laura, you said earlier you had a weird feeling before going to bed. What made you feel weird?"

I explained, "Oh, yes. It was the strangest thing. I was in our bedroom that night about to change out of my clothes, and I had the feeling that someone was watching me. It was like a sixth sense had been triggered and I could feel someone or something there with me. I even jerked back the window blinds to see if someone was outside looking in, but there wasn't anyone. I just figured that I was being paranoid with Chris gone. But the feeling was so strong that I changed clothes in the adjoining bathroom instead of the bedroom, something I never do. And I put the little bar latch on the bedroom door. It's just a flimsy thing but that eerie feeling made me want to latch the door before going to bed."

"It sounds like you were listening to your intuition that night."

"I guess, but now I'm *so sensitive*. Before, I dismissed that weird feeling, but now I pay attention to it *all of the time*."

I exhaled. I couldn't hold it back—my eyes began to tear.

How can I be crying in front of a total stranger?

Dr. Cole spoke in a soothing voice. "That's quite normal."

The tears were starting to roll down my cheeks. I confessed, "It's exhausting—and it won't stop."

She nodded. "There is a lot of psychological distress that comes with the trauma you faced, and it doesn't just disappear once the threat is gone. Your sensitivity may be what is called hyper vigilance."

"Hyper vigilance? I've never heard of that," I said. "My husband thinks I have PTSD."

"Well, hyper vigilance is one of the symptoms of PTSD, but I'd need a better understanding of all of your symptoms before we make that diagnosis."

Maybe I did have PTSD? Part of me was scarred, but I wasn't sure how badly.

Dr. Cole handed me a tissue and I wiped my face.

"How do I get better?" I asked.

Dr. Cole smiled. "Laura, dealing with your feelings is the first step in the process of recovery and that is something we can work through together, if you like. The good news is that the worst part, the actual attack, is over, so now you can begin the recovery."

"I don't know," I replied. "The recurring nightmares make it seem like it's not over. Nearly every night I've been reliving what happened."

Dr. Cole jotted a quick note. "Can you tell me more about the nightmares?"

I thought back to the terror of the preceding night.

"Usually, I dream about the attack. It's not much different than what really happened. I see his dark silhouette in the doorway and he pounces on me. Usually Chris wakes me up because he says I'm screaming in my sleep. One time I was even scratching the bed post when he woke me."

"I see," she said. "The nightmares are your mind's way of processing the trauma. When you feel threatened, your mind tries to cope with the situation subconsciously. Having nightmares is actually a good sign that you are struggling to make sense of a horrific situation."

"But why don't they subside? It's been over a month."

"You said your husband wakes you each time?"

"Yes."

"Well, I can't say for sure, but it could be that your unconscious self wants to be heard. If you don't pay attention to it, if you resist it rather than accept what it is trying to tell you, it will keep trying. It may sound counterintuitive, but if you listen to the dreams, if you embrace them instead of suppressing them, your unconscious self will feel that it is being heard."

I gave that hypothesis some thought. I would often "sleep on a story" if I was getting writer's block and let my subconscious work on it. Though this explanation wasn't exactly the same, it made sense.

Dr. Cole continued, "Once you pay attention to the dream or, in this case, the flashback nightmare, your unconscious self will likely work with you to process the information."

"So, should I tell Chris not to wake me?"

"You could try asking him to just hold you, to comfort you as you process the images but to let it play out. Once your unconscious self knows you are embracing the experience, the energy may shift. It's a bit like a child who wants your attention. If you ignore the child, he will keep acting up."

I shifted uncomfortably; I didn't know much about children or how they behaved. That could be a whole separate therapy session on why Chris was stalling.

Before the attack, I rarely remembered my dreams. Now, they were on vivid replay and I couldn't press the stop button. I had never considered that trying to suppress them might make them want to be heard even more. Though I didn't relish the idea of letting it play out, I was willing to try anything that would make the nightmares end.

I asked, "If I let them play out, how long before they stop?"

Dr. Cole smiled again. "I'm afraid the mind isn't that precise. Have you ever dreamt about the part when he retreats?"

"No. He's always still there."

"Well, once you let it play out, you might be surprised how quickly it dissipates, especially because you were able to fight back."

The pillow behind my lower back had sunk into the couch. I adjusted it to try to get more support.

Dr. Cole jotted a note on her pad. "Laura, is there more you'd like to share?"

"Well…Dr. Cole," I began.

"Please call me Barbara. That's only fair since you have allowed me to call you Laura."

"Okay, Barbara. You said I was able to fight back. I did. I fought him so hard. From the minute he broke into my bedroom to the minute he left, all I could think about was getting him away from me. But because I wasn't raped, I think people expect me to be instantly okay—like it doesn't count that I was attacked.

"My friend, Heather, said I should consider myself lucky because I wasn't raped. Lucky! Now that it's over, I certainly don't feel lucky. I mean I'm afraid to go in the house alone now. I'm afraid all the time, even when the alarm is on."

Barbara nodded. "Sometimes people are inconsiderate or at the very least uneducated about trauma. Just because you were not raped does not mean that you don't feel similar insecurities, just as someone who is robbed feels violated. From my experience, I have seen that the reactions of people are very much the same. It is the length of time to heal that can differ, depending on the severity of the crime. Like I said, you were able to fight back, which brings you a step closer to healing, to feeling secure again."

"Maybe you should give Heather a call," I huffed.

Barbara jotted another note and then glanced at her clock. "Laura, our time is almost up. I think I can help you with your recovery, but only if you like. I know you said your husband made the appointment so it is up to you if you would like to return. If you need to think about it for a while, that's perfectly fine."

Without hesitating, I replied, "I think I'd like to come back."

I could already hear the "I told you so" from Chris. No matter; I beat him at basketball at the state fair. He could be right this time.

"Okay, good." Barbara's voice became slow and deliberate. "You've told me a few things that have changed in your life over the last month. For your next visit, would you be open to writing them down as you think of them?"

I nodded.

Barbara started the list, "You mentioned earlier that you are now having nightmares, that you have an alarm system and that your sense of being watched is more acute. I suppose we could start with that."

"I said all that? I sound like a basket case."

Barbara shook her head. "Not at all. And I'm sure there are more changes in your life as well. So, as you think about them, even if they seem small, please write them down. We'll look at them together next time. Okay?"

"Okay."

We stood; I was surprised by the fact that I wanted to stay and talk longer.

"Well, good. Why don't you set up an appointment with Alisa on the way out?"

I shook Barbara's hand and made my next appointment for the following Tuesday. As I shut the office door behind me, I couldn't remember which way to the elevator. Was it right or left?

I glimpsed the back of someone opening the door to the stairs and remembered that the elevator was in the other direction.

FROM THE DESK OF
BARBARA COLE

July 7, Visit 1
New Patient - Laura Holland

Husband made appt, did not make appt herself
  * Speak to Alisa about appt policy

Husband - Chris, Neighbor - Troy, Mother, Sister, brother-in-law
  • No mention of father?

Attacked at home during night, attempted rape, bitten
  • Other injuries? Does she have full recollection?

Had premonition - changed clothes in bathroom, latched bedroom door
Attacker had a knife (not known until after)
Destroyed wedding album - took her photos
Broke in through kitchen window, neighbor's (Troy) finger prints there?

Symptoms:
  • Recurring flashback nightmares
  • Hypervigilent
  • Afraid to go into house alone

—BAC

 # Friday, July 7 afternoon

Since it was a beautiful, summer day and parking in midtown was never easy, I decided to walk the few blocks to Chris' office. We could pick up my car on the way to dinner. Besides, getting Chris out of work before 6:00 p.m., even on a Friday, would be difficult. I was anxious to tell him that I liked Barbara Cole, even though I would have to endure his gloating.

For the first time in a while, I felt optimistic. Maybe there was a way to return to my "before" life. As I walked down Peachtree Street, the sidewalk was coming to life with people eager to leave work and embark on the weekend. I thought about the last time we really celebrated—New Year's night at the St. Regis. After the party, we went for pancakes at 2:00 a.m. I'm sure we looked funny sitting in that corner booth, Chris in his tux and me in my black evening gown, eating blueberry pancakes with thick maple syrup and whipped cream. We each stated our resolutions for the coming year. Chris' was to exercise more. He was concerned that he'd lose his toned, athletic body now that he was over 30. Mine was to do more charity work.

BLAM

"Excuse me, ma'am," was all I heard. I felt like I had walked into a concrete wall.

I looked up and saw a dark face inches from mine. A tall black man was nearly on top of me.

"Did I hurt you?"

What is he saying? Why are his hands on my shoulders? Why is he touching me?

"Get away from me!" I shrieked.

I jerked backwards, escaping his grasp and ran the last two blocks to Chris' building, glancing over my shoulder to be sure he wasn't chasing me.

Once inside the lobby of the Colony Square building, I tried to calm down. My heart was racing and I was out of breath. I thought back to the collision. Would he come after me in broad daylight like that, with so many people around? I replayed his words, "Excuse me ma'am." He had a thick southern drawl and a meek little voice. It wasn't his voice.

Now that I was calmer, I realized it was probably an accident. That young man meant me no harm. I couldn't continue to be afraid of every tall black man that I came in contact with. But I couldn't control my panic either.

This would definitely have to go on "the list."

I stopped in the bathroom to towel off my face before heading to Chris' office. The reception area had pictures of X-ray tables and computed tomography scanners, all featured with beautiful, young nurses and smiling, happy patients.

Linda, his administrator, sat dutifully at her desk typing faster than I could imagine. She had been deemed a risky hire by Chris' counterpart, Dan Mallory, the regional service manager. Though it was not at all appropriate, Dan had even voiced his concerns about her being a single parent returning to work after her separation.

"We need someone who can be dedicated to this business," Dan had preached. "Our customers are more and more demanding. We have to be on the job 24/7 and so does she! We're running a business here, not a charity house."

Frankly, I couldn't stand that Chris tolerated Dan's chauvinism and exaggerations. Because they were childhood friends, Chris has a warped loyalty where Dan is concerned. And it was my husband's clout and reputation that got Dan his fancy service job in the first place.

Not that Dan will admit it, but Chris' instincts about Linda had been right. She was efficient and courteous, never letting her personal life interfere with her job. I wondered how she managed to stay late some nights with two young children at home, but didn't dare ask. At last year's Christmas party, Linda had brought her two boys. They were the spitting image of her—blonde hair, happy, round faces and bodies, and very well mannered.

"Good afternoon, Miss Laura," said Linda. She forced a cheerful smile. "Chris said you would be stopping by today. It's good to see you."

Linda's eyes were red and puffy—she looked like she had been crying. Had Dan said or done something mean to her?

"Are you okay?" I asked.

"Oh, just my allergies," she replied. "Thanks again for the books you sent over. The boys really liked them."

"You're welcome. Since we don't have our own kids yet, we'll spoil yours."

She forced a smile.

I really wanted to ask what Dan had done to her, but didn't want to make her feel worse.

"Your timing is perfect. Your husband just got back."

"Is he in a good mood?" I asked. "He doesn't like the long wait at Houston's."

"I think so. The meeting went well."

I walked with Linda to Chris' office. The full length glass window behind his desk displayed a stunning view of the Atlanta skyline. After verifying that Chris had no more work for the day, Linda said goodbye.

Once we were alone, he asked, "So, how was your visit?"

I knew he would ask.

I replied, "Good, but I'll tell you more at the restaurant. We had better get going to get a table. We need to pick up my car on the way, too."

"It must have gone well," he said. "Otherwise you would be expounding here and now on the many reasons why you should not have gone and why I had made a mistake in setting up the appointment. Am I right?"

He flashed his silly coy smile at me.

I might as well face it now.

"Okay, you were right. It was a good visit. I am going back next Tuesday. Now, can we go?"

Chris' arms rose in the victory pose I knew to expect.

"I knew you'd do that," I said.

"You know me so well, my dear."

He flashed that smile at me again. It was sweet and smart-ass at the same time. He leaned over and kissed me on the forehead and then reached for his computer bag.

As we passed Dan's office, I asked, "Where's Dan?"

"He went home after the meeting."

"Of course he did. Why should he come back to work when you can cover for him?"

"Let's pick up your car afterwards. I'm hungry."

Chris had both ignored my jab and changed the subject, typical when the topic of Dan came up.

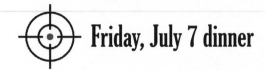 # Friday, July 7 dinner

We took Chris' Infiniti toward Buckhead and Houston's restaurant. People were already waiting outside at the top level, so he dropped me off at the door to reserve a table while he went in search of a parking spot in the open lot below.

Inside the bar, the cool air conditioning was a relief to the hot Atlanta July night. The dark brick walls with dim lighting made it feel cozy. I savored the smell of steaks grilling on an open flame. The restaurant was festive, buzzing with laughter and conversation. I ordered a vodka cranberry and a Tanqueray and tonic for Chris.

Chris arrived, lifted his glass and asked, "To what shall we toast?"

"Well, did you make the sale?" I asked.

"Not definite yet, but I could tell they were impressed with the images. I'm betting they'll order at least two systems within the next few weeks."

"Did Dan help or is he still trying to figure out how a CT scanner works?" I smirked.

"Laura, lay off, alright?"

Discussing Dan never had a good ending, but I couldn't just ignore how he treated Linda.

"Did you notice that Linda had been crying?" I asked.

"She looked okay to me."

"How could you not notice?"

Chris' hand twirled his Tanqueray glass, a nervous habit.

"Probably the soon-to-be ex-husband," he said. "It's been going on for a while now. He's trying to get custody of the kids. I don't think he even wants them—he just doesn't want her to have them. Spiteful bastard. It's okay, though, I got her a good lawyer."

"How can she afford one of your lawyers?" I asked.

"It's taken care of."

Taken care of? Is Chris paying for her divorce lawyer?

I wanted to ask but his reply was so terse that it didn't seem like a good idea. But, I wasn't going to let him drop the subject of Dan.

"Are you sure it wasn't Dan that upset her?" I asked. "He's not nice to her, you know."

"He wasn't even there this afternoon, Laura. Anyway, tell me about your doctor's visit."

There he went, changing the subject again. Well, if he could be terse, so could I.
"It was fine."

"And …" he prodded.

I just looked at him for a moment. He leaned over and kissed me on the cheek. "Come on, tell me about your day. I really want to hear."

I relented. "Well, I pretty much just told her what happened and she listened."

I told him about Barbara's hypervigilance theory and that I was to make a list of everything that has changed in my life since that night.

"So I'm writing things down like the nightmares," I said. "Oh, and she said I should embrace the dreams rather than trying to stop them. Once I embrace them they might go away. So, you can't keep waking me up."

Chris looked perplexed. "What? I'm just supposed to let you scream all night?"

"Yes, you have to let me process the dream."

"Maybe you should stay at Troy's."

He glanced at my face, and quickly apologized.

"I'm sorry. I didn't mean it that way. It's just how am I supposed to listen to your moans all night and not do anything about it? That would be torture."

"It's more torture having them, I assure you."

There was silence between us until Chris broke it.

"Well, I'm glad you agreed to go."

He twirled his empty glass again.

One of the bartenders asked if we wanted refills. Chris ordered another Tanqueray but I declined.

"Maybe you should add that to the list," Chris suggested.

"Add what?" I asked.

"You wouldn't even look at that black guy. If that waitress over there had asked if you wanted another drink, I bet you would have said yes."

I glared at Chris. He was right, of course, but I didn't need him micromanaging my therapy homework assignment.

"I'm fine with black men," I lied. "I just didn't want another drink."

We waited an hour at the bar before the buzzer went off for a table. Like the bar, the restaurant was also lively—as if everyone had exhaled and was ready to enjoy the weekend. I knew that Chris didn't like waiting so long for dinner, and that a Houston's hickory burger was his bribe in case today's session had been a disaster.

 # Friday, July 7 evening

My white Audi sat all by herself in the parking garage at the Georgia Building. I felt a pang of guilt for leaving her all alone.

For Heaven's sake, it's a car. It can't feel.

Still, I thought she might have been afraid there all by herself. I jumped in the driver's seat and patted the dashboard.

"I'm here now," I said to my car. "I'll take you home."

I pulled out of the garage and followed Chris up Peachtree Street to our house in Brookhaven.

He unlocked the front door and quickly punched in the alarm code; we had only forty seconds before it would sound. The code was the first four digits of his quarterly sales goal. Chris had said it would be a good daily reminder of the work ahead of him. He also did not want to use anything that could be easily guessed, such as a birthday or anniversary.

Since my attacker had ravaged our wedding album, there was no telling what he knew about us.

Chris changed into a cotton T-shirt and boxers. Before the attack, I used to wear bikini panties and one of Chris' T-shirts. But ever since that night, wearing so little made me feel vulnerable. Now, I wore pajamas with a top and bottom. I missed the smell of Chris' T-shirts so I kept my pajamas in his T-shirt drawer.

Chris finished brushing his teeth and walked into the adjoining bedroom—I was already on the bed waiting for him. He left the bathroom light on with the door open. I knew he preferred to sleep in complete darkness, but I was not ready for that.

He climbed into bed and first set the alarm for 7:00 a.m. and then decided to not set it at all to try to catch up on his sleep. He turned to me, wrapping his arms around my waist as we lay next to each other.

"I have to go to work for a few hours in the morning," he said. "How about we have lunch together and go to the driving range in the afternoon?"

I immediately frowned. The weekends were the two days that I didn't have to worry about being alone. He knew that.

"Come with me if you like, but I have to go in. I'm way behind."

"Fine," I retorted. "Vicki wants to go shopping so I'll go with her until you're done."

Vicki Roberts was my best friend; she and her husband, Kevin, were the other half of our golf foursome.

Chris pulled me closer and I laid my head on his chest—this was the place where I felt the safest in the world.

"Vicki told me last week they are thinking about having kids."

Chris didn't reply.

"Are you listening?" I asked.

"I heard you. Vicki is thinking about having kids."

There had been no question in my mind that we would have kids; for me, it was a question of when. Chris had always said that I'd be a great mom. But, with his career on the rise and the many hours he spent at work, he didn't seem able to envision a child now. He was thirty-one. Five years ago, he had said he would be ready at thirty. Now he just avoided the subject.

I couldn't help thinking what our child would be like. Though not born yet—or even conceived, I could already sense my baby's spirit. He would be a boy, a blend of each of our strengths. He would have Chris' warm brown eyes, his brunette hair, light tanned skin and athletic body. He would have my straight, white teeth, ski-jump nose, and my heart-shaped face. I hoped he would not have my feet, especially my overly large big toe inherited from my father, or my pale skin that never tanned.

Enough daydreaming.

I feared that if I thought about it too much the child might be deformed, kind of God's way of punishing me for asking too much.

I looked at Chris. These thoughts of children made me at least want to practice. We had not made love since the attack. Though it had been a month, it didn't seem that long. For the first few weeks, it wasn't even on my mind. All I wanted from Chris was to be held and protected.

Chris said goodnight and kissed me softly on the lips. He began to sink his head into his down pillow when I stopped him and kissed him again. I moved from his lips to his cheek to his earlobe, the spot I knew he couldn't resist. I alternated nibbling on and blowing in his ear and began to caress his body with my hands.

Chris didn't respond as usual. I thought he would be pleased that I was taking the initiative. We were good together and he must have missed having sex.

To my surprise, he pulled me off of his ear. I climbed on top of him and tried to kiss his lips but he responded half-heartedly.

"What gives?" I asked.

He took a deep breath and rolled me off of him. He then reached for my left hand and examined it closely. I could tell he was looking at the crescent moon shaped scab that covered my ring and pinky fingers. It was now beginning to heal though the scab was still quite thick.

"What's wrong?" I asked.

"I just want to give you some time. Let's not rush anything."

"It's been a month. I'm ready," I assured him. "He didn't change my feelings for you. What's wrong?"

Chris stroked my hair and looked into my eyes. He started to speak, but sounded like he had a lump in his throat. "There is something we didn't think about."

"I'm still taking my pills. I didn't stop taking them just because we haven't had sex in a while."

"No," he said. "It's not that. It's something else. I should have thought of it earlier but everything has been so crazy lately. I would have thought the police would have at least suggested this, but Dan's the one who made me think of it."

"What are you talking about? Why are you talking to Dan about us?"

"Well, first, this is nothing to be alarmed about. Okay? You promise you'll hear me out on this?"

"Ok," I said uneasily.

Chris continued, "The other day at work, Dan asked how you were doing …"

"Since when is Dan concerned about anyone besides himself, especially me?" I snapped.

"Just listen, please. I told him that you were coping pretty well, all things considered. He asked what your doctor said about the bite and it occurred to me that we never took you to the doctor."

"It's healing fine," I said. "You give doctors too much credit."

"Laura, just hear me out. After I realized that we hadn't checked you out yet, I called the health department just to see what might need to be done. I knew you'd kill me if I called your own physician directly. The woman at the health department suggested you get some tests, just to be cautious."

"What kind of tests? It's not infected. See?" I lifted my hand to show him the scab.

"The women said that human bites can be more dangerous than animal bites. There are more bacteria and yeasts. There are some diseases that can be transmitted by saliva like Tetanus."

He paused and seemed to check my expression.

"Like Hepatitis."

He paused again.

"Like AIDS."

AIDS!

Before I could even put that thought in perspective, Chris tried reassuring me.

"Then, I called the Atlanta AIDS Project to get more information. They said there is only a very, very slim chance you could have contracted HIV from a bite. They said anytime bodily fluids are exchanged there is a chance, but blood to blood or blood to semen exchanges are the most likely. Saliva to blood could be possible, but it's very, very remote. And he would have to be HIV positive, which he may not be. The pragmatic thing to do, though, is to be on the safe side and get you tested."

Chris finally stopped talking. We stared at each other.

During the attack, I had thought if I could just get away from him, it would all be over. Until now, my worst fear was his parting threat. My only worry was that he would return. Now, a whole new devastation was gnawing at me. By a single bite, I could never cleanse myself of him.

"You okay?" Chris asked. "Really, it is just a precaution, the chances are extremely low."

I burst into tears, burying my head into Konk's fur. I imagined waiting together at the doctor's office and the nurse handed me HIV positive test results. Five minutes ago, I was thinking about a pregnancy test—now, I had to think about an AIDS test?

I pulled my head up and wiped my eyes. One of my favorite poems, *Desiderata*, was hanging on our bedroom wall. I liked it there. The words always brought me comfort. I mumbled one of my favorite lines out loud.

"*…do not distress yourself with imaginings. Many fears are born of fatigue and loneliness. Beyond a wholesome discipline, be gentle with yourself.*"

Chris nodded, and added, "Neither of us has been getting any sleep. You're tired. Let's not overreact."

Slowly composing myself, I asked, "What tests do I have to take?"

"The women at the AIDS Project suggested that you take the HIV/AIDS test. I think we should go to the health clinic to remain anonymous. I don't want our insurance policy trying to cancel you just for taking the test."

"Could that really happen?" I asked.

"I'm not sure, but I don't want to take any chances."

"That's so unfair."

"Fair or not, we need to be smart about it."

Chris explained that the clinic would take a blood sample and do an ELISA test to check for antibodies developing in my body to fight the disease. If the ELISA test came back positive, then they would do a second test called a Western Blot to check for HIV. The worst part was that there was a "window period" of about three months from the time of exposure to detect the antibodies.

"But it's only been a month," I replied.

"I know. So we need to wait another two months before you go in, if we want to be sure of the results."

He paused, looked for my reaction, then continued.

"That is why I didn't want to say anything yet. Why should you worry for the next two months? I'm sorry. I should have waited to tell you, but I didn't want you to think I wasn't interested, you know?"

I realized the burden that Chris had been carrying, and appreciated his efforts to spare me the anxiety. I wanted to show him that I could carry the burden, too. "Well, let's put the test on the calendar for two months from now, in September. I guess no more earlobe kisses for a while?"

"Now what kind of salesman would I be if I didn't have a plan B?"

Chris flashed a smile, reached into the nightstand and pulled out a pack of condoms.

<u>Desiderata</u>

Go placidly amid the noise and haste, and remember
what peace there may be in silence.
As far as possible without surrender be on good terms with all persons.
Speak your truth quietly and clearly; and listen to others,
even the dull and ignorant; they too have their story.
Avoid loud and aggressive persons, they are vexations to the spirit.
If you compare yourself with others, you may become vain and bitter;
for always there will be greater and lesser persons than yourself.
Enjoy your achievements as well as your plans.
Keep interested in your career, however humble; it is a
real possession in the changing fortunes of time.
Exercise caution in your business affairs; for the world is full of trickery.
But let this not blind you to what virtue there is;
many persons strive for high ideals;
and everywhere life is full of heroism.
Be yourself.
Especially, do not feign affection.
Neither be cynical about love; for in the face of all aridity
and disenchantment it is as perennial as the grass.
Take kindly the counsel of the years, gracefully
surrendering the things of youth.
Nurture strength of spirit to shield you in sudden misfortune.
But do not distress yourself with imaginings.
Many fears are born of fatigue and loneliness. Beyond
a wholesome discipline, be gentle with yourself.
You are a child of the universe, no less than the trees and the stars;
you have a right to be here.
And whether or not it is clear to you, no doubt
the universe is unfolding as it should.
Therefore be at peace with God, whatever you conceive Him to be,
and whatever your labors and aspirations, in the noisy
confusion of life keep peace with your soul.
With all its sham, drudgery and broken dreams, it is still
a beautiful world. Be cheerful. Strive to be happy.

MAX EHRMANN, 1927

 # Tuesday, July 11

The weekend had passed quickly—shopping, the golf range, a Net-flix movie and relaxing at home. I didn't mind being home when Chris was there.

After the *Atlanta* magazine story, I had not taken any new assign-ments, which meant a lot of free time. Though I wasn't much of a cook, I decided to make dinner for Chris and Troy.

I made the grocery list according to the exact layout of the store and was off to Kroger. As I drove south down Peachtree Street toward Lenox, I rolled down my windows and enjoyed the beautiful, sunny summer day. It was ninety-two degrees with heavy humidity, but I didn't mind. I loved the fresh air.

I stopped smiling when I realized how much I missed the fresh air at home. I was no longer able to enjoy the fresh air at night. There was no way I could sleep with the windows open. That was how he got in.

Now, all doors, all windows, everything had to be shut and locked before going to bed. There was no more fresh air, no more sounds of crickets chirping outside as we slept. To build a fortress, it had to be sealed.

I pulled into a parking spot at the store, reached into my purse and grabbed a folded sheet of paper. It was titled, *Changes to my life.*

I added to the list, *"Won't sleep with the windows open."*

I tucked the paper back in my purse so it would be handy for my afternoon visit with Barbara. I was surprised at the number of changes to my life and probably would have never thought about them all had Barbara not asked me to make the list.

With each addition to the list, I became angrier at him for disrupt-ing my life.

I finished my grocery shopping, checked out and returned home. The front of our single story home looked innocent enough—light blue exterior, grey shutters and matching grey roof. Three potted ferns dan-gled from their hangers on the right side of the porch. A white rocking chair invited you to sit for a spell and enjoy the lazy summer with a cool glass of iced tea. The grass was green, the flowers were blooming, and a slight breeze danced through the leaves of the large pecan tree in the front yard. Everything outside was peaceful and cheery.

Then, I pictured him crouched in the closet waiting for me. Somehow he had gotten inside while I was gone. He had deactivated the alarm and was waiting for me to come home.

"Stop it!" I said out loud. "The alarm is on. He couldn't possibly get in. This was a random attack. He is not coming back, certainly not in broad daylight. Just go into the damn house."

Still, I sat glued to the car seat, hands stuck to the steering wheel, unable to garner the courage to get out. I stared at the front of my house trying to reassure myself that it was safe. But, as much as I tried to suppress it, I was unable to erase the image of him reveling in delight as he waited silently in my closet.

All of the sudden, I caught a glimpse of a dark figure standing at my passenger window.

He's not inside. He's right here!

I screamed and instinctively threw my body toward the side of the driver's door. I crushed my elbow into the armrest and it started to throb with pain. I scrambled to grab the door handle, pulling the lever but it didn't budge. The door was locked. I frantically fumbled for the switch— my hands were shaking. I couldn't make my body move fast enough.

A hand reached through the passenger window and unlocked the doors. It was a white hand. Then a face appeared—Troy's face.

"Oh my God, you scared me," I cried as I tried to catch my breath.

"Sorry," he replied sheepishly.

Troy had obviously seen me pull into my driveway through his kitchen window. When I stayed in the car, he probably figured I was afraid to go in.

Troy opened the passenger door. He was dressed in blue jeans and a T-shirt. This was standard work attire as his family owned a profitable dry-cleaning chain and he never needed to dress up to check on the stores. When his father turned 60, Troy's parents retired to Florida and left the daily oversight of the business, as well as their large home on the golf course, to him. Each store had its own manager so there really wasn't much work for Troy to do other than an occasional drop-in.

I noticed a big delivery truck in his driveway. "What's going on?" I asked.

"I'm getting a waterbed. Jeannie never wanted one, so with her gone, I figured I'd indulge myself. If I get one now, my next wife won't have a say 'cause it will already be there, you know?"

I just shook my head.

At least he was opening up to the idea of another wife, if even a joke. For the first six months after his ex, Jeannie, left, he had been a basket case—not going to any of the dry-cleaning stores, not getting dressed, overeating and moping around the house. Chris and I had tried to take care of him, tried to cheer him up, but nothing seemed to help. After about eight months, he suddenly improved. He decided not to let her ruin his life and that it was time to move on. He agreed to the divorce, threw out her pictures and pulled his life back together.

Luckily, the house was in his parents' name so he was able to keep it. She moved to New York and they didn't talk again other than to finalize the divorce. Since then, he has dated every now and then, but nothing serious.

I figured he was gun shy. From what I gathered, Jeannie had left Troy because she was restless. She had gotten tired of the average American life, of a dependable, but unexciting husband. They had married young and she missed her chance to be wild. Troy, who was completely devoted to her, never understood what he had done wrong and tried desperately to hang on. Finally, he gave up and let her go.

He looked into the back seat of my car and saw the groceries. "Want some help carrying them in?" he asked.

He always seemed to show up when I needed him. I didn't feel like being brave, not today, so was more than willing to have him escort me into the house. He grabbed the four plastic bags in one hand and took them to the front door, unlocking it with his free hand. He was such a burly guy—what would have taken me two trips, he handled in one. Once inside, he tucked his copy of our house key in his jeans pocket and extended his hand to deactivate the alarm. I instinctively reached for the alarm at the same time and our arms collided.

He brushed me away. "I've got it," he said, and then walked to the kitchen to plop the grocery bags on the counter.

"I'll check the place out while you put them away," he said. I thanked him. He always seemed to offer what I was afraid to ask, knowing that I was still afraid in my own home.

"Okay," I agreed. "Hey, I bought these groceries for you, too. I am actually going to cook a real dinner tonight. Want to come over around seven?"

"Sure. Just the *three* of us, right?" Troy asked.

"Yes, just us three." I knew why he was asking. I had tried to play matchmaker before with my friend, Denise, a photographer from the newspaper.

I had thought they would be a good match, so Troy reluctantly agreed to be set up. Denise was petite, cute and seemed ready to date more seriously. The first evening actually went well and Troy asked her out again. For once, Chris had to remain silent rather than express his pessimistic views on blind dates. On the third date, however, the relationship ended. Troy was at Denise's condo when she proposed the idea of photographing him in the nude, one of her hobbies. The last straw for him was when Denise opened her closet door and showed him about thirty pictures of her nude ex-boyfriends.

After checking the house, Troy walked back to the kitchen.

"How was I to know she wanted to photograph you?" I continued. "Besides, you could think of it as kind of a compliment."

"Yeah, right. Meet Troy Shepard, the latest prize photo of psycho Denise, displayed prominently on the lower left-hand corner of her closet."

"Next time I'll find a better match for you," I offered.

Troy cocked his head and gave me a sharp glance.

"Okay, okay. No next time. Are you coming for dinner or not?"

"Sure. Hey, I'd better get back to the delivery guys. Don't need them flooding mom's priceless Persian rugs. I'll see you tonight."

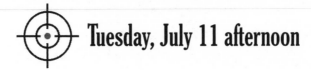

Tuesday, July 11 afternoon

I walked into the kitchen to start preparing the evening's feast—a chicken casserole. It wasn't exactly glamorous, but it was the comfort food I was craving.

I was relieved that Troy had searched the house so I wouldn't have to. I took the celery from the plastic shopping bag, washed it and grabbed a cutting board. Then, I reached into the drawer next to the sink to get a knife.

I looked at the knife's sturdy wooden handle and sharp, serrated edges.

I hesitated to pick it up, and then, became upset that something as mundane as chopping celery should stand out to me now. I reached for my purse, pulled out the list again and wrote, "*Afraid of knives.*"

I forced myself to take the knife and cut the celery, and then finished making the casserole and put it in the refrigerator. At first, I left the cutting board and knife in the sink with the other dishes to wash later, but the thought of a knife out in the open, so easily accessible made me feel uncomfortable. So, I rinsed everything and put the knife in the dishwasher, as far back as I could reach.

A few hours later, I made the journey to Barbara Cole's office and entered the familiar, masculine waiting room. Alisa greeted me and not long after, Barbara opened the door to begin our second session.

"Hello, Laura. How have you been doing?"

"Pretty much the same, thanks. I did write that list of the things that have changed in my life since the attack."

I pulled out the sheet of paper from my purse and unfolded it. When I tried to hand it to Barbara, she asked me to keep it and read it aloud instead. I looked down and began.

Changes to my life:

- Wouldn't go in house alone, at first
- Afraid to be left alone, at first
- Won't wear Chris' T-shirts to bed anymore
- Sleep with bathroom light on
- Nightmares about the attack
- Rearranged bedroom furniture so don't have same view of the doorway
- Bought alarm system for the house
- Sense I'm being watched
- Search the house when I go in
- Afraid of black men
- Won't sleep with the windows open
- Afraid of knives

"How did it make you feel to write this down?" Barbara asked.

"I'll admit I was surprised at how many things I wrote and I'm sure I haven't captured them all. I just thought of those last two today. And for the one about the knives, I never thought of our knives as anything but kitchen tools. Not anymore."

"I see. Were some things harder to write than others?"

"I don't think so, not as far as writing them. Some things are harder to live with than others. I'm still having nightmares. I'm trying to embrace the dreams like you said last time, but they aren't going away. And, I'm still paranoid that *he's* gotten into the house, even with the alarm on."

"Was there anything you felt you couldn't write down? You don't have to tell me what it is. It's perfectly fine if you can't address everything just yet. It can be overwhelming."

I thought for a moment about the possibility of contracting HIV.

"I don't think I've missed anything," I lied.

"Was there anything that you wrote down that made you feel better?" Barbara asked.

I scanned the list again. "Well, rearranging the furniture made me feel better. We changed the room around so when I wake up, I don't see the doorway and start thinking about his silhouette there. Instead I see the dresser and the wall. We even talked about selling the house and moving, but I can't handle any more disruption to our lives."

"How did you come up with the idea to change the room?"

"I've been reading a book about recovering from rape. It said that more women are raped in their own home than any other place— almost thirty percent. I read that even if you move, the fears don't really go away, even in a new place. It suggested rearranging the furniture for a different feel, so we did."

"It sounds like you are already making changes to help you feel secure again," said Barbara.

"Oh, I didn't mention adding new locks to the doors in addition to the alarm. We put a deadbolt lock on the bedroom door and reinforced the window locks. The bedroom already had a small bar lock that was there when we moved in. It's an older-style house and didn't have any sophisticated locks. I think I told you at our last visit that I felt so strange the night of the attack that I actually used that feeble latch for the first time. Now, when I think back, it saved me. It really saved me."

"How is that?" asked Barbara.

"Well, it was enough to keep him from quietly opening the door and sneaking up on me. Instead, he had to force the door open, which made enough noise to wake me up. It gave me a few seconds to realize what was happening and to react. I can't imagine what it would have been like if the first moment I realized he was in my room was with him on top of me with a knife at my throat. I don't know if I would have been able to fight back."

I felt my eyes welling up with tears but tried to fight them off.

"I'm sorry," I said.

Barbara handed me a tissue and spoke softly. "Crying is part of the healing process, Laura."

I was surprised that crying came so easily in Barbara's office. I tried to push back the tears and speak which resulted in choppy, broken sentences about how *he* could have killed me if he had wanted. I told Barbara how I felt lucky for not being harmed, but at the same time, so incredibly scared. I could hardly believe that something so awful could have happened to me and wondered what I could have done differently to prevent the attack.

Once my sobs turned to sniffles, Barbara asked, "Laura, are you blaming yourself for the attack?"

"Well, I don't think I did anything to attract him. I don't dress provocatively. I don't go out alone at night where he could have spotted me and followed me home. I lock the doors. It's just that Chris and I had talked about buying an alarm system before and never did. If we had only bought one, he would have never made it through the kitchen window."

"I see." Barbara paused for a moment. "And what if you did dress provocatively? Would you have deserved this unwanted attention?"

I shook my head. "No, of course not. I didn't mean it like that. But why did he target me?"

"We may never know, unless he's caught. Laura, what else makes you feel better?"

I looked at the list.

"Well, it's kind of a silly thing but I started wearing pajamas to bed. The night of the attack I was wearing only Chris' T-shirt and my underwear. I can't really explain it, but I feel better having pajama bottoms on, something to provide more protection even if it's just cloth."

· · · 32 · · ·

It would have been so easy for him to have ripped off my underwear leaving me completely exposed. I shuddered and continued explaining.

"In the book, it said that most women won't wear the same or similar outfits as the one they were wearing during the attack. But then it said not to develop a false sense of security just because I was avoiding the items that replicated that night. Logically, I know I could wear Chris' T-shirts and be just as safe or just as vulnerable, but I just don't want to wear them anymore."

"That makes sense. I wanted to ask you about one of the first items on your list. You noted that you were afraid to be left alone or go into the house alone, *at first*. Do I interpret your statement to mean that this is no longer true?"

"That's right. For the first week or two, I couldn't stand to be left alone, even in the daytime. It was just too scary. Chris took some vacation days and we went to St. Simons Island. It really helped for me to get away for a while. After that, I would leave in the morning when Chris did and spend the whole day at the newspaper, mall or Starbucks until he came home. I needed to be around people and my freelance writing kept me home alone. I was getting behind in my deadlines so my mom came to visit for about a week so I could stay at home during the day and write. Finally, I realized that I'd have to face staying in the house by myself. By then, we had the alarm and the new locks and Mom had to go back to South Carolina. I learned to live with being alone."

"It's a normal reaction. Most women do not want to be alone for the first few weeks. Many actually stay with friends or relatives, away from the environment where the assault occurred. Laura, between the alarm system and the trip, I'd say you are doing many of the right things to heal."

I just smiled and nodded.

Barbara asked, "How was it having your mom stay with you?"

I supposed every therapist had to bring up that topic at some point. It was the ultimate cliché—here I was sitting on a therapist's couch about to discuss my mother.

"Oh, my mom was wonderful. She tried to balance being helpful without getting in my way. She'd make dinner, but then retire early so as not to disturb me and Chris in the evening. Or, she would just sit in the same room with me during the day and quietly read so I could work without being disturbed. I'm sure she would have stayed for weeks if I had asked her to."

"And your father, is he involved in your life?"

"We lost him to a heart attack seven years ago."

I thought about how my dad would have reacted. He probably would have hired a personal body guard for me if he were still here.

Barbara jotted a quick note. "And how do you feel now about being alone?"

"Sometimes my imagination gets the best of me."

"How is that?"

"Like today. I went to the grocery store and when I came home I was afraid he had gotten into the house and was waiting for me. I just got so scared and panicked. I know it's not possible with our alarm system, but sometimes I can't convince myself with logical reasoning."

"I see. When you felt panicked, where did you feel the tension in your body?"

I raised my hands to my shoulders and chest. "I guess my shoulders were tense and my heart was beating faster. Why do you ask?"

"It's important to be aware of your body. We tend to be more rational than experiential. We want to solve problems with our logic and reasoning and from what you've shared, you are particularly pragmatic. But we also need to listen to our body to heal. When you came home today and were feeling panicked, what did you do?"

"I was lucky this time. Troy was home so he checked out the house. I think he enjoys the chance to take care of me. It was safe, of course, but sometimes I just can't get past my panic attacks."

We sat for a moment of silence.

"Laura, why don't we try an exercise together? It should help you deal with the panic attacks like the one you had today. It's a simple relaxation exercise."

"Okay."

"To begin, I'd like you to make sure you are comfortable on the couch and then shut your eyes." I repositioned myself slightly, leaned back into the couch and closed my eyes.

"Are you comfortable?" Barbara asked in a soothing, soft voice.

I nodded.

"Now I'd like you to think of a place where you are at peace, where you feel calm and safe. It doesn't have to be a place you've actually been to but a place where you feel totally serene."

I thought for a moment. I had always liked the mountains. I pictured myself on the top of a huge, bare mountain peak, like Stone Mountain but higher and deserted. There were dark green tree tops below me in the distance and a blue clear sky above. From my high vantage point, I could see in all directions, which made me feel especially safe, as I could see if anyone was approaching.

"Where are you?" Barbara asked.

"On the top of a mountain."

"Okay. Stay there and we are going to progressively tighten and then relax your muscles."

Barbara took me through an exercise where I would tense and relax my body from my head to my toes, breathing deeply the whole time. When we were done, she gave me a CD so I could practice at home.

Just when I was starting to feel comfortable, Barbara looked at her clock. Our time was up.

FROM THE DESK OF
BARBARA COLE

July 11, Visit 2
Laura Holland

Positive Changes: Alarm, Locks, Moved furniture
Progressing to be alone, Changed night clothes
Concerns: Hypervigilant, Nightmares

Blame: could have bought alarm
Does husband (Chris) blame himself?
 • monitor husband's coping

Parents: Mother - supportive
Lost father, heart attack, 7 years ago
 • still keeping com , significant event in her life

Relaxation exercise - succumbs quickly, good candidate for EMDR
Place: Mountain top
 • continue to practice, build trust

—BAC

 # Tuesday, July 11 evening

I drove the familiar path north on Peachtree Street back home. Troy met me in the driveway and checked the house like before.

I figured that I had better call Chris to be sure he would be home at a decent hour. Just as I reached for my cell phone, it rang.

"That's funny. I was just going to call you," I said.

"Yeah, what's up?"

"I've made dinner and Troy is coming over. Can you be home before seven?"

Chris replied, "I'm sorry. That's why I'm calling. I've had a meeting come up in Nashville tomorrow morning. I have my spare bag here at the office so I thought I'd just drive from here unless you want to come with us?"

I was used to these impromptu meetings popping up, though this was the first one since my attack. I felt a brush of fear—but then I remembered Troy was coming over.

"That's okay. I don't want to go to Nashville with you and Dan. I'll save you some leftovers, assuming Troy doesn't eat everything."

"Actually, Dan isn't going. I'm dropping off Linda and her boys in Chattanooga on the way."

"Why?" I asked.

"She's going to stay with her mom for a bit. Her ex has been harassing her so we thought it was a good idea for her to get out of town for a while."

We?

"Why doesn't she just get a restraining order?" I asked.

"She has but she doesn't have any proof of some of the stunts he's been pulling."

"How's she gonna get back to Atlanta? Do you have to go pick her up, too?"

"No. Her mom will drive them back. It's just a few days," he said. "Will you be alright tonight?"

I could hear the concern in his voice.

"Sure, I'll be fine." I was already contemplating asking Troy to stay over.

At 7:00 pm, Troy showed up promptly and did a really poor job pretending to be surprised that Chris couldn't join us. I bet Chris already called him and asked him to stay over. After dinner, Troy suggested we go out for a drink.

"But it's a week night," I protested.

"What do either of us have to do tomorrow?" he retorted. He had a good point. I didn't have any new work and he never had much work. We decided to go to Red Martini to listen to a jazz band. We had already finished a bottle of wine with dinner so Troy offered to drive. We spent the evening listening to music and I tried to pick out potential dates for Troy. If a cute girl passed by, I would ask what he thought and Troy would critique her. He seemed to like the petite brunettes best, though I knew he wouldn't dare go talk to any of them.

It was approaching midnight when I took the last sip of my cosmopolitan—I wasn't drunk but I wasn't really sober either. Troy had been drinking beer nonstop.

"Let's go," I said. "We'd better call a cab."

"No. I'll drive," he said, slurring his words with an unwarranted self-confidence. "I can't leave my Explorer here overnight."

"I'll drive you back here first thing tomorrow to pick it up."

The alcohol had slowed his speech and his reactions. Before he could protest, I had already requested an Uber.

The black limo arrived shortly thereafter and we were home within 15 minutes, an advantage of living inside the perimeter, or "ITP," as Atlantans call it. When the car stopped outside of my house, I awoke the sleeping giant next to me. We climbed the porch stairs arm-in-arm. I tried to help him maintain his balance but he was like a clumsy bull, swaying from side to side as we mounted the stairs. The fresh air had helped me sober up a little.

Once inside, I reset the alarm and put my purse on the kitchen table. Troy had wandered off into the next room. When I returned to the den seconds later, I found Troy lying on his back in the middle of the room.

"I'm going to sleep here," he muttered not opening his eyes. "And tomorrow we are going to get my truck."

I knelt down beside him. "Okay, but why don't you sleep in the other room on the bed? It would be more comfortable. And you can check the house on your way."

"No."

I grabbed his arm and tried to pull him up. "Come on, Troy. Get up." I had no success in moving him. He was a lead weight. Instead, he clasped my hand tightly and pulled me toward him, almost making me lose my balance.

"I'm going to sleep here outside your door and guard you," he said, with eyes still shut.

He clasped my hand tighter and took a deep breath. "I have to tell you something," he said.

"What?"

He paused and then spoke. "I love you."

I patted him on the stomach with my free hand. "I love you, too, Troy. You're the brother I never had. Now, come on. Get up."

All of the sudden, his eyes opened and he looked at me intensely. "No. Not like that. I'm in love with you."

I froze. He didn't sound so drunk anymore. My hand now felt trapped by his grip.

He continued, "I won't do anything about it. I can't. Maybe if I didn't know Chris, it would be different. Why can't there be two of you?"

"Troy, you're drunk and you're talking crazy." I snatched my hand away from his grip. "I'll check the house myself."

I stood up and walked toward the guest bedroom. I shut the door behind me and leaned back against it. I mustered the courage to fling open the closet door—no one was there—nor were there any monsters under the bed, but I still had to check.

When I returned to the den with a blanket and pillow, Troy was fast asleep, snoring rhythmically. That was a relief. I slowly covered him with the blanket and put the pillow beside his head. I didn't dare lift his head to slide the pillow under and risk waking him to continue the conversation.

I then tiptoed to my room, changed clothes, and climbed into bed. I thought about Troy. I wondered if I should tell Chris what he had said. No, he wouldn't understand. Even if I could pretend it never happened, Chris would never pretend. Maybe it was the coward's way out, but I decided to ignore everything. I could feign a drunken memory loss and I would.

The alcohol and late hour were making me drowsy. I closed my eyes praying not to have another nightmare.

 # Wednesday, July 12

The next morning, there was good news and bad news.

The bad news was that I had dreamt of the attack and was quite panicked when I awoke in the night without Chris to cling to. I had peeked out of my bedroom door and saw Troy still asleep on the floor.

The good news was that Troy didn't remember much of the night. He had forgotten that he left his truck at the bar, and didn't seem to remember our later conversation, which was fine with me.

Later that evening, Chris returned home from Nashville.

"I can't believe Troy!" Chris exclaimed as he stepped out of the kitchen and faced me on the couch.

"What?" I asked.

How did he know?

"He ate all of the chicken casserole. Didn't you tell him to save some for me?"

"Oh," I said, relieved. "I'll make another one."

 # Saturday, July 15

"Holland/Roberts, first tee," a voice announced over the loud-speaker. Chris and I had a standing 8:17 a.m. tee time every other Saturday with Vicki and Kevin Roberts. I was the novice of the group, having picked up my first club only six years ago.

We sounded like a mercenary of marching soldiers as the plastic spikes of our golf shoes clicked on the gravel outside the Capital City Clubhouse. We loaded our carts and drove to the first tee. Rather than teaming up as husband and wife pairs, the girls shared a cart and so did the boys.

As we rode along, I took a deep breath and turned to my best friend.

"I'm thinking of buying a gun," I said, watching for Vicki's reaction.

"You're what?"

"I'm thinking of buying a gun for protection. I'd take lessons to learn how to shoot it, but I'd feel better if we had a gun in the house."

"What does Chris say?"

"You know Chris. I don't think he would like the idea. He grew up with golfers, not hunters."

"You haven't asked him?" she asked, in a hushed voice.

"Not yet. I don't think he would agree so I need to figure out how to bring it up."

Vicki jumped out of the driver's seat, grabbed a three iron from her golf bag and walked to tee off. Her shot went straight down the fairway. I took my turn, hitting the ball not far from Vicki's and then I drove us back to the cart path until we were parallel to the boys. We watched Kevin take a swing. Vicki leaned over, whispering so the guys wouldn't hear.

"Well, I think you have to talk to Chris before you do anything else. If he doesn't want a gun, then I don't see how you'll be able to get one."

I couldn't disagree. "Maybe I should see if I even like to shoot one before I get a veto. Hell, maybe I won't even like it and that will be the end of the story."

"Have you ever shot a gun before?" Vicki asked.

"No, have you?"

"No."

"Well, you're the journalist," she said. "Why not do some research first? Interview the police chief or something like that."

"Yeah, that's a good idea. I haven't read many articles on women and guns. Might be an interesting angle."

"That could work. Do your research and get a story out of it," Vicki suggested.

"Yeah, but none of my regular magazines would want a gun story. I'd have to cast a wider net to publish it."

"What would you write about exactly?"

"Maybe the pros and cons of women owning guns. I like your idea of interviewing the police chief. I'll try to set that up. So, what's going on with you?"

Vicki had a devilish smile on her face. "We decided that I should stop my birth control."

"You did!" I exclaimed, forgetting I was on the golf course. "Are you sure you're ready?"

"I am. You know I show all these houses with these cute little nurseries and I just want one for myself. I'm ready and Kevin is, too."

I tried to feign excitement for my friend but couldn't help but feel that she was getting ahead of me. I had always hoped that we would have kids around the same time, to share the experience together. But how could I bring a baby into my troubled world? And what if I had AIDS? I couldn't endanger an innocent child. It was too much—too much to think about right now.

 # Tuesday, July 18

One week had passed since my second visit with Barbara. I was headed back for my third session. Barbara was always on time, a courtesy I thought no longer existed in the medical profession. The doctor's wardrobe was beginning to show a pattern—long, loose flowery skirts with a knit blouse and solid colored jacket. She wore big necklaces and earrings to match and had her bifocals dangling in front of her necklace on a thin chain. Her salt and pepper hair was pulled back off her face

"So tell me, how have the relaxation exercises been going?" Barbara asked.

"Pretty well. I've listened to them almost every day and am getting a little more brave about going into the house alone."

I paused and then admitted sheepishly, "But if Troy or Chris are around, I let them check out the house for me."

"How would you feel if you went in the house and no one checked it, not even yourself?" asked Barbara.

"Oh, I couldn't do that."

"Are you afraid that he will return?"

I looked down at my hands. Tears started to well up out of nowhere. It was time to share the rest of the story.

"That night, he said something to me. Something I haven't told you about yet."

I took a deep breath.

"Yes?" she encouraged.

"Right before he left…"

The floodgate opened. I broke down. I had cried more in the last month than in the last five years, and most frequently on this couch.

Barbara leaned over and gently rubbed my arm.

"Did he threaten you?" she asked.

I nodded. "Right before he left, he whispered, '*You win for now, but don't you forget Sweet Sam.*' He told me his name. He told me not to forget him. I think he's coming back."

It had taken me three visits to Barbara Cole before I was able to share his threat. I wiped my face and let out a long exhale. Strangely, Barbara did not seem surprised.

"Laura, this is a very common theme I hear. Actually, the most common intimidation tactic by a rapist is retaliation toward the victim or her loved ones if she tells anyone. The next most common threat is that he will return and repeat the act. I'd say over seventy-five percent of my rape patients convey one of these same messages. But, I can tell you that none of my patients have ever been raped a second time, once they reported the incident, and none have ever had the attacker return. This doesn't mean I don't want you to be careful, but it's important for you to know that the rapist rarely carries out these threats."

I replied, "But your data is of rape victims. The rapists didn't come back because they got what they wanted. What about me? He didn't get what he wanted. Won't that make him more determined to come back?"

"If he plans to strike again, which I'm afraid he will—most rapists are serial in nature—he will probably look for what he deems an easier target. You weren't."

I wasn't convinced.

"I still have this vivid picture of him running away. I could see a red circle on the back of his T-shirt. It was like a bull's eye that I wish I could have shot."

"Why?"

"So he wouldn't have gotten away. So he wouldn't be free to come back to hurt me again."

"How do you think you would have felt if you had shot him?" Barbara asked.

As I sat on the couch I envisioned the scene. It was one I had pictured many times. I aimed the gun toward the bull's eye on his shirt, fired a shot, and watched his figure fall to the pavement. I took quiet satisfaction in the thought.

Barbara watched me, still waiting for my answer.

"I don't like to admit it, but it would have felt good. I felt so helpless standing on my porch with a can of Mace watching him run away. If I'd had a gun, I would have stopped him. I'm not a violent person. I don't even like to kill insects that get in the house. But this was different."

"But if you had shot him, you would be dealing with a lot more than you are today," she replied. "If you killed or even wounded him, there could have been other ramifications, don't you think?"

"It would have been self-defense. He attacked me, remember?"

"Yes, I know, and I'm not a legal expert, but I believe if you had shot him when he was *leaving*, you couldn't claim self-defense."

"No reasonable person would have blamed me," I said.

I thought about the old saying, 'If you shoot someone outside, just be sure to drag the body inside.' I wondered if Barbara was right about claiming self-defense. I had better find out before trying to convince Chris to own a gun. Though he was an engineer, he could debate like a lawyer and would surely use this point in his anti-gun argument.

We sat in silence. Then I admitted my intentions.

"You see, I am thinking about buying a gun and I need to know the laws and my rights."

"You're thinking of buying a gun?" Barbara asked.

I thought I detected disapproval in her voice.

"I am—for protection," I replied.

"Have you ever owned a gun before?" Barbara asked.

I shook my head.

Barbara spoke carefully, as if she was throttling her response. "Well, if you are considering gun ownership, maybe you should investigate first. Maybe ask a criminal defense lawyer about the rules of self-defense."

"Yeah, you're right. I want to understand the boundaries of the law. It's kind of amazing how little I know about the criminal world, the guns, the laws, the prison sentences. I really don't even understand the difference between first and second-degree murder, even with all these cop shows on TV. I guess it's because my writing has never crossed into those areas and my family has never owned guns. Speaking of which, Chris is really opposed to our buying one. That's why I need to gather some facts first, or I'll never convince him. You have a good point. I should ask a lawyer."

"Laura, I'd like to switch gears if that is okay with you?"

"Sure."

"How are you sleeping now? Are the nightmares still occurring?"

"Yes, but not every night. Maybe the relaxation CD is helping. Is there anything else we can try?"

"We have a couple of other options. There is hypnosis or EMDR."

"I'm not into hypnosis, but what's EMDR?" I asked.

"It stands for Eye Movement, Desensitization, and Reprocessing. EMDR was discovered by a woman named Francine Shapiro in the late 80's. It seems to work by helping the mind process disturbances that are blocked or trapped in the nervous system. More therapists are being trained in this technique and it's proving to be quite effective."

"I don't think I can be hypnotized anyway," I said.

"Why not?"

"Well, Chris and I were in Vegas a few years ago for one of his work conferences. They had a hypnotist act and, as my bad luck would have it, he picked me to come on stage to be part of the show. There were ten of us, and he sent three of us back to our seats. I was one of the three."

"Did you want to be hypnotized?"

"Lord, no! We were in front of all of Chris' work colleagues. There was no way I wanted to make a fool of myself and embarrass him."

"Well, that explains it," said Barbara. "You can't be hypnotized against your will. I'm surprised the fellow picked you. They normally want volunteers who are already open to the idea."

"He had a few volunteers, but not enough to fill all the seats. I guess no one else wanted to look like a fool either."

Barbara laughed.

"How does EMDR work? If it's effective, I'd like to try it," I asked.

Barbara explained, "Well, the mind is naturally configured to process information. A trauma, however, can disrupt the normal processing patterns. Sometimes trauma becomes blocked in the central nervous system in the same form in which it was initially experienced. Think of it like having the memory stuck on an island in your mind with no bridges to access it. Because the trauma is trapped, it cannot be associated with other more adaptive, positive information, so it cannot be processed. EMDR is believed to assist in both accessing and processing that isolated information. The actual practice, however, is further advanced than the clinical science, so no one really knows for sure why it works."

"I think I understand, but what will we actually be doing during the session?"

"Basically, I will have you concentrate on an image that represents the disturbing event. That image is called the target. I'll ask you to follow my fingers as I sway them back and forth about a foot away from your face. At that point, your mind should take over and you'll just go with the flow of what you experience. The image will probably change or shift as your mind starts to link it with other experiences, which indicates that you are unlocking the trapped, disturbing memory."

"That's bizarre. Why would moving my eyes have an effect on my mind?"

"That's a good question. There are a few theories out there, though the one I believe has to do with REM or rapid eye movement sleep. During REM sleep, the mind processes information. We know that because, when subjects are awakened from REM sleep, they can usually recount a dream they are having.

"Also during REM sleep, the eyes are moving back and forth. We don't know why, but it appears that the eye movement and the processing of information are somehow connected. EMDR uses the eye movements to assist in processing information, but the difference is that you are awake—I know that's a lot to take in."

"It is, but it's fascinating. I want to try it. I need these nightmares to go away for good, and I'm sure Chris wouldn't mind either."

"How is he dealing with the attack?" asked Barbara.

I thought of my husband. "He's been an angel. He has been so understanding and patient. I'm sure he feels guilty about having been out of town that night, too."

"I see. Family members can experience a significant response, especially guilt, like you said, for not having protected their loved one. They are, however, much more likely to deal with the pain in isolation. I'd be happy to talk to your husband if you think that would help."

I knew Chris had no problem making the appointment for me, but asking him to come was another story.

"Maybe," I replied. "I don't see him coming here unless I really begged him or told him it was necessary for me to heal."

"It may be beneficial for him to understand more of your healing process, especially if we do EMDR treatment. But it's your choice of course."

"Maybe later, although I tell him about our sessions and he always listens. But I'm not sure I'd get him here personally."

Barbara didn't press further.

With the remaining 20 minutes we had left, Barbara showed me more relaxation techniques. Before leaving, I booked a two-hour appointment for my next session where we would try the EMDR.

FROM THE DESK OF
BARBARA COLE

July 18, Visit 3
Laura Holland

Hyper-arousal, self-protection instincts revved up in the fight or flight mode
Manifests in need to check the house each time she enters
  • Not yet at the level of impairing basic functioning,
  continue to monitor

Fear attacker will return, to finish the job, he verbally threatened her
before retreating "You win for now, but don't you forget sweet Sam"
  • He told her his name, real name?

Considering buying a gun, husband (Chris) objects
Motive for gun? - Self-defense, does not appear to be suicidal/homicidal
  • Ask Thomas about legal ramifications

Nightmares subsided but not over
  • EMDR candidate
  • Tell Alisa to schedule 2 hr session next time

Husband (Chris) feeling guilty for not protecting her, likely suffering
  • Joint session, he might resist, continue to probe on
  his condition

                              —BAC

Barbara Cole

Barbara finished her notes on Laura and to quell her curiosity, did some research on gun ownership and self-defense. She waited until about 7:30 p.m. to leave the office—about the time when Thomas would be leaving the building as well.

Thomas S. Bennett was a criminal defense attorney who had opened his own practice two years ago on the eighth floor of the Georgia Building. Before that, he had spent three years as an assistant district attorney for Fulton County, so he had the advantage of understanding the prosecutor's angle in most criminal cases. He had graduated from Morehouse College with a degree in political science and then earned a scholarship for law school at Duke University. After graduating, he decided to return to his hometown of Atlanta and passed the Georgia State Bar soon after his arrival.

Thomas and Barbara had often seen one another in the elevator at the end of a long day. They both left work late as neither one had anyone waiting for them at home. They had begun to talk and over time grew to be friendly.

She dialed his phone, "Are you still working?"

"I'm done. Meet you in the lobby?" he replied.

The elevator opened and Barbara saw her lawyer friend standing under one of the huge chandeliers. As usual, he was dressed impeccably. He could have been mistaken for a model in his shiny gray Tom Ford suit and coordinated purple and gray tie. His white teeth contrasted his chocolate brown skin and eyes.

Though Barbara rarely took anything outside the boundaries of her office, her internet search on self-defense left more questions than answers.

"Thomas, I have a legal question for you, if you don't mind?" she asked, as they walked across the lobby. Barbara had never asked for legal counsel before.

"Yes?" he asked.

"Suppose a man breaks into a woman's house and unsuccessfully tries to rape her. What would happen if she shot him as he left her home?"

"Where's this coming from?" Thomas asked. His voice remained calm but his face showed concern.

"Suppose I had a colleague who had a patient who needed to know."

"Barbara, does your colleague have knowledge of a shooting? Even with patient confidentiality, that would have to be reported."

"No, no. No one was actually shot," she reassured him. "The patient was wishfully thinking, mental revenge if you will, but probably doesn't understand the trouble she'd be in if she had actually shot the guy."

"Do you mean what would legally happen to her?" he clarified.

"Yes."

"It depends. You're asking what if she killed the guy?"

"Suppose she did."

"Did she kill him in her house?"

Barbara remembered that Laura had envisioned shooting from her porch as he fled down the street. "No, I guess it would have been outside."

Thomas held the front door open and they walked toward the parking deck. The guard waved as they left.

Thomas continued, "If the shooting had been in the house, it's a pretty clear case of self-defense. End of story."

"But since it was outside the house?" Barbara prompted.

"Yeah, that makes it more complicated. Without knowing the specifics, it's hard to say. I'd have to know more. For example, how far was he from the house? Where was he shot? Did he have a weapon or a history of prior assaults? Did they know each other? More importantly, what exactly do you mean by an unsuccessful rape? Did he physically harm her or just scare her? You see, all of this information would be provided to the grand jury when they assess the state's case. Then, they would make a ruling on whether the case had prosecutive merit."

"You mean they may not prosecute her?"

"Well, maybe, maybe not. If I was the DA, I'd be thinking about how the jury would react. I'd evaluate what would be the likelihood of conviction. The jury may say, 'I would have shot the S.O.B., too'. In that case, as the DA, I wouldn't want to try the case with the feeling that the jury wouldn't convict. On the other hand, I'm fairly sure the DA couldn't let a murder go uncharged."

"But it's the grand jury that makes the call?"

"Yes, if it's a murder case. They may say she was justified and let it go. They may say she should be charged and let a jury sort it out. It could go either way."

"If they did prosecute her, what would the charge be?" asked Barbara.

"She would probably be indicted with murder and voluntary manslaughter."

"Both?"

"Probably," he assured.

"Why both?"

"Well the DA likes to throw everything applicable and see what sticks. So, if he couldn't get murder, then he could try for manslaughter. It's hard to say without really knowing the details of the specific case."

By then, they had reached Barbara's tan Volvo. She unlocked the doors with her remote and Thomas opened the driver's door for her.

"Thanks. This was helpful," she said.

"I'll send you my bill," he said with a big smile.

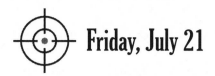 # Friday, July 21

I went the remainder of the week with fewer nightmares, but now I was waking up every night around 4 a.m. and couldn't go back to sleep. It was as if my body clock knew the time I needed to be awake to protect myself.

Though I was tired, I didn't want to disappoint Chris by canceling our Friday night dinner date. He usually picked out a trendy restaurant in Buckhead or Virginia Highlands, but tonight he wanted to go to Fat Matt's Rib Shack—we had loved going there during college. Just down the road were the risqué nightclubs of The Gold Club and Tattletales. In their day, these clubs were hotspots for frat boys with dollar bills. I had been a good sport letting Chris' best man and college roommate, Mark, take him and the other groomsmen there for the bachelor party—as long as it wasn't the night before the wedding.

I remember pleading with Mark, "I just want him to look rested in the pictures." So, to appease me, Mark took Chris out a good week before the wedding. The 8x10 photo that Chris kept on his desk at work showed me in my white lace gown with my handsome, rested groom in his flashy tuxedo.

Chris brought the only remaining photo of our wedding home and placed it on the left side of the mantle. On the right side was a wedding picture of my sister, Lucy, and my brother-in-law, Ben, taken two years earlier. A large burgundy vase with white silk lilacs, a wedding gift from Ben and Lucy, was placed in the middle.

I glanced at the photo and then the alarm before heading to our bedroom. It was an off weekend for golf with Kevin and Vicki and I relished the thought of sleeping in on Saturday.

"No nightmares, just a pleasant night's sleep," I said aloud.

Chris asked, "Do you want to try a sleeping pill?"

"You have sleeping pills?"

"Yeah, I can't sleep with so much light so I bought some. They help."

"I'm sorry," I said. "How about we crack the bathroom door? It would be good for me to try sleeping in the dark again."

"You sure?" I could hear the hesitation in his voice.

"I'm sure," I replied. "Let me try one of your pills."

Chris went to the bathroom and returned with a white oblong pill and a glass of water.

"Where's the bottle?" I asked. "I want to see how potent they are."

"This is the last one. I threw the bottle away. They're normal potency. I don't wake up groggy or anything."

I popped the pill in my mouth and threw back my head to swallow it whole.

Chris cracked the bathroom door halfway and made sure I was comfortable with the reduced lighting. I kissed him goodnight and rested my head on the pillow. I could slowly feel the medicine taking affect. It was as if the drug wanted to turn off my brain against my will. The more I fought it, the more I was thrust into a lightheaded drowsiness. I didn't like it, but it was in my system now.

SQUEAK...

There was the faint sound of the bedroom door hinges moving. I looked toward the sound. Did I really hear something? My head felt like I had cotton balls in it. I heard a shuffle. Someone was there. I looked toward the door, where I had heard the sound.

His amorphous silhouette was standing there.

I gasped quietly.

It's happening.

He hadn't made his move yet. Could he tell I was awake or was he taking pleasure first in watching me sleep, savoring the moment when he would pounce?

I reached over to Chris to wake him. Chris would be able to fight him off.

I felt for my husband in the bed, but the only thing my palm touched was the mattress. I reached further over in the king-size bed to find him. Unlike that night, my husband was home with me this time. He would protect me. But, as my hands scrambled across the bed, I felt nothing.

Chris was gone!

I looked back at the figure in the doorway. He was moving. This was not a dream. He had done something awful to Chris and now was coming back for me!

I screamed in terror, just like that first night. My heart was pounding in my throat. I instinctively retracted to the far side of the bed.

What weapons did I have? What means did I have to protect myself? I screamed even louder, remembering how my voice had unnerved him before.

The figure raced toward me at full speed, leaping on the bed landing on his knees. His body was directly across from me and he firmly grabbed both of my shoulders and pulled me toward him. I slammed my palms into his chest, using all of my strength. To my surprise, he staggered backwards off the bed.

I didn't have the strength for another fight, especially if he had already killed Chris.

"Laura, it's me. It's just me!"

All of the sudden, the lights flicked on, nearly blinding me with the brightness. As I squinted, I saw the familiar face of my husband, though I had never seen him so panicked before. The adrenaline rush pierced the grogginess I had felt from the sleeping pills.

"I'm sorry!" he shouted, half out of breath. "I didn't mean to scare you. Man, you scared the hell out of me!"

I replied, "I thought you were him! You looked just like him standing in the door like that."

"I didn't mean to scare you. The ribs made me thirsty. I just went to the kitchen to get some tea."

Chris walked over to the bed and pulled me into his lap. He hugged me tightly—my heart was still beating furiously. He brushed the hair off of my face and looked into my eyes.

"This is what it was like for you? God, I'm sorry. I'm so sorry I wasn't here to protect you. If I'd only been home, you wouldn't be going through any of this."

I hugged my husband tightly.

"It's not your fault," I sighed. "Don't blame yourself."

"But I do."

"Barbara said sometimes we blame ourselves when we shouldn't. We try to find something that we could have done differently so we can make sure it won't happen again."

I paused and then continued, "You know, she mentioned that you might want to talk to her?"

"You think I should visit your psychiatrist?"

"Psychologist."

"Whatever."

"Well, she said that you may be going through some difficult times, too. You just said you felt guilty for not being here to protect me, and every time you go on a trip, Troy is always over here. You wouldn't have something to do with that now would you? You wouldn't be overcompensating for your guilt, would you?"

"Hey, don't play therapist with me. Just because I ask Troy to keep an eye on you doesn't mean I need to talk to her."

Here was the double standard I already knew to expect. "So it's okay for me to see a therapist, but not for you?"

Chris paused and then replied. "Laura, honey, I have a million things to do at work. If I really thought I needed to see her, I would go, but right now it's just not on my list of priorities."

"I'm not a priority? You're the one who asked me to see her. And now, here I am going for you and you won't go for me?"

He sighed.

I pouted.

"Alright," he said. "I'll think about it."

 **Tuesday, July 25**

"4 @ Dr Cole dont 4get"

I texted Chris to remind him of our joint appointment with Barbara.

I arrived at the Georgia Building early, so I bought a cup of tea at the coffee shop and sat at one of the small, wooden tables to wait for my reluctant husband.

As I read the newspaper, something felt wrong. Someone was watching me. I abruptly looked up and scanned the lobby. It wasn't very crowded. A few people were entering and exiting the building, but I would be able to see if anyone was watching me. I noticed the guard in a blue uniform sitting behind his desk by the front door. He was black, but he was short and heavy. There was no way *he* could have shrunk a few inches and put on 50 pounds. I looked back to my paper, but would glance up nervously every once in a while. There was definitely someone watching me. I could feel it.

You're being hyper vigilant. Barbara said that was a symptom of PTSD. There is obviously no one here.

I refocused on my paper determined not to look up until I had read the entire article. Just then, I felt a presence in front of me.

It was the guard. He was standing too close, but his demeanor certainly wasn't threatening.

"Hi," he said. "I couldn't help but notice you looking around. Is there something I can help you with?"

I tried to brush him off. "Oh, I'm fine. I'm just waiting for my husband for an appointment."

"Uh huh," he muttered. "What's he look like? I'll keep an eye out for him."

I reluctantly obliged. "He's six-foot-two with brown hair."

"And his name?" he asked.

Not hiding my annoyance, I replied, "His name is Chris."

"Last name?"

"Holland," I snapped.

"Okay, I'm on it, Mrs. Holland."

He smiled with such enthusiasm that my annoyance dissipated. This was probably the only excitement he would have all day, guarding this mundane office building. It was unkind to be short with him.

Noticing the "M. Howard" on his gold nametag, I said, "I appreciate the help, Mr. Howard."

"Oh, call me Mike."

"Okay. Thanks, Mike. I'm Laura." I extended my arm to shake his hand.

"*Little House on the Prairie* had a windmill," he said.

"Excuse me?" I asked.

"It's how I remember names. Laura Ingalls was on *Little House on the Prairie* and windmills are in Holland. Now, I'll remember your name."

He was an endearing little guy, obviously quirky, but likeable. Just then, Chris walked up. We looked at him at the same time.

"I bet this is your guy," Mike said proudly, as if he had solved a great mystery.

I just smiled and nodded. Poor Mike's excitement had ended so quickly. I said goodbye and directed Chris to the elevator, which we took to the 10th floor. I checked in with Alisa, and we waited just a few minutes before Barbara opened her door and I introduced Chris.

We sat on the couch together and I could tell he was regretting giving in to me. Though he was cordial to her, he was perturbed.

Barbara opened the session by casually chatting with Chris—asking him about his background and how we met.

"May I call you Chris?" she asked.

"Sure," he replied.

"Chris, thank you for coming here today. I wanted you to know that I always invite the spouse or partner of my client to have at least an introductory meeting. We don't have to take the full hour. It's really up to you how much time you'd like to spend. I often find that when one person in a couple goes to therapy, it can affect the dynamics of the relationship. Therefore, I wanted to give you a chance to understand my work with Laura and to see if you have any questions or concerns."

"Okay," he replied.

"My goal is to support Laura, as well as her relationship with you. So after this session, if you want to come back at some point, you are more than welcome. You wouldn't be my patient, of course, but it would be in the context of supporting her."

Chris just nodded. I knew this visit was a one-time deal.

"Chris, do you have any questions for me?" Barbara asked.

My husband looked at me, somewhat caught off guard. It was one of the few times I had ever seen him ill-prepared. As if by instinct, he regained himself and quickly took control.

"Well, I guess the obvious one. When will she be better?"

"I don't mean to avoid your question," said Barbara, "but what to you is better for her?"

"Well, she used to be so carefree. It's like part of her innocence has been taken away. She's more timid. I mean she's still *my* Laura, but she's not quite herself."

Chris turned toward me and scanned my face, trying to judge my reaction.

"Chris, there's not really a time table for healing, but Laura is doing exceptionally well. The most horrific feeling in the world is to have your life threatened and to feel powerless. Because she was able to fight back, she kept some of her sense of power. But it takes time and every person is different in how he or she deals with trauma. She's reading about rape, which is helpful and you both are making changes to your life, like the alarm system, that make her feel more secure."

Chris didn't reply.

Barbara asked, "Chris, do you blame yourself for her attack?"

After a pause he said, "Well sure I do. If I had been home, it would have been me who fought him off, not her."

"But don't you think she would still be frightened? The fears she has now may have still arisen, even if you had been there."

"Maybe so, but I don't think she would be as bad off. And if I had been there, he wouldn't have gotten away."

Chris clenched his fists as he spoke.

"What would you have done?" Barbara asked.

"Who knows, but I'd like to get my hands on him now."

He hesitated.

"But, since we don't know who he is, there's really not much I can do. Sometimes, I look out the window late at night when Laura's asleep to see if anyone is out there lurking around. I'm hoping he would be crazy enough to come back so I could take care of him."

I looked at Chris with surprise—I had no idea he was doing this.

Barbara counseled, "Just remember, Laura is counting on you for support now. You need to keep yourself available for her, which means avoiding any incidents that would give her another crisis to overcome. If you were hurt or in jail, you wouldn't be much help to her."

"I know. It's just a fantasy. I don't think he's coming back."

"Do you treat her differently now?" asked Barbara.

Chris thought for a moment. "I don't know. I guess I take better care of her. I do more to make sure she is safe."

"Could you give me an example?"

"Just the normal things any guy would do. I watch out for her."

I chimed in, "What aren't you saying?"

"Nothing," he deflected.

"Tell me," I insisted.

He looked at Barbara instead of me when he replied.

"Well, I've cancelled a few trips so I can be home. And I've asked our neighbor to watch out for her if I'm not there, that's all."

I knew he was sending over Troy, but I didn't know he was avoiding his work trips to be home. That couldn't continue.

I interjected, "Chris, you can't keep cancelling your trips for me. That's going to affect your job."

"It's alright. I've got it under control," he replied, almost dismissively. "I don't want you waking up scared and by yourself."

"Well, I don't want you getting fired because you've stopped traveling. When is your next trip? I want you to promise me that you'll go."

Chris just looked at me in silence.

"Well, when is it?" I asked again, "When?"

"There's a show in Tampa next week, but I've decided not to go."

"Why not? You don't have to stay home and babysit me. If you need to go, I want you to go."

"Alright. I'll look into it," he said.

I knew what that meant.

Chris turned to Barbara trying to change the subject. "There is an area where we could use your help. It's been …." Chris quickly did the math in his head. The attack was on June 7. Today was July 25. "…a month and a half and she still isn't sleeping well."

"Yes, Laura and I talked about that during our last visit. We are going to try a technique next time that may help release some of her pent up emotions. It's good that you are here today, Chris, because I wanted to tell you about it. Because this technique, called EMDR, helps Laura process the memories of that night, she may be more disturbed than usual for the next few weeks. I wanted you both to know that it's completely normal and a sign that she is healing. If this treatment is successful, the nightmares will go away. Laura, that reminds me, we should schedule two hours for next time."

I nodded.

Barbara turned back to Chris. "What else is on your mind today?"

"Well, what are the odds of this guy getting caught? I mean, she fought him off and I'm sure he was stronger. Do you think this was his first attempt and when it didn't go as planned, he aborted or do you think he's a serial rapist?"

"Chris, what do you know about the profile of a rapist?"

"Not much. I guess he rapes out of anger at women."

"That's true in part, but it is also to gain a sense of power and worth. Through the destruction of a woman's feelings of personal power and self-worth, he hopes to take from her what he does not already feel in himself. It is not an act of sexual gratification, but an angry expression of the rapist's desire to dominate someone else.

"Rapists are likely to be angry men unable to deal with their emotions effectively. They are often ineffectual in other relationships as well. A small percentage of them could be considered mentally ill or criminally insane, but most of them appear to be basically normal people. You cannot pick them out in a crowd. However, no matter how they appear, they are not normal, healthy men or they would not be raping women."

"Anyone who is prowling around at 4 a.m. certainly isn't normal in my book," he sneered.

Barbara continued, "As far as why he stopped the attack, or if this was his first attempt, we don't know. I'm sure Laura fought back more fiercely than he expected. You should be proud of her."

"I am," Chris said, smiling at me. "But I already was." He gave me a quick wink and squeezed my hand.

"Are there any other questions or concerns you have?" Barbara asked.

Chris didn't have any other topics, so he thanked her and we wrapped up the session early.

FROM THE DESK OF
BARBARA COLE

July 25, Visit 4
Laura Holland joint visit with Husband (Chris Holland)

Background
Met in college, married 8 years
Bachelors/Masters in Electrical Engineering from Georgia Tech
31 yrs old, oldest of 3 boys
Region Sales Mgr, Medical equipment

Him
Protective body language, arm around her, touching her
Feels guilt - should have been there, didn't have home alarm
Wants revenge
Changing his patterns - not traveling, sending over the neighbor (Trey)

—BAC

August

 # Wednesday, August 2 afternoon

After several attempts, I was finally able to get an afternoon appointment with *the* police chief. I figured he was dodging calls from a journalist and half expected him to cancel on me.

I drove to Tucker, the location of police headquarters and was surprised to see a modern glass building. I had expected something more dilapidated. After passing through security, I walked up to the front reception.

"I'm Laura Holland. I'm here to see Captain Mickey Renante. He's expecting me."

The woman behind the desk called for Captain Renante. A few minutes later, a young sergeant arrived to escort me to the captain's office. The security was tight, with key card access required for the elevator ride. When the doors opened on the fourth floor, we walked down the hall and the sergeant pointed to an office surrounded by glass walls.

A husky Asian man leaned back in his chair, talking on his cell phone. He held an unlit cigar in his right hand and gnawed at it while bellowing orders into the phone. Occasionally, he waved his hand into the air as if he needed it to help articulate his directives. He looked like a miniature tyrant—so animated and bullish. I waited for him to finish his call and then knocked firmly on the glass.

"Hello Captain Renante. I'm Laura Holland, the journalist. We spoke on the phone last week."

"Yeah, come on in. Have a seat," he said, as he pointed to a leather chair on wheels in front of his desk. His strong southern accent clashed with his obvious Asian features and Hispanic last name. I wondered if he was Filipino. He had dark circles around his eyes making him look overworked and tired. His jet-black hair was receding at the temples and his thick neck looked constricted by his tight collar and outdated tie.

"Thanks for agreeing to speak with me," I said. "I'm doing some research for a self-defense story centering on women. I'd specifically like to take the angle of whether a woman should or should not own a gun. I'd like your perspective, if you don't mind."

Captain Renante began to speak in a harsh, matter-of-fact tone, as if he had delivered this speech many times before.

"Miss Holland, let me tell you some facts. There are about a thousand officers on the force for the seven hundred thousand civilians in DeKalb County alone. Lack of funds has prohibited me from hiring new policemen. Attrition, resignations, and such have reduced our ranks over the past few years by eight percent. There is no humanly way possible for my officers to be there all of the time to protect every person. I know this is not what you or the general public likes to hear, but it's true.

"Therefore, I recommend that every responsible citizen, male or female, own a gun for protection. You see, I'm not one of those self-righteous, pompous officers who thinks that only the police can handle guns. We're just human beings like you and your readers. The difference is that we appreciate the responsibility of owning a gun and take proper care and training. If every citizen would do the same, there would be a lot less crime on the streets."

"Why do you say that?"

"Miss Holland, you might say I believe in werewolves. I believe in them because I've seen them. We just caught a rapist based on the DNA he left when he bit his victim's nipple off. I've seen the face of the enemy and I know that criminals are deterred by only two things—big, vicious dogs and armed citizens who are prepared to kill them if they don't cease and desist."

My face must have revealed my disgust.

"I'm sorry ma'am to give you such a graphic example, but it's better for you and your readers to learn the truth here and now, in time to protect yourself, than for you to find out the hard way."

Little did the captain know that I had already found out the hard way.

"How long will that monster be behind bars?" I asked.

The captain grimaced. "He had some fancy legal connections. He's out on bail, but we're watching him."

How could this violent rapist be on the loose? All the more reason to own a gun.

"What else would you like to know?" he asked.

"Do you think that women are more reluctant to own guns than men?"

"No offense to you, sweetheart, but the view of most women toward self-defense is pathetic. They read those magazines providing bullshit suggestions for self-protection, none of which give the best advice—to own a gun."

This was indeed a different kind of interview. He had no qualms about telling me a gruesome story but I appreciated his candor.

"Can you give me some examples of what those stories recommend?" I asked.

"Sure. They tell you that all manner of worthless household items will save you from a vicious attack by a person much bigger and stronger than you."

He was still being vague. I pressed, "So, can you give me some specific examples of these household items that you don't endorse?"

"Take a whistle, for example. Women are told to keep a whistle handy and blow it if they are in danger. When most people hear a police whistle, they assume the police are already there and don't bother to assist."

"What about screaming?"

"You think that would deter him? As soon as you open your mouth, a hardened mugger or rapist will slash your throat."

I thought about the knife that *he* had brought into my bedroom. Why hadn't he used it on me? He could have so easily. And when he does come back, he will be better prepared to silence my screams.

I looked up at Captain Renante. He just stared at me, waiting for my next question. I couldn't think of one.

He continued, "Those magazines tell you to do the old standby of kicking him in the balls. Won't work. If your assailant knows anything about attacking a woman, he is waiting for you to do just that. The moment you try, he'll grab your foot and flip you on your back."

I looked at the captain in disbelief. It was if he had a play by play of my attack and was explaining, in hindsight, why my attempts at self-defense had failed.

"Then they say jab him in the eyes. This is a common move he'll expect. The minute he sees your hands in his face, he'll probably break your fingers."

I moved my iPad over my left hand to hide the bite marks. I knew all too well that this tactic didn't work. I thought of my upcoming AIDS test. My body shivered. I forced the thought out of my mind.

"What about Mace or tear gas?" My voice cracked slightly at the end of my question.

"The formulas in Mace or any supposedly incapacitating aerosol have been watered-down to the point that they are ineffective. Since the complaints about suspects' eye damage, all the formulas sold to civilians have been substantially weakened. And any smart criminal will grab the canister and use it on you."

I instinctively held my breath.

"Here at the department, we issue Curb 60, the most potent one. I got sprayed with it once by accident. I held my breath and immediately went to the can to wash it off. My skin felt like it was burning and my eyes stung, but it wasn't incapacitating. Forget Mace. Sprayed into your face, and you won't be able to breathe enough to scream or resist."

"So, you are saying the only way to protect yourself is to buy a gun?" I asked.

"Yeah, that's what I'm saying, but you have to learn how to handle it, or it could be taken and used on you, just like the Mace."

"But what about all the statistics that say you are more likely to accidently shoot someone you know, like your spouse?"

"Yeah, yeah. They say you'll shoot yourself instead of the attacker. You'll shoot your husband. Your kids will get hold of the gun and accidentally shoot themselves. It's bullshit. Complete bullshit. If you buy a gun, store it properly and get the right training. It's the only way to be safe, especially for a woman."

The sergeant who had greeted me poked his head in the door. "Excuse me, sir, it's urgent. Line two."

Ignoring me, the captain picked up the receiver of his office phone, punched line two, and listened intently. I hadn't expected to make it through the interview uninterrupted, but thought he could at least say excuse me.

He bellowed into the receiver, "Well, if they didn't see a getaway vehicle, lock down the area. How far can the guy get on foot for Christ's sake! He probably lives close by. Bring over patrol from Decatur if you have to."

He slammed down the phone and started gnawing on his unlit cigar.

I thought of my own case. I hadn't thought about it before, but I hadn't seen him run to a car. He ran down the street and disappeared. Did he have a car hidden further away or did he live close enough to retreat on foot? But how would someone like him be able to afford a place in my neighborhood?

I couldn't help but ask, "Do most criminals live close to the crime scene?"

"They do. They don't have the good sense the Lord gave them not to shit where they eat. And this idiot was dealing in broad daylight. He can't have run too far, though. We'll get 'em. Look, I need to go."

"Sure. Just one last question if I may? If you are endorsing women to own guns, how do they know what kind to buy and where to get training? Do you offer classes here?"

"Not for civilians. Too much liability. Most shooting ranges should have some type of instruction or can at least tell you where to look. I have a buddy who is a retired police sergeant who works part-time at Sandy Springs Gun Club & Range. He mostly trains security guards, but he'll take on beginners."

"Could I have his contact information?" I asked.

The captain was getting restless. My one question was turning into more. He pulled open his desk drawer and filed through a stack of business cards, pulling out a tattered one which he tossed at me.

"You can take his number, but leave the card. Was nice chatting with you, ma'am."

With that, the captain got up and walked out of his office, leaving me alone.

"I guess the interview is over," I said out loud but of course no one was there to hear me.

I looked at the card and quickly entered the information into my iPhone.

SECURITY GUARD INSTRUCTION • PERSONALIZED PISTOL INSTRUCTION

John Stires

404-555-4815
john.stires@aol.com

GA Certified Security Guard
NRA Certified Pistol Instructor
Master Pistol Shooter

I stood up in the empty office and let myself out. The captain hadn't even asked when or where my article would be published.

I had also planned to ask him for a reference for a criminal defense lawyer, but he left too abruptly. No matter; I had another idea.

 # Wednesday, August 2 evening

I remembered seeing a lawyer's name who practiced criminal law on Barbara's floor at the Georgia Building. I couldn't remember his name so tried to look him up on my phone, but couldn't find anything. I had time before I was meeting Chris downtown for dinner so I drove over to the building. I entered the lobby. It looked haunting in the evening with no natural light. I said an obligatory hello to Mike the guard. His face lit up like we were old friends. I walked over to the building directory, which was to the right of the coffee shop and started scanning the list.

"Hello, Mrs. Holland."

The voice out of nowhere startled me. I looked up to see Mike.

"You're here later than usual today," he said.

"Yes. I am." I didn't elaborate and looked back at the directory.

"Are you looking for someone in particular?" he asked eagerly.

Why not? He seems to know everyone's business.

I replied, "I'm looking for a lawyer. A criminal defense lawyer for some research I'm doing."

"Oh, that's easy." He started to rattle off names. "There's HH&M, Heying, Hillewaert and Mougin on the third floor. They seem to have a lot of clients. Then, there's a group of independent lawyers on the eighth floor. I think Andy Hayes and Thomas Bennett do defense work. You could try the Levines, a father and son team, but I think they do more injury stuff."

After naming the first few people, Mike started to scan the directory himself to find others.

The elevator doors opened on the other side of the lobby and Barbara walked out, chatting casually with a young black man. I slid behind Mike. It wasn't that I had anything to hide, but it would have been awkward running into Barbara in the lobby.

Mike pointed toward them as they walked out the front doors. "That's Mr. Bennett right there, speak of the devil."

"Oh. Who was he talking to?" I asked innocently, wondering what Mike would have to say about Barbara.

"That's Dr. Cole, a psychologist. They're friends, usually the last two to leave the building. I'd pick him. He must work hard 'cause he's always here late."

Jackpot!

 Friday, August 4

On Friday afternoon, I entered a large reception area on the eighth floor of the Georgia Building. Though Thomas Bennett wasn't the lawyer I had originally targeted, knowing that he was friends with Barbara was a stronger endorsement.

I walked up to the receptionist, a lady in her fifties with short brown, bobbed hair. She was impeccably dressed with a colorful peacock pendant on her lapel. Behind the reception area, there were large, dark wooden shelves stacked with law books. It reminded me of a library, but with modern furniture and real plants. It also lacked the stale smell of old books and hushed silence.

"Hi. I'm Laura Holland. I'm here for a 2:30 appointment with Thomas Bennett."

"Yes, Ms. Holland. Let me tell him you're here."

The receptionist picked up the phone and pressed one of the buttons. "This way, please. Could I offer you some coffee?"

"No thanks."

The receptionist tapped gently on the dark wooden door and a voice said to come in. She opened the door and respectfully said, "Mr. Bennett, this is Laura Holland for your appointment. I'll hold your calls."

I looked at the young lawyer sitting slightly reclined in his chair. I knew he was African American from seeing him with Barbara from a distance, but I hadn't realized how I would feel being up close.

As he rose to his feet, I felt like I was shrinking in size.

He was at least six feet tall with a strong, athletic build. His dark brown eyes were so piercing they looked almost black. He looked like *him*. I meekly shook his hand and listened intently to his voice when he introduced himself.

It was the same voice. My mouth went dry. My heart started beating uncontrollably.

"Please, have a seat," he said.

I tried desperately to reason with myself.

This is the first black man that looks like him that you've had to speak with since that night. It is natural that he will make you uncomfortable. There is no way this could be him. This is a young lawyer and, more importantly, a friend of Barbara's. There are many black guys who fit his description. You are being ridiculous.

As I sat down in a large leather chair with an oak desk separating us, I couldn't stand the thought of being alone with him. I needed some-one else in the room.

"You know, your receptionist offered me some coffee. I've changed my mind. I think I'd like some."

"Sure." He pushed the intercom, "Joanne, could you bring us two cups of coffee. How do you take yours?"

"Just cream," I lied. I didn't even drink coffee.

"Ms. Holland will have hers with cream." Joanne took less than a minute to deliver the mugs while he commented on the hot August weather we were having.

I knew that he sensed my nervousness, but hoped he attributed it to the fact that something stressful in my life had made me seek a lawyer.

Joanne delivered the coffee. I wanted to beg, "Stay in here. Stay with us. Don't leave me here alone with him." But she was gone as quickly as she had come and we were alone again.

"So, Ms. Holland, how can I be of assistance?" he asked.

I spoke with a slight quiver. I would see if he recognized my story.

"I'm here because I need clarification on a question that I have, one involving shooting a fleeing criminal." I stopped. I needed to catch my breath and calm my voice. I could feel that I was on the verge of a panic attack.

"Go on," he said.

I concentrated on my heartbeat, mentally forcing it to slow down. I managed another sentence. "If a guy broke into my house and attacked me, could I legally shoot him as he ran off?"

Mr. Bennett squinted and cocked his head slightly, never taking his intense stare off of me. He spoke slowly.

"You know, I had that exact same question asked of me not long ago by a colleague who is a therapist. She was asking on behalf of a patient. Isn't that a strange coincidence?"

Oh, no.

Instead of answering my question, he was directly confronting my relationship with Barbara. I had never expected Barbara to ask him about my situation, which allowed him to make the link.

To my surprise, I responded matter-of-factly, controlling my voice much more than before.

"Yes, very strange since I would assume a therapist wouldn't break a patient's confidence."

Thomas stared at me for a moment, and then spoke. "Ms. Holland, did you shoot someone?"

"No, I didn't shoot anyone."

"Then why are you here?" he asked.

"The rest of the story is real. Earlier this summer, I was attacked. I was in my bedroom asleep. I awoke to the sound of my bedroom door being forced open. This guy was standing there. He grabbed me. He tried to rape me. I was able to fight him off and finally, to my surprise, he ran out of the house."

I looked for signs of recognition of my story in his face. He didn't react.

I continued, "If I had owned a gun, I would have shot him. Instead, all I could do was run to the door after him and stand there helplessly on my porch as he escaped. Now, I'm wondering if I could have legally shot him as he fled. I would have considered it self-defense, but if the law says it wasn't, I want to understand why."

He grew agitated.

"With all due respect, Ms. Holland, why do you care? There's not a real case here," he said, not hiding his annoyance.

He paused. "Unless you are *planning* to shoot this guy who attacked you and I certainly can't give you legal advice on how to get away with a future murder."

"I'm not planning anything of the sort," I said defiantly. "I don't even know the guy and I never got a good look at him. I just wanted a legal opinion. I'd be happy to pay you for your time if you would just explain the legalities to me for my own education."

He seemed to settle down.

Because I offered to pay him or because I admitted that I couldn't identify my attacker?

"My fee is $200 per hour if you would like an hour's time today," he said.

"That's fine," I replied.

"Okay. Before we start, I need to reconfirm. You have not committed a crime, you are not asking for someone else who has committed a crime, and you are not planning a crime?"

"Of course not," I snapped.

Maybe this was a mistake. Maybe I should just leave.

Before I had time to say anything further, he started talking.

"Well, to start, I need to be clear in conveying that how the law would be interpreted depends on a number of circumstances and is different for every case. I know you are looking for a definitive answer here. Guilty or not guilty, self-defense or murder, but there's not a clear answer."

"But for my case, what do you think would have happened?"

"I'd have to know all the details."

"That's fine. What do you need to know?" I asked.

"Well, if you were really my client, I would start by having you write down everything that happened that night."

"I can do that. But for time's sake, can you just ask me what you need to know?"

He took a deep breath. His chest heaved up and down as he looked at me with those hawk-like eyes.

I wondered what he was thinking. I couldn't read him. Was he annoyed? No, it wasn't annoyance. It was something else—but what?

"Where would you have shot him?" he asked abruptly.

"In the back," I replied.

"Outside of your home?" he clarified.

"Yes, as he was running down the street."

"Describe where he was in relation to you."

"He would have been about thirty feet away. I was on the front porch of our house and he would have been in the middle of the street."

"How many shots would you have fired?" he asked.

"I don't know. I guess as many as it took to kill him."

"So you would have killed him, not just injured him?"

"Yes, let's say he was killed. Could I have claimed self-defense?"

He shook his head. He seemed agitated again.

"What you claim as your defense comes later. What you are charged with comes first, and I suspect you would have been charged with murder."

"Murder! But he attacked me," my voice rose.

"Yes, but he's the one who's dead in the street, shot in the back, possibly several times. Would you have called 911?"

"I suppose."

"So the police would have shown up and, at a first blush, they might have assumed you were an upset girlfriend who murdered her lover."

"Lover! I'm happily married. I didn't even know the guy."

"They won't know that. And your chance to prove it wouldn't come until much later."

"So when is it ever a clear case of self-defense?" I asked.

He leaned back in his leather chair and crossed his right foot over his left knee, revealing a well-shined black wing-tip.

"Self-defense in the form of deadly force can only be used as long as you reasonably feared pending death or great bodily harm. It would not be permissible for you to respond with deadly force if that specific fear no longer existed."

He continued, "From what you have said, you pursued him outside of your home. In that case, you would not be responding to the initial confrontation, but creating a new one. Even worse, you would now be considered the aggressor, not him."

"That's absurd," I replied. "Everything had happened so quickly. How could anyone have time to think through such distinctions during a panic situation?"

"There's more," he added. "Because you pursued him, he would have legally possessed the privilege of self-defense. He could have turned around and killed you and possibly gotten away with it. The way the law could be interpreted is that he was trying to avoid the confrontation and you were the one escalating the fight. You see, the past incident does not give you the right to deadly force in the immediate present, no matter how recently it occurred."

"But it wouldn't have been two separate events. He had just attacked me and I was fighting back."

He shook his head. "Shooting a criminal after the offense has been committed, no matter the time interval could be interpreted as avenging the crime. Your motivations might have been interpreted as a spiteful and unlawful execution."

"You mean after he attacked me, all I could do is let him get away?"

"You could have chased him until he was no longer a danger but you would have been wise not to shoot."

"So if I had shot this guy, you are saying the courts would have found me guilty?"

"Not necessarily. What I just told you was the strictest interpretation of the laws of self-defense. Whether you were actually prosecuted and found guilty as a result of this incident is a completely separate matter.

That would be up to the district attorney and possibly a jury. And, if you had a sympathetic jury, it is possible they would have interpreted your actions as self-defense. They may have said that since he broke into your home, you were completely justified. They may have put themselves in your shoes and decided that they would have done the same thing. Again, every case is different and every case depends on state laws, precedents, and the general mood of the courts."

"But there is a chance the jury's verdict could go either way?"

"Sure." He shrugged his shoulders.

I asked, "If I was tried and found guilty, what would my sentence be?"

"It depends. You could be indicted for several offenses including malice murder, felony murder and/or voluntary manslaughter."

"He caused this, not me. How could I ever be found guilty?"

"I think your views represent many of the misconceptions of the American public. Many people who own guns don't know their legal boundaries and many gun shops don't inform them of their rights or obligations. Sometimes I think we do a better job of licensing people to drive cars than to own guns."

"I'm still amazed. I would have shot him and I, the victim, could have been punished. If this had really happened, and I had hired you as my lawyer, what would you have done?"

"Picked a white female jury and prayed a lot," he said, sarcastically.

The muscles in my neck instantly stiffened.

"How did you know he was black?" I asked.

"I didn't."

"You said a *white* female jury."

"Oh, not necessarily because he was black, but because you are white. The best jury would be one who empathized with you, one who was most like you."

My neck relaxed a little. I could feel my journalistic instincts coming alive.

"Wouldn't that be interesting? To try a hypothetical case like this to see if I would be legally exonerated."

"I suppose, but there is quite a bit of information that we don't know. After all, you said he escaped."

"True, but it could be done. Better yet, it could be published. I am a journalist, you see. Obviously this is something that people need to know. I'm sure I'm not the only person ignorant of the laws, like you said. This could be a real eye opener—taking this hypothetical case through a trial and verdict."

My direction was set. I had found a new project and my desire to write had been rekindled. I would write this case, whether Thomas Bennett was interested or not. There was no denying it would be helpful to have him on board—he was knowledgeable, already knew my story, and was trusted by Barbara.

I was ready to offer a deal.

"I'd like to pursue this story to show what would happen to a woman if she shot an attacker outside of her home. I'd start with the attack and end with the court verdict. It could be really powerful and informative. Are you interested in helping? I'd write the story but would need your legal counsel."

I watched him as he thought over my offer. Maybe he already had a full plate and didn't want to be bothered.

"It sounds interesting, but I am a bit unclear on how much of my time you would need," he replied.

"Well, at first I would need you to walk me through the legal process. Just act as if this incident really happened and that I have hired you to defend me."

"If you were really my client, I'd require a $25,000 retainer," he said.

I stopped. My enthusiasm waned. I couldn't pay him. Journalists don't pay their sources, surely he knew that. Then again, why would he agree to help me? Any time spent with me would be time he wasn't billing real clients, and from the looks of his clothes, he cared about money.

"I could give you a by line?" I offered, already realizing that was a feeble enticement. I started thinking about who else I could ask to help for free. Did I have any uncollected favors?

To my surprise, he countered. "I'd have the right to review the article before publishing, especially if my name is mentioned, and I could only meet a few hours a week."

I nodded.

He continued, "You realize that the hypothetical nature will make this more difficult than a real case. You'll have to invent all of the details?"

"I understand," I replied. "But in the end, I want to be found innocent."

He chuckled. "Well, that's what every client says. We will have to let the case unfold before we can pronounce the verdict."

I liked that comment. It proved that he was already invested in the story.

But can you stand to be around him? Would it get better in time? Would being around him actually help you overcome your fear of black men?

I closed, "So, you'll be my lawyer?"

"You'll be my pro-bono quota," he clarified.

"Is there anything I can start reading to get me up to speed? I don't know much about the legal system."

"Sure. Look up the *Official Code of Georgia* on the Internet. You should find the Georgia statutes. Title 16 covers crimes and offenses. You might want to read the sections on murder, manslaughter and the use of force in defense of self or others. It may be a bit dry, but it has some good information to get you started. I'd suggest you skim it and then we can meet again next week."

"Okay. I'm out this way on Tuesday afternoons."

I stopped myself.

Had I just given away the Barbara connection? Too late now.

"Joanne can confirm a time with you on your way out," he said.

 # Tuesday, August 8

The following Tuesday rolled around quickly. I had a full afternoon planned. I had my second meeting with Thomas Bennett and would begin my first EMDR session with Barbara afterward. I debated if I would tell Barbara that I was working with her lawyer friend. I could always tell the truth that Mike the guard had recommended him, but would Barbara be able to sense there was more to the story?

Better not say anything for now.

I debated what to wear. I wanted to look professional for the legal meeting, but Barbara wouldn't expect me in a business suit. I opted for a gray pants suit with a white silk blouse, accented with amethyst and diamond earrings, an anniversary present from Chris.

I said hello to Mike when I entered the building, and took the elevator to the eighth floor. When I arrived at the lawyers' offices, Joanne once again led me down the corridor to Thomas' office. Looking at him for a second time, I couldn't ignore the resemblance. As much as I had prepared myself to face him again, I briefly panicked.

You're the lamb walking into the lion's den. Why tell him the story? He knows it as well as you. He was there.

Again, I talked myself out of being afraid of him just as I had to do for every black man who fit *his* description.

Come on. You're being crazy. Work with him. He's about to help you publish what could become a very compelling story. Besides, this project was your idea, not his, so get used to being around him.

Thomas greeted me, more friendly and enthusiastic than the first visit.

"Good afternoon. I thought over your project some more. I must admit, I had some reservations after you left. The hypothetical part could be too speculative to formalize, but you're the writer so I decided to give it a shot." Thomas continued with a smile, "No pun intended."

I smiled at the irony. I had my own reservations about working with him.

He continued, "I drafted a brief agreement based primarily upon what we discussed last time. I'd like you to read it and let me know if you concur."

He handed me a one-page document, which I quickly skimmed. The agreement covered the project description and duration, stating each party's obligations. I hadn't expected a formal agreement. Then again, he was a lawyer.

I replied, "On the proofing rights, I can't guarantee that my editor won't cut and rearrange what I submit. And the copy editor will check for accuracy of the facts."

Thomas replied firmly, "I don't believe your copy editor has a law degree."

He swept his hand across the wall behind him which looked like a shrine of his accomplishments. There was his diploma from Duke, his Member of the Georgia Bar certificate, and a certificate that stated he was admitted to practice in the Georgia Court of Appeals and Supreme Court of Georgia. Each document was matted and framed. To the right of the shrine was a photo of a little boy surrounded by four older girls. I wondered if that was Thomas as a child and if they were his sisters. Then I noticed a more current photo of him on his desk, surrounded by three women.

"Fair enough. I'll ask if you can have the final proofread," I replied. "I'm aiming to complete this by the end of November. I'll plan to have the galley to you by, let's say, mid-November?"

There was an awkward pause, which luckily was broken by Joanne entering the office with two cups of coffee, this time without asking. At least I wasn't mentally begging her to stay in the room as I had done last time. I thanked her and took a sip of the coffee. I didn't like the taste or how antsy it made me feel. How was I going to explain my dislike of coffee when I had already requested a cup during the first visit?

Well, you see Joanne, I really didn't want that coffee. I was just so sure that Mr. Bennett was a violent rapist that I wanted you to come back in the room so I wouldn't be left alone with him.

I shook off that thought and got back to business. "So assuming we have our housekeeping done, where do we begin?"

"Well, let's start with some basic questions about that night," he said, while pulling out a notepad. "Can you describe for me again, in detail, what happened?"

I repeated my night of terror, just as I had done for Troy, Chris, my mother, my sister, my close friends and Barbara Cole. I began with the figure standing in my bedroom doorway and ended with me running to the front door after him. I didn't tell him about the parting threat, just as I hadn't told Barbara at first. I could tell almost anyone the story…except those last words.

"Now, instead of watching him get away as I stood on the porch with my can of Mace, let's say I had a gun and I shot him as he was leaving. Let's say the shot killed him. Legally, what would happen to me?"

"Why don't we begin with the perpetrator's name?" Thomas asked.

I froze, his voice suddenly playing in the back of my mind, '*You win for now, but don't you forget Sweet Sam*'.

Why was his name important to Thomas Bennett?

"I don't know his name," I said defensively.

Thomas pressed his lips together and stared at me. Maybe he knew I was lying?

He spoke, "Well, since he is a major component of the story, we need to call him something rather than your attacker or the perpetrator. He needs a name."

"You give him one, then." I realized Thomas was just trying to formulate the characters of the case. My anxiety eased.

Thomas looked around as if he was expecting to find a name written on the wall. He then pointed to his navy suit jacket hanging on the wooden stand at the corner of his office. The label read Perry Ellis.

"Okay, let's call him Perry. That should suffice, for now. Next, we need to start at the scene of the crime. We need to walk through what happens when the police arrive after you've shot Perry. I assume you called 911?"

"Yes. Actually, the first person I called was Troy, my neighbor. He came over and called the police."

"Okay. So a policeman shows up and sees Perry lying lifeless in the street. There's no threat there. He wouldn't touch the body except to do a cursory inspection. He would get on the radio and call for a bus …"

"A bus?"

"An ambulance. After that, all of his attention would be on you. Because of the time of the night, he'll likely be a relatively young, inexperienced patrol officer. The experienced ones don't want to work the night shift. And because of his inexperience and the seriousness of the situation, the officer will be nervous and overly precautious."

"Would he be by himself? I thought policemen worked in pairs?" I asked.

"Not always. He will likely be alone but will immediately radio for backup. Once he calls out the code for a suspected homicide, it will trigger a caravan of people showing up at your house. He will probably handcuff you and your neighbor against the cop car while he waits for backup."

"But I'll explain what happened."

"Save your breath. You'll hear sirens and several police cars and ambulances will arrive. More than likely, a higher ranking, more experienced officer will take over. He will talk to the patrol deputy first to find out what happened. Then, he'll consult with the EMS and determine that the guy on the ground looks DOA."

I typed furiously but Thomas was talking too fast.

"Can I record this?" I asked. "Just so I can capture the details?"

"Go ahead."

He leaned back in his chair placing his elbow on the armrest. As he pushed back his shirt sleeve, I noticed the thick muscles of his forearms. *He must spend all his spare time working out.*

I pulled a small recorder from my purse as Thomas continued with the story. "The patrol deputy will put up crime scene tape and block off your house and maybe the entire street. I'm sure that, by then, your neighbors will be outside gawking and trying to figure out what's going on. Then, a homicide or major crime scene detective will come over to talk to you. I assume you would do the talking instead of your neighbor?"

"Yes. All Troy knows is that this guy, um, Perry, broke in and attacked me. And then he called the police."

"Hypothetically, Troy knows you shot the guy as well?"

"Oh, yeah. He would know that, too."

"The detective will ask you if you know Perry and will give you a chance to explain what happened. Would you talk to him?"

"Yes, why not?"

"So, legally, there's a gray area here. Are you in custody? Are you under investigative detention or under arrest? The detective will probably take off your handcuffs and start chatting more casually with you. With the handcuffs off, I suspect you won't consider yourself under suspicion and will talk more freely. If he had left you in handcuffs and read your Miranda rights, what would you have done?"

"I would have asked for a lawyer," I replied.

"Exactly. But if you aren't cuffed and don't hear your Miranda rights, you aren't thinking you're in trouble."

"Right."

"But as soon as you tell your story, that you were attacked in the house and then followed Perry outside and shot him, you are confessing your guilt. You see, there was a period of time between the attack and the shooting called a *cooling off period*. That time between what happened in the house and what happened in the street took away your claim of self-defense. The detective will immediately take a stance that you are a murderer. And, he will want to keep you talking because you are confessing. What you won't realize is that by confessing, you have just become nonhuman in his eyes. His demeanor will change but you'll miss all the social cues.

"Next, the detective will tell you that he needs to talk to you further at the station. He will realize from your story that your neighbor is not involved so he'll put the handcuffs back on you and probably let your neighbor go after taking his information and a statement. As for you, you will be put in the back of the patrol car."

"Why would he cuff me? I'm not dangerous."

"You just admitted to killing a guy."

"Wouldn't he let me at least get dressed before taking me to the station?"

"He might take you out of the car so you can show him where things took place in the house. He will look for evidence to corroborate your story, like the knife…

Knife!

…on your bedroom floor or a forced entry, but then he will put you right back in the patrol car. You're a murderer so why would he care if you are dressed or not?"

The knife. He just mentioned the knife on my bedroom floor. I never told him about that. I'm sure of it. I didn't know about the knife until we went back inside and I hadn't told him that part yet. How did he know there was a knife? Oh my God, I was right about him.

I need to get out of here…now. But I can't let him know that I'm on to him. I just need to keep my head together. But I've got to get out of here.

I slowly shifted my body in the chair, allowing my legs to point toward the door so I could make a run for it. At the same time, I couldn't resist asking. I couldn't resist ensnarling him with his own words.

"I don't recall telling you about the knife?" I said, as matter-of-factly as I could muster, though my voice was quivering.

I looked at the door. I reassured myself.

Joanne is just down the hall. If he jumps at me again, I can scream. This time, people will hear me.

Thomas leaned across his desk and nonchalantly pulled out some stapled pages from a manila folder. He tossed them at me.

"It's in the police report," he said. "Those pages recount what really happened at your house the night of June 7th."

"How did you get this?" I asked, stunned. My body was still pointing toward the door.

"It's a matter of public record," he replied. "I had Joanne pull it so I could have a read. I was hoping there'd be some angle that would turn this case into self-defense, but I didn't find one."

My head was spinning. I took a deep breath. How could I go from feeling such mistrust and fear to feeling so foolish in a matter of seconds?

I slowly turned my legs back toward his desk. My heart started to return to its normal beat. I wondered if he noticed my suspicion. I mean, it certainly wasn't obvious how he would have known about the knife.

I took another deep breath and began to regain my composure. I glanced at the cover page of the police report and put it back on his desk.

"So where were we?" I asked.

"You're back in the patrol car, still in your pajamas."

That night I was actually in Chris' T-shirt and my underwear. I only switched to wearing pajamas after the attack.

See. He didn't know what you were wearing. He wasn't there.

Thomas continued, "While in the car, you will hear the police sharing information about your case on their radio. We can ask for the recordings and listen to what the police have assumed. Part of my job is to discredit the police assumptions in front of the jury. For example, the police may quickly decide that this is a domestic dispute and the entire investigation could be based on that. It won't be until months later when we are preparing for trial that we can show that you and Perry didn't know each other. I'm assuming you didn't know him, right?"

"I told you last time that I didn't know him."

"Good that you are able to stick to the same story," he smirked, and then continued.

"So you will be sitting in the patrol car for a while as the police talk to any witnesses. They'll take Perry to the ER, even if he is already dead. Would he have any ID on him?"

"Probably not. I'd presume he wouldn't bring his driver's license on his nighttime hunts."

"Okay. You'll have to work on how much they learn about him, and if he can even be identified. Then, they will drive you to the police station and put you in a holding cell. It could take anywhere from 40 minutes to 4 hours before anything more happens, and I'm sure you will be wondering what in God's name is going on."

"A holding cell? You mean I would have to go to jail?"

"Technically, it's not jail, just a holding cell, but it would look similar, bars and all."

I had never done anything that would even remotely cause me to see the inside of a jail. The worst crime I had ever committed was borrowing my sister's ID to get into the college bars before I turned 21.

I repeated, "So I would have spent the rest of the night in a jail cell?"

"Considering that Perry was spending the night in the morgue, I would say that you got the better deal," Thomas chuckled.

Not amusing.

"I'd assume my neighbor, Troy, would be trying to get ahold of my husband so he could get me out of there."

"Easier said than done. I'll explain. So after your four hours or so, you will be taken from the holding cell to an interview room. It's a plain room with a table, two chairs and a clock on the wall which is also a camera. A detective will come in to talk to you. He'll probably take an initial approach of befriending you, taking off the handcuffs and offering you some coffee or water. You may feel relieved that finally someone is listening to you but that's a mistake. You'd be missing all the interrogation tactics. He would ask you in a kind voice to tell him what happened. Would you have told your story?"

"Is this the same detective that was at the scene?"

"Probably."

"Well, I'd just be repeating my story to him, right?"

"Yes, but here's the catch. At some point, he would pull out a document and say something like, '*Before we go any further, I want to be sure you are aware of your rights.'* He will pull out a Miranda Rights waiver for you to sign. It's so subtle that most defendants miss the fact that they are waiving their right to remain silent. You'll be thinking, '*I'm not in trouble. I'm not a suspect. I have no reason not to talk.'* But that's all wrong."

"Why?"

"After you've waived your rights, he will get you to confess it all over again. You will feel like you are just repeating your story but he will be capturing your post-Miranda statement."

"You know, I hear police say the Miranda rights on TV. Do we hear the full version or are they abridged for TV?"

Thomas searched through one of his desk drawers and pulled out a small card which he handed to me.

---

1. You have the right to remain silent.
2. Anything you say can and will be used against you in a court of law.
3. You have the right to talk to a lawyer and have him present with you while you are being questioned.
4. If you cannot afford to hire a lawyer, one will be appointed to represent you before any questioning, if you wish.
5. You can decide at any time to exercise these rights and not answer any questions or make any statements.

I turned the card over and read the back side while he hummed to himself.

WAIVER

After the warning and in order to secure a waiver, the following questions should be asked and an affirmative reply secured to each question.

1. Do you understand each of these rights I have explained to you?
2. Having these rights in mind, do you wish to talk to us now?
   Prosecuting Attorneys' Council of Georgia
   3951 Snapfinger Parkway
   Decatur, Georgia 30035

"I'm not so sure I would talk after hearing my rights. I might ask for a lawyer," I said.

"Hey, it's your story. If you ask for a lawyer, they will cuff you and take you back to the holding cell. And they won't spare their feelings of how pissed they are that you aren't cooperating."

He looked at his watch as if mirroring their irritation.

"Okay. So for argument's sake, assume I'm foolish enough to waive my rights and keep talking. What happens next?"

"Well, you would talk to the detective for a while. If he is experienced, he may try to flush out the self-defense part of your story. He would painstakingly go through your every action because he will know the thing that you don't. He will know that every decision you made, from grabbing your gun, to going outside, to taking aim, to shooting, all of these actions are individual, independent decisions that would negate a plea of self-defense. On the other hand, he may gloss over scrutinizing your self-defense claim and just arrest you for murder."

"So he would want to prove that I had time to think and stop before I took a shot?"

"Exactly. He might also tell you that he doesn't think this is self-defense, but say it's up to the DA to decide, in essence passing the buck. Of course, he has the power to influence the DA, but he may choose to let the DA sort it out. But worse than passing the buck, he might tell you that you are going to court in the morning for your first appearance hearing where the judge will set a bond. That's a lie. He would know that for a murder case, you most likely will be denied bond."

"Really?"

"Afraid so. He may lead you to believe that everything will be straightened out in the morning, but that's not reality. Next, you would be taken for booking-in, which can take up to 24 hours."

"24 hours!" I repeated.

"That's the rule in DeKalb County. Depends on how busy they are. You could be waiting in the holding cell for at least a day. Eventually, someone would come for you. You would be strip searched and given a prison uniform worn by thousands of other inmates before you. Instead of shoes, you would be given socks with flip flops. They don't give shoelaces for fear you would hang yourself. The guards, who for the most part are lower middle-class workers collecting a modicum of a salary, would be indifferent toward you. If they sense you putting on any airs, they might even be mean."

Thomas paused, "Still wishing you had shot this guy?"

I had to admit, he was painting a grim picture. I asked, "Don't I get a phone call?"

"Not at this point. Your chance for a call comes a little later. Worse, your husband won't know where you are. He'll be calling all over DeKalb County, running into bureaucracy and getting nowhere. He will have no clout. He's just the husband of a murderer. They would treat him just as badly as they are treating you."

I protested, "He would pull strings to get me out."

Thomas replied with such certainty, "You would be lost in an abyss. He wouldn't be able to find you."

I frowned.

Thomas continued, "The guard will handle the booking-in process, obtaining your pertinent information, fingerprints and mug shot. Then, you will get your phone call, but it's not like you are handed a telephone. You'll be in a holding cell with a communal phone and have to wait your turn. When you try to call your husband collect, it will likely be blocked because most cell phones have a collect call blocking feature. So you may not get through to anyone right away which I imagine will be terribly disheartening."

"Why would I call him collect, it's local."

"Every call out of jail costs money—local or not," he replied.

Thomas reached in his pocket, pulled out his cell phone and offered it to me.

"Call your husband," he commanded.

"What?"

"One hundred dollars says you can't."

I looked at his phone but didn't take it. I quickly realized that Chris' cell and office numbers were programmed into my phone. I didn't actually know his numbers.

Thomas just grinned, and continued.

"By then, you'll probably go to sleep out of sheer exhaustion. You'll sleep on a metal bench in the holding cell. If you need to use the toilet, there's a communal one with no privacy. Around 5:00 a.m., you will be awakened by all the jail noise. The guards will come for you and put you in shackles with a chain around your waist and feet. They will herd you and the other inmates onto a big school bus and take you over to the courthouse where you will wait in a holding cell in the basement. Eventually, the guards will take you and the other inmates on a huge freight elevator to a waiting room upstairs where you'll have your first appearance."

I tried to picture myself in an abrasive jumpsuit and cold, metal shackles binding my wrists. I had my own starring role in *Orange is the New Black*.

"At this point, I imagine you'll start paying more attention to what the other inmates are saying. Some will be whining. Others will be flippant, trying to show that they're comfortable with the whole jail scene. Others will be trash talking, especially throwing jeers toward the guards when they're out of earshot. They won't care what you're in for as they will only be concerned about themselves. Invariably, you'll get pulled into the conversation. They'll tell you that you aren't getting a bond for murder and that you were a fool for talking to the detective. It will probably be the first time that the enormity of your situation sinks in."

"Will Chris know when my hearing is?" I asked.

"Maybe, maybe not. Someone may take pity on him and tell him that you have a bond hearing at the courthouse that morning. He would frantically go to the courthouse and try to find what room you're in. It's such a big bureaucracy."

I probed further, "But if it has already been twenty-four hours, Chris would have hired a lawyer who could find out where I was, right?"

"Good point. Does he have $25,000 cash to put into my hands to get me started on your case?"

"Yes, if that's what it would take."

"Really?" he challenged.

"Of course he would find a way."

Thomas continued, "Okay. Assuming Chris has hired me, then I would have the chance to talk to you in the courtroom—during your first appearance. The state would probably have an experienced DA, because this is a murder case. And the detective who first investigated the case would be there as well."

"Would I get to talk to my husband?"

"No. I would start by stating your name, your age, that you are well-educated, married, have always lived in Georgia, have never been charged with a crime, etc. Basically, I would paint you to look like Mother Theresa. I would affirm that you had been attacked and shot the perpetrator in self-defense."

I nodded.

"The judge would then ask the state what they have to say. This is when the DA would say that this was a violent crime of revenge, that the victim was found dead, shot in the back in the middle of the street. He would say that they are investigating the relationship between you and the deceased."

My mouth dropped open.

"Yes, you would be flabbergasted, just as you are now. And that nice detective who took off your handcuffs and brought you a cup of coffee will be nodding his head in agreement with the DA."

"That's insane," I interjected.

"That's the legal system. Now, maybe you are starting to realize that this is bad. Really bad. As your lawyer, I will request a bond but it will depend on whether the judge would allow it. For a murder charge, he will most likely deny bond. I suppose there is a slim chance, but he'd set it so high that you'd be hard pressed to come up with that kind of money."

"How much?"

"Maybe $500,000."

"Wow. We'd have to mortgage the house."

"That or you could use a bonding company, but they will charge you about twelve percent of the bond amount, which they keep. So, that's $60,000 down the drain."

"And if he denies bond?" I asked. "What exactly does that mean?"

"That means that you are sitting in jail for up to ninety days until your arraignment. What you wouldn't know is that your trial date could be three to four years away."

"What happened to innocent until proven guilty? What about our constitutional right to a speedy trial?"

"That's how it works," he said, as he shrugged his shoulders.

"So, for my story, let's say bond is denied. I just go back to jail and wait for my trial?"

"Yes. You'd be housed with other high-security female inmates, some pretty rough customers. They'd probably try to scare you, telling you that you'll be there for life. And let's hope none of the black ones find out that you shot one of their own."

I had no reply.

"Next, I'd prepare you for what is called a preliminary hearing, which would happen in about three weeks. At the preliminary, it's the chance for me to listen to the state and find out their version of what happened. The state will call your friend, the detective, who will paint a sad picture. He'll say something like, '*We found poor, young Perry Smith, dead, lying in the street, shot in the back.*'

"The prelim will be a bombardment of detailed accusations. Everything you told them while in custody would be extrapolated. The detective may even say that you confessed that you planned to kill Perry and made sure that you got close enough to ensure your aim was true."

"That's a lie."

"It's his interpretation of your words. The detective won't necessarily give just the facts. He may embellish the story quite a bit. Remember, it's not his job to show you're innocent. That's my job. Meanwhile, you are going to be wondering why I'm not objecting or countering what the detective is saying, but at the prelims, we don't do that. As your defense counsel, my role is to just listen to the state's case and to start mentally forming your defense."

"So you won't try to correct anything he says? Doesn't that imply that you agree with him?"

"I won't waste objections here. I'll just take notes. Objections come at the trial, not the prelim. In the meantime, the DA will decide what he plans to present to the grand jury as far as charges."

"And the grand jury decides if we go to trial?"

"Right. The grand jury is composed of sixteen jurors who meet to determine if a case merits an indictment. There has to be at least twelve who think there is probable cause for the case to proceed. If there aren't at least twelve votes, then you would not be criminally liable."

I asked with a glimmer of hope, "So there's a possibility I would never be charged?"

Thomas shook his head. "Your confession alone is substantive evidence, and it's not a clean case of self-defense."

"But it was self-defense," I protested. "The whole episode was self-defense. From the moment I struggled with him on my bedroom floor to the moment I would have shot him from my porch, it was all one event."

"That's what we will have to prove to the trial jury, but not the grand jury. The grand jury only decides if the case is worth prosecuting. The trial jury decides your guilt or innocence."

"So you think the grand jury would indict me?"

"Afraid so. The next step would be your arraignment and we would start preparing for trial."

I looked at my watch. I needed to leave for my 4:00 p.m. appointment with Barbara. Besides, my head was beyond full.

"I'll have to go in a minute. What do we cover next?"

"Next, I can explain the arraignment process. When are you thinking of meeting again?"

I had a thought, but wasn't sure how receptive he would be. "Do you think you could show me what a jail cell looks like? So I can describe it realistically for the story?"

"I doubt it," he said. "It's not like CNN—they aren't open for tours."

I rolled my eyes … then pressed again, "But could you at least ask?"

Tuesday, August 8 late afternoon

I sat in the familiar waiting room of Barbara's office, trying to clear my mind of all the information Thomas had just laid on me. Thomas had exceeded my expectations with the detail he provided and his willingness to jump into this hypothetical case. I was eager to organize it all and start writing. As usual, I didn't have to wait long before Barbara invited me into her office.

As we started to sit down, Barbara commented on the last visit. "I enjoyed meeting Chris. He seems very supportive."

"Yes, he has been. He didn't say much about the session afterward, but I think it was helpful for him. We ended up going to Tampa together, kind of a compromise."

Barbara nodded and smiled.

"So, are you ready to begin the EMDR session?"

"Sure."

Though I had done some research on the Internet on EMDR, it was still a mysterious black-box. I knew I would have to experience it to really understand.

"Remember from before when I explained how EMDR works? What we will try to do is take the traumatic memories stored in your nervous system and accelerate the processing of that information. If it works, those memories will become desensitized and restructured within a more positive framework. We talked about the idea of your traumatic memory being stuck on an island. Think of EMDR as a bridge to that island. You'll be able to access the memories and process them to what we call an adaptive resolution, one that places the trauma in context.

"Also, when we met with Chris, we talked about the possibility that your disturbance level may actually rise during this session and in-between sessions. That is completely normal and a sign that you are processing the information and healing. Because you've learned how to use your relaxation CD, you can use it during this session or between sessions to help you feel calmer."

I nodded.

"Now, with EMDR, it is different for each person. It may take several attempts to have your mind start flowing with the image. I may have to change the direction of my hand movement or change the pace for it to work. There is no right or wrong method and there is no timetable for it to work. Just tell me what you are experiencing so I can make the proper choices on how to proceed. And, if you need to stop, just raise your hand and I'll stop immediately. I want you to know that you are in complete control of this session."

"Okay."

Barbara moved her chair closer to the couch so she was positioned off of my left shoulder.

"For starters, let's see what eye movement feels comfortable. Just try to track my hand movement."

Barbara moved her pointer and middle fingers about twelve inches from my face and began to sway them back and forth like a pendulum.

My eyes moved back and forth like I was watching a tennis match. It actually felt kind of silly.

"Is that comfortable for you?" she asked.

"It's fine."

"Okay. If you have any eye pain or if you want me to stop, just raise your hand. Let's practice that."

I raised my right hand and Barbara stopped the pendulum motion.

"Okay, good. Now I'd like you to think of your safe place from the relaxation exercises we've done before. What is the name of your safe place?"

"My mountain top," I replied.

"Good. During our session today, if you are ever too overwhelmed, you can go back to your mountain top. But before you retreat, if you can, try to stay in the moment. Think of yourself on a moving train. You are watching the scene through the train window. You are an outsider passing by, so no matter how afraid you may feel, remember that you are passing by what you see and it won't harm you. If you can stay in the moment without retreating, you'll allow the image to process and heal more quickly.

"Now, I'd like you to picture the night of your attack. Form an image in your mind that represents the most upsetting part. We'll call that your target. By picturing this image or target, your conscious mind is forming a bridge to where the disturbing information is stored."

I immediately thought of his dark silhouette in my doorway. I remembered sensing pure evil before I had even realized what was happening.

"What do you get?" Barbara asked.

"I see him standing in the doorway of my bedroom."

"Okay. That image may morph or change. Just notice it and follow the flow. Now tell me a statement that expresses a negative belief about yourself or your situation today."

"What do you mean?" I asked.

"To go with the target image, what is a belief you have today that is harmful? It could be something like 'I'm powerless' or 'I'm worthless' or something else you currently feel."

I replied, "I'm not safe."

"Where do you feel it in your body?" Barbara asked.

"I'm not really sure. Maybe my chest and my throat."

"Okay, after we go through the process, we'll be able to see if any of these baseline feelings change. Let's start with the eye movement that we practiced. Remember, it is your own mind that is doing the healing and you are in control. I'd like you to focus on your target image and follow my fingers with your eyes. The image may shift. Just witness what is happening and we'll talk afterward. Even if something seems unimportant, don't discard it. As new information surfaces, it is usually connected in some fashion. If it gets too intense, just raise your hand and go back to your mountain top."

Barbara held her pointer and middle fingers together and began swaying them back and forth in front of my face like before. As instructed, I pictured his image in my doorway as I followed the doctor's fingers.

Nothing happened.

I wasn't even sure what was supposed to happen but I just watched her fingers and felt silly.

"Really concentrate on your target image," she said.

I'm not sure how much time passed but eventually I stopped noticing her fingers. I was too busy watching him in the doorway and wondering what he was going to do. He didn't rush at me, which is what I was anticipating. Instead, his dark figure slowly glides around my bed, like he is on a merry-go-round. He is prolonging the anticipation of the attack, getting pleasure from my fear. I just sit in my bed, frozen, as he spins around me. It isn't as dark as it was that night. As much as I'm afraid to look, I strain to see his face. I need to get that right this time so I can describe him to the police. So he won't be a faceless, black silhouette in the night. But then, when he comes closer, I *can* see his face.

He is Mr. Riley. The image flashes and is gone and I notice Barbara's fingers again but can't follow them. I'm still trying to figure out what just happened.

Barbara asked me to explain what I saw, which I did.

"Who is Mr. Riley?" she asked.

"My fourth grade teacher. He never liked me—and I knew it. I was a good student and didn't cause any trouble but he was so mean to me. In fact, he would make up reasons to punish me. My mom must have noticed a change in my behavior and my grades and pulled me from his class."

"Go on," she said.

"I remember sitting in my childhood classroom in one of those small, wooden desks. My parents and the principal came in to the room and pulled me out. My mom leaned down and told me that I was going to a different class. I was so happy and relieved."

I paused, feeling like a little girl for a brief moment.

"But Mr. Riley was an angry, old white man," I said. "How did his face show up on my attacker's body?"

"Why do you think he showed up?" asked Barbara.

"I don't know. Maybe because he's the only other person who's ever tried to hurt me? That's funny. I haven't thought of him in years. He must be dead by now. He was ancient back then."

"Why do you think he treated you badly?"

"I truly have no idea. I was a good kid. Thank goodness my mother stepped in. She knew something was wrong. That was so bizarre."

"How do you feel now?"

"I don't know. Do you think my brain bundled my attack with how I felt in fourth grade?"

"We don't really know how it works, but your most recent trauma can attach itself to earlier traumas. It's kind of like dominos, when one falls, the others start to fall. Do you want to try another set?"

"Okay," I said with some trepidation.

"Let's go back to the original target." Barbara raised her hand and started the pendulum motion.

Like before, it took a few tries before the image started to morph. As I watched his silhouette in the doorway, he didn't circle the bed this time. Instead he comes straight for me and starts to choke me with both of his hands. I try to scream, but he is constricting my windpipe so no sound can come out. I try to pry his hands from my neck with my fingers when I see my dad standing behind him. My dad grabs him and does the Heimlich maneuver on him and he collapses to the floor. He shrivels into a black heap like the wicked witch in the *Wizard of Oz* after Dorothy poured water on her.

I explained to Barbara what I had just seen. Though she didn't ask for an interpretation, I wanted to make sense of it.

"When I was about eight years old, my parents had the Evans family over for dinner at our house. We were having steak and a piece of meat got stuck in my throat. I couldn't breathe. I got up and walked over to my dad who was at the head of the table. I tapped him on the shoulder and started to tell him that I couldn't breathe, but no words came out.

"He immediately knew I was choking, turned me around and did the Heimlich maneuver on me. A big chunk of steak popped out of my throat and I could breathe again. I started crying and wouldn't eat the rest of my dinner. My parents let me go to my room.

"If my dad hadn't known the Heimlich maneuver, I probably would have died. Afterward, he started passing out pamphlets about it at his store to every customer who came in. I was so embarrassed when he told the story encouraging everyone to learn the procedure."

"Why do you think that memory came up?" asked Barbara.

"I'm not sure. The Heimlich maneuver is supposed to help you, but instead it injured him."

Barbara asked, "What physical sensations did you feel?"

"I felt my throat closing. I felt my air passage being blocked. I felt panicked because I needed to scream when he was choking me and I couldn't get a sound out."

"When you were a child and were choking, why did you go to your father?"

"I don't know. It turns out he was the only one at the table who knew how to save me. I guess it's pretty obvious in all of these memories that my parents are the ones who keep saving me."

Barbara nodded. "Do you feel less fear now?"

I thought about it. "I guess it doesn't feel as intense as before."

"What about the idea of feeling safe? How does 'I am safe' sound to you, with ten being completely true and one being completely false?

"It's hard to say. I don't feel as afraid. I'd give it maybe a six."

"Now, I'd like you to take note of your body from your head to your toes. Do you feel any tension anywhere?" Barbara asked.

"In my hands."

I made claws with both of my hands to demonstrate.

"Okay, I'd like to address that, but want to make sure we have adequate time. Let's try to do some relaxation work on your hands today, and we'll pick up that tension next time. We can also reassess your original target to see if it is still as intense. Right now, I'd like to take you back to your mountain top and start to relax."

We did some more relaxation exercises over the next 15 minutes, particularly focusing on my hands and throat.

"Laura, do you remember how you kept a list of changes in your life after our first visit?"

"Yes."

"Well, I'd like you to keep a new list of any memories, dreams or thoughts you have over the next week. Jot down anything that is disturbing and also anything that is positive. You don't have to write a lot of detail, just enough to help you remember what happened. You had quite a few things to process during this session, so don't be surprised if it continues in between sessions. If you become afraid or tense, use your relaxation CD. In fact, you may want to use it every day. And you'll want to remind Chris that you could have some bad nights before it gets better, so he isn't alarmed. If you have any issues where you need my help, just give my office a call. Do you have any questions for me?"

"If this works so well, why didn't we do it sooner?" I didn't mean to sound critical, but it was obviously working so why had she waited?

"Well, to have a successful session, we needed time to build trust. And you needed to be able to relax in your safe place first. I don't think it would have been as beneficial as what you experienced today if we had tried this therapy any sooner."

That made sense.

I left Barbara's office exhausted. Seeing Thomas Bennett and Barbara Cole on the same day was not a good idea. It was too much to handle. As I waited for the elevator, I wondered what hidden monsters I had unleashed and if they would show up in my dreams over the next week.

FROM THE DESK OF
BARBARA COLE

August 8, Visit 5, EMDR Session 1
Laura Holland

EMDR - engaged quickly, eager to heal

Opened 2 channels from childhood:
1) abusive teacher (Mr. Riley, 4th grade, a white man?)
2) choking at dinner (8 years old)
— parents saved her both times

Tension in throat, chest and hands
Vulnerable without air / without voice
  • choking as a child, attacker choking her in the session
  • other instances of no air / no voice?

—BAC

 # Friday, August 11

On Friday morning, I awoke early, partly because I was anxious about going to the jail with Thomas—he had finagled a visit. But also because I had a disturbing dream involving Chris and never fully went back to sleep. I wrote down the details in my journal so I could share them with Barbara.

I showered and dressed before Chris was awake and was finishing some cereal when his alarm clock went off. He shuffled into the kitchen still in his boxers and T-shirt to make coffee.

"Good mornin'. Did you have a bad dream?" he asked me, as he rubbed his eyes. I had briefly awakened him during the night.

"Yes."

"But Dr. Cole said to expect that, right, after the EMDR session?"

"Yes, she did so maybe that's a good sign," I said half-heartedly.

"Was it the attack again?" he asked.

"No. I was with my mom. We were being chased. I don't really remember it all," I lied.

"You're burning the candle at both ends," he commented. "Maybe you should try to get some more rest."

I had been staying up late all week writing my story. For some reason, I was more inspired to write at night than during the day.

"Maybe," I agreed. "I'm going to see the jail today with Thomas."

"With Thomas? So you're on a first name basis now?" Chris asked. He spun the Keurig carousel looking for his dark roast and then popped it into the machine.

"You jealous?"

He walked over to me and encircled my waist with his arms. "Should I be?"

"Don't be silly."

"What's at the jail?" he asked. I could see he was still groggy from another restless night.

"I just want to see what it looks like, so I can describe it in the story."

"Is this going to be a magazine story?"

"No, I think it has more of the makings for a short TV movie. My editor and I were just talking about that the other day."

"That's a first for you," he commented, letting go of my waist and reaching for his coffee mug

"Yeah. Wouldn't it be cool to have a TV movie?"

"Do I get to play myself?" he asked smiling.

"How's your acting?"

"Depends on who plays you," he said, grinning. It was the same dev-ilish grin I had seen in my dream, which frightened me a little.

I looked at my watch. "I'd better get going," I said, and started to leave the kitchen.

"Where's my goodbye?" Chris walked over to me, coffee mug still in hand, and gave me a peck on the lips.

I pulled back. "Coffee breath," I stammered.

Before he was even dressed for the day, I was in my Audi driving down Peachtree Street to Thomas' office. When I was about halfway there, my cell phone rang.

"Hi, it's Thomas Bennett," the voice said. He sounded different over the phone—more like a generic Midwest TV anchor voice than a southern black man voice.

"Hi," I replied. "I'm on my way to your office now. Is there a prob-lem with going to the jail?"

"No, not at all. I was just going to ask if you minded driving? I can meet you out front of the building."

"Oh. No problem. I'll call you back when I'm close. It should be about fifteen minutes."

I couldn't help but feel a twinge of relief that, if I had to get into the car with Thomas, I would be the one driving and in control.

Thomas was waiting on the curb outside the Georgia Building when I pulled up. He jumped in my car, dressed in a dark blue designer suit, white shirt and a blue, gold and silver striped tie.

As we pulled onto the highway, his cologne permeated the car. It made me think of the beach and cocktails and wealth.

I asked "So is there any jail etiquette I need to know?"

"Not really. Try not to stare, and if anyone does anything shocking, try not to act shocked. Just follow my lead."

"Okay," I said as I continued to look forward, keeping my eyes on the traffic. "I was thinking about the whole bond process and have a question for you. If they wouldn't let me out on bond, isn't there any-thing else we could do to speed up the trial? I mean it's crazy to think I'd be sitting in jail for years. What if I used my media contacts to bring visibility to the case so I could get a faster trial?"

Thomas was quick to reply. "That could backfire on you. The more media attention, the more vigorously they will prosecute. Your case won't be just one they want to win, but one they *have to win* because of the publicity. Not to mention, if we bring in the media, that would really open the door to character attacks. The DA will try to find every ex-boyfriend you've ever had to discredit your character, and they'll be ruthless. Do you really want any misstep you've ever made played out in front of all your friends and family?"

"I've got a pretty clean record," I countered.

"Who's to say some narcissist wanting his fifteen minutes of fame doesn't come forward and say he's having an affair with you? It would be your word against his."

"He'd have no proof," I countered. I glanced at Thomas and noticed that he was eyeing my bare legs. I was wearing a tan skirt and black heels. My calf muscle flexed as I pressed the gas pedal. His gaze lasted a little too long. I shifted uncomfortably.

"You should have worn pants," he said bluntly.

"Aren't we going to the women's section?"

"The women can be worse than the men."

I shrugged my shoulders. There was nothing I could do about my outfit now. His words hung between us for a moment.

"Is there no other option, other than being stuck in jail without bond?" I asked.

"We could petition for a speedy trial, but I'd want to see your indictment first." Thomas pointed to the exit lane. "You're going to get off here on Moreland."

"How does the indictment work?"

"So, assume the grand jury decides that your case was worth prosecuting. The DA would prepare the charges, probably listing more than we expected. For example, I would think he would charge you with malice murder, felony murder and voluntary manslaughter, but he may add on a few more like possession of a firearm during the commission of a felony, aggravated assault and aggravated battery."

"What are the last two?" I asked as I glanced over my shoulder before merging into the exit lane.

"Aggravated assault is when you threaten another person with a deadly weapon. Aggravated battery is when you cause serious bodily injury using a deadly weapon."

"So death is considered a serious bodily injury?" I asked, with sarcasm.

"They will indict you for any charge that is applicable. Of course, if you are convicted of murder, the lesser charges merge under the more serious one. The positive element, if you can call any of this positive, is that by having so many charges, the jury has more options. Say they don't want to convict you of murder, they can opt for the lesser charge of manslaughter thinking they are giving you a break."

"Some break."

Thomas continued, "So you'll be in jail and one day an envelope will arrive with a list of the charges. You'll probably be shocked that there are so many and the verbiage will seem like a foreign language, but I'll be able to visit you and explain each count. Then, probably a few weeks later, you'll get another envelope with your arraignment date. That's where we enter your plea. Many lawyers have their client waive attendance, but I don't."

"Why?"

"First, I'd want to give you a break from jail, if only temporarily. Also, it would let you see that something is physically happening with your case. Finally, it would give you a chance to see your husband."

"Can't he visit me at the jail?"

"Yes, but you'd always be behind glass."

I pictured sitting in a chair with Chris across from me, separated by a glass barrier. We'd have to talk via a phone and everything would be recorded. It would be horrible. This was making for a good fictional story, but I couldn't imagine it being my reality.

"So what exactly happens at the arraignment?" I asked.

"You'd be brought to the courthouse and the judge would review your charges. He would ask you if you understand the charges, and ask how you plead. I presume you'd want me to say not guilty."

"Yes. Do I have to give a reason why I'm pleading not guilty?"

"No. Not at this point. The arraignment is really the official start of your case. It also starts a time period of ten days for me to file any motions asking for information from the state and any motions to suppress."

"What would you want suppressed?"

"Definitely anything you said at the crime scene pre-Miranda, and potentially information in the interview room."

"How could you suppress that if I signed the Miranda waiver?"

"We'd challenge how the Miranda process was executed. After the arraignment, you'd go back to jail and wouldn't have another court date for potentially years, unless we file the speedy trial demand."

"Well, we'd file the demand right away, wouldn't we?"

"We could, but there is a downside."

I rolled my eyes. There always seemed to be some kind of downside.

Thomas continued, "Having a waiting period can help you. That zealous cop may have moved on. The DA may have gotten promoted and a new person is in place. Your file could become what is called an old fish file, one that isn't easy to win and one that no one wants to touch. If you wait it out awhile, anyone new on the case won't have as much personal investment and pride to win. If you wait for turnover in the DA's office, the new DA can treat the case as someone else's mess that he or she is just cleaning up."

"So it's a catch-22. If I try for a speedy trial, the current prosecutor would be more eager to win. If I sit around in jail, I may get an easier, less engaged prosecutor but am wasting my life away."

Thomas just shrugged and nodded. "And if we file for a speedy trial, we may not have time to see all of the state's evidence, which could leave me unprepared in court."

Thomas pointed to the jail parking lot and I turned in. I pulled into a visitor parking spot in front of a tall, tan brick building. When we walked in, there were rows of plastic chairs that formed a waiting area and a metal detector behind them.

It was not at all what I expected: the room was clean and orderly. Thomas approached the clerk and explained that he had arranged for a private tour with Lieutenant Charlie Parsons. We were instructed to go through the metal detector, and told that he would meet us on the other side.

The lieutenant was a short, stocky man with light brownish-gray hair that matched his beige uniform. He seemed very eager to have an author in his presence, as that is how Thomas had described me.

I shared a little background on my story and then asked if we could see the facility. Lieutenant Parsons appeared pleased to have the chance to show off his well-run jail.

We proceeded to the booking-in area so the lieutenant could show the process from the beginning. He pointed to a closet with a stack of orange jumpsuits.

"Those are for minimum or medium security inmates. The red

ones over there are for maximum security. We don't blend the inmates, meaning we'd never put a minimum security inmate with a maximum security one. Someone would get hurt."

"So you classify by the crime, not the temperament of the inmate?" I asked.

"Right."

That didn't sound so good.

As we walked down the hall, four male inmates dressed in orange were being escorted by two guards along the same corridor.

One inmate eyed Thomas fiercely.

Thomas stared him down.

I was surprised by the unspoken hostility in the exchange.

Did they know each other?

When the lieutenant passed, the guards forced the inmates to put their hands behind their backs and face the wall.

"I demand that they show me respect," he boasted. "That's why most criminals don't want to come here. I see to it that they follow the rules and learn to respect authority."

Suddenly, the guy who had been eyeing Thomas broke from the guards' grip and lunged forward, shouting, "Yo, brother, share what you got!"

The guard snatched the prisoner and pushed him to his knees. Lieutenant Parsons marched over to the guy and jammed his face into the wall with his left hand while he spoke into his radio with his right. Two more guards promptly appeared and escorted the inmate away.

"He won't do that again," the lieutenant assured, as he returned to us.

What was that all about?

I had felt safe until now.

Next, we were shown where the inmates were patted down, fingerprinted and photographed—an open, clean space, yet chillingly featureless and sterile.

The lieutenant explained, "After we book an inmate, we do a screening to see if she is on any meds, has any diseases or is suicidal. Then she would be doused with Betadine to get rid of any lice and given her jumpsuit."

From the booking-in area, the lieutenant walked us down another corridor to see actual cells.

"Did you know that guy?" I whispered to Thomas.

He didn't answer, staring straight ahead. Before I could ask again, we entered an octagon-shaped room, with a guard's station in the center. The fluorescent lighting was dim and the walls were a neutral brown. Seeing the lieutenant, a female, African-American guard quickly stood up. "Is there something you need, sir?" she asked.

"No, thanks, Chelsea. I'm just giving a tour," he said, with a touch of self-importance.

Chelsea sat back down in front of a panel of monitors. Around the central station, there were windows into eight different pods. In each pod, there were long tables where the inmates could mingle. Behind the tables were four cell doors, which meant that eight inmates shared the common area. There were a few inmates dressed in orange jump-suits sitting at the tables. They appeared to be having casual conversations, like girlfriends out to lunch except that there was no leaving this party. Contrary to what I had expected, it didn't feel dirty or violent. Instead it was incredibly confining and impersonal.

Lieutenant Parsons explained the surroundings, "Like I said earlier, there are two inmates to a cell. They can come in the common area for two hours a day and they can take a shower there in the corner."

I hadn't noticed the shower. Though it was in the corner of the open space, there was no curtain and no privacy.

"You can't see inside the cells from here, but there are two bunks, a sink and a toilet. If they want to go outside, they can go in that room for up to 30 minutes a day."

He pointed to a room adjacent to the guard's station. The only difference between it and the common area was that it had a long horizontal window at the top.

"They don't get to actually go outdoors?" I asked.

"That *is* outdoors as far as they're concerned," he retorted.

The window was so high that it was impossible to see out. The only advantage to that room over any other was that a small amount of sunlight shined in.

He continued, "If they want to go to church, they can go down there."

He pointed to another smaller room next to the guard's station with a row of pews. I was beginning to understand that every part of life for these inmates existed inside this brown octagon.

"What about meals?" I asked.

"They get twenty minutes. The food trays are brought inside the common area."

"There's no central cafeteria to eat?"

"Nope. Avoids fights. They don't leave this space unless they need to see a doctor."

The walls around me started leaning inward. There wasn't enough oxygen in the room for all of us to breathe. I took a deep breath to stave off the claustrophobia and looming panic attack.

Luckily, the tour was over and the lieutenant walked us back to the front reception. We thanked him for his time and walked outside.

Before he could get in the car, I turned toward Thomas. "Did you know that prisoner in there?"

Thomas shrugged. "No."

I didn't quite believe him.

"Well, then, why did he talk to you?"

Thomas laughed. "Are you serious?"

"Of course I'm serious."

Thomas crossed his arms and asked me slowly, "What do you *think* he meant?"

"How would I know?" I replied. "Is there something you're not telling me?"

Thomas shook his head and chuckled.

"He wanted me to share you. That outburst back there—it wasn't about me. It was about you."

"Oh," was all I could manage to say.

As we drove back to Thomas' office, he informed me that one of his trials had been moved up and that he couldn't meet the following week. I wondered if this was his not so subtle way of retaliating for my accusatory behavior.

 # Tuesday, August 15

Back at Barbara's office, I readied myself for my second EMDR session. As predicted, there had been some strange nightmares since the last session, but not one of them was a flashback of the attack. As I sat down on Barbara's couch, my dreams were the first topic of conversation.

"So, Laura, how was the past week for you?" she asked.

"I kept the log like you suggested. I didn't have the same nightmare of the attack, but some new weird stuff came up."

"Anything in particular?"

"One dream was the most disturbing. It happened last Thursday. I was at my childhood home with my mom and I knew someone bad was coming to get us. We had to leave the house before he arrived and I was trying to get dressed and out of there in time. My mom wasn't the least bit concerned and was slowing us down. For some strange reason, she wanted to give me her heirloom rings and she wanted me to wear all of them before we left. I didn't want to put them on as that would waste time, but it was the only way to get her moving. The problem was that I couldn't get them on my fingers because they were all too small.

"I finally shoved as many rings on my fingers as I could and we were rushing to leave through the kitchen door when I noticed the back door, which was across the room, opening. Someone was coming in. I was terrified. We hadn't gotten out in time. And then I realized in our rush to leave that I had left my gun in the back bedroom.

"Then I saw it was Chris coming through the back door. I was surprised to see him because I had already sent him away to his parents' house to be safe. I asked him why he was here and he said that he was here for me. He had a funny smile—not a good smile. For an instant, I didn't know if he was there to protect me or if I should be afraid of him."

"Did it feel like Chris was the bad guy?" Barbara asked.

"I'm not sure. I wish I hadn't woken up so I could have seen what happened next. When I first saw him in the dream, I was afraid for him. I had sent him away to be safe. But, it was the way he said, 'I'm here for you,' that frightened me. Was he here to save me or to hurt me? It was terrible."

"Did you tell him about the dream?" she asked.

"No. I've never had a dream where I was afraid of Chris. I couldn't even think about how to bring it up."

Barbara replied, "Well, being chased is one of the most common dream types. The most likely interpretation is that you are trying to escape a person or situation in your real life but there could be a number of reasons why Chris was there. More importantly, dreams are not always literal. For example, a masculine figure in your dream like Chris may not be Chris himself, but your masculine self."

"My masculine self?"

"Yes, the night of your attack, Chris was not there to protect you. You haven't had to play the role of protector in your life before because you've had your father or Chris. That night brought out a required masculine side of you for your own self-protection."

"I hadn't thought of it that way. As a child, my father always took care of me, like with the Heimlich maneuver. And I wasn't in college long before I met Chris and he took over that protector role. Here I am at thirty years old and this is the first time I've ever had to protect myself," I said.

"That's true. And if you choose to tell Chris about your dream, it may help both of you to know that there are many interpretations. He shouldn't jump to the conclusion that he is the bad guy."

"I don't know. We're going away for Labor Day. It's our wedding anniversary. I'd hate to bring up something like this. Chris could brood over it for weeks, even if I reassured him."

"Has there been any friction between you two lately?"

"Not really." I thought for a moment more. "I told Chris that I wanted to take a gun class, and he did not approve. That's really all we've disagreed about lately."

"Didn't you say in your dream that you had forgotten your gun?"

"Yes. I was distraught that I didn't have it with me when I saw the back door opening. Maybe I was getting vibes from his disapproval."

"I suppose that's possible. In any case, the dream is a sign that you are still processing and purging disturbing information. Are you still having the flashback nightmares of your attack?"

"No, thankfully."

Barbara nodded. "Was there anything else that came up?"

"Nothing on the scale of that one. For a few nights, I don't think I dreamed at all. I was at the jail for a story on Friday and thought that would trigger something really awful, but it didn't."

"You were at the jail?"

"Some research for a story."

Barbara jotted a few notes, then asked, "Is there anything else you wanted to address before we try another EMDR set?"

"I don't think so."

"Okay. Last time we didn't have enough time to address the tension in your hands. If you are able to think of that as your new target, we can try a set and see where it goes."

I nodded.

"And like last time, if you need to stop, just raise your hand. Now, try to form an image of how the stress in your hands feels."

Barbara lifted her hand and began the tick-tock motion. At first, I couldn't get the image to move, but when it did, it seemed to go faster.

I started by picturing my hands curled like claws, my fingers laden with the heirloom rings from my dream. Then, slowly, as I look at my hands, I am unable to see them anymore. Instead, there is a black blob over my left hand. At first, I imagine it is covered with ink—the smell is so strong, almost nauseating. But then I notice two dog ears pointing up from the black mass. It transforms into a dog's head, a Great Dane, who is biting my hand.

He's piercing my skin to the bone. It hurts. I'm afraid if I pull away, he will tear off my finger.

I'm outside at my childhood home and know if I can just get inside, I'll be okay. I try to pull away from him, and finally do. I'm on roller skates, but instead of skating, I run across the grass in my front yard and into my house. I lock the door behind me so he can't get in.

The image fades.

I explained the weird story I had just watched.

Barbara made the obvious link. "Your attacker bit you."

"Yes, when he bit me, my fingers scabbed up and I couldn't take off my rings. Maybe that's why there were rings in my dream?"

"It could be." Barbara smiled.

"And that smell. That was the same awful smell from the night of my attack. I don't know if it was bad cologne, or if he worked with chemicals, but I would recognize that horrible smell again."

Barbara nodded. "Sensory information can be locked in your

memory just like an image. It's not uncommon to have smells, sounds and other physical sensations appear in EMDR. I noticed this time that your house was your safe haven."

"Yes. That really happened when I was a kid. Our neighbor had this huge, black Great Dane. They kept him caged, but he would break out and chase us. One time, my friend, Rachel, and I were on roller skates and we ran across the grass to get away from him because we couldn't skate fast enough. But, he never bit me. He just chased us. Thinking back, he was probably just a puppy having fun, but because he was so huge, we were terrified of him."

"How do your hands feel now?"

I looked down at my hands. The bite had healed leaving a scar on my ring and pinky fingers.

"They're not as tense, though there's one last thing to do to really feel better."

"What's that?" asked Barbara.

I hesitated. "I'm going to take an AIDS test in a few weeks. Everything I've read indicates that it would be really hard to contract AIDS from a human bite, but I just want to be sure."

"It sounds like that test is troubling you?" she asked.

"The waiting is hard. It takes three months to detect the virus. I guess I've tried not to think about it because there's nothing I can do but wait to take the test."

"I've never heard of anyone contracting HIV from a bite, but I suppose it can't hurt to be safe."

I nodded and pushed it out of my mind.

Barbara continued, "I wanted to go back to the house in that last set. It was the place that made you feel safe. Up until now, your house hasn't necessarily felt safe to you."

"Yes. But this was my childhood home, not the one we're in now."

"The same one as your dream?"

I paused and then realized why Barbara had asked. "Oh, I see. My childhood home wasn't safe in my dream. We had to leave. But just now it was where I retreated from the dog. It's the same house."

Barbara asked, "Do you want to try to go back to your original target and see what happens?"

"Okay, if you think we should."

I became more nervous about going back to my original image of him in the doorway. But, this time, it wouldn't move. Even the image felt more remote. The best way I could describe it was that it had been neutralized.

Barbara explained, "With EMDR, since you are processing disturbing thoughts and images, after they start to restructure in a more adaptive framework, they can fade. In fact, I've had to wait to do EMDR with a client who was a witness for a police line-up. We couldn't risk that her image would diminish, which it did after treatment."

I was amazed. It was as if Barbara had inserted years of healing between my attack and the present day. For the first time, the threatening image of him standing in my doorway felt like it was years behind me. How was that possible?

Barbara continued, "Since this image has seemed to fade, are there any others that come up from that night?"

I thought for a moment. I recalled the weight of his body on top of me. Because of that last set, I remembered his nauseating smell. I thought of his first words, "If you shut up, I'll leave." I remembered him running away down the street, the helpless feeling that I couldn't catch him. But, there wasn't a single striking image like the one in the doorway, and there wasn't anything substantial that I wanted to bring up.

"Does that mean we're done?" I asked.

"Not necessarily. Let's continue to discuss your dreams if you can continue to log them."

Barbara concluded the session like last time with me on my mountain top and relaxed.

I wondered if my dream was a sign that I should cancel my gun class with Sergeant Stires. The appointment was in two days. Then again, I very much regretted forgetting my gun in the dream so decided to stay the course. I hadn't yet told Chris that I was taking the class, opting to save that argument for another day.

FROM THE DESK OF
BARBARA COLE

August 15, Visit 6, EMDR Session 2
Laura Holland

New dream - with mother, trying to put on rings, trying to flee "bad guy", husband appears
- masculine self appearing?
- actual unconscious fear of husband?

Flashback nightmares have stopped - progress

Talked to police chief
Wants to take gun class
Visited the jail
- new energy channeled here, discuss further next time

EMDR set 2 - hands become dog biting/chasing her,
escaped to childhood home
After actual attack, her fingers scabbed up, couldn't take off rings
Recognizes smell - cologne or ink

Stress in hands & fingers
- apprehension over AIDS test from bite?
Research: Contracting AIDS from human bite
Can't recapture original target of attacker in the doorway - progress
Still missing complete serenity, feels unsettled
- monitor dreams, review next time

—BAC

 **Thursday, August 17**

As I walked up the sidewalk to the gun shop, I could hear the booms from the range inside. I entered the shop and approached the counter where a heavy-set man was finishing with a customer.

"Can I help you, miss?" he asked.

"Yes, I'm looking for Sergeant Stires."

The clerk pointed to a man standing in front of the glass windows watching the other shooters practice. He looked to be in his sixties, about 5'10" and 180 lbs. He wore brown slacks, a tan Oxford shirt and had on brown heavy-duty boots. Next to his boots was a large black leather bag.

I walked up to him and introduced myself. "Hi. I'm Laura Holland." He turned to face me.

"John Stires," he said in a commanding, deep voice. I couldn't help but notice his intense blue eyes. Though his wrinkled face showed his age, his eyes were young and alert, the kind of eyes that absorbed every piece of data around them.

"Nice to meet you," I said as I shook his hand. It was a firm grip, though I could tell he was holding back as to not crush my fingers.

"Are you ready to get started?" he asked.

"Sure," I replied, though I was totally out of my element.

He waved for me to follow him toward a side classroom. As he shut the door, the noise from the shooting range subsided, which was a relief.

"Please have a seat," he directed, pointing to one of the tables in the room. It was set up like a classroom with several long tables and folding chairs. I wrapped the strap of my purse around the back of the cold metal chair and sat down, as he pulled up a chair directly across from me.

"Let me start by telling you a little about myself. I'm a retired police sergeant and have been teaching pistol safety and shooting techniques for about thirty years. We'll spend about two and a half hours together today, first here in the classroom and then I'll take you out to the practice range. Have you ever shot a gun before?"

"No," I replied.

"And what is your motivation for learning about guns? Is it for personal safety, for marksmanship or something else?"

"It's for safety."

"Okay. Now, let me say right now that if you plan to buy a gun, one lesson is not enough. And I encourage you to come to the range on a regular basis to maintain your skill level. It's kind of like exercise. You can't quit or you'll get out of shape. Also, every gun has a different feel so you should purchase one that fits you, that's comfortable. They'll let you rent different types here so you can best determine which one suits you."

I nodded. I wouldn't buy a gun right away. Chris would have to agree first.

"Next topic," he continued. "When should you use your gun?"

I hesitated, unsure if his question was rhetorical.

"The answer is that the ultimate purpose of a gun is for your defense. It is not a warning or intimidation instrument, but a tool of destruction. If you cannot accept this, you have no business owning a weapon. We all know the Second Amendment gives all law-abiding citizens the right to bear arms. To be worthy of this privilege, you must be competent and use good judgment."

I nodded.

"Let me give you some examples. Never use your gun during a robbery or carjacking unless you are in absolute fear of your life. Only then, would the taking of another life be justified. There is a term called deadly force, which describes the intensity of attack that would put your life at risk. Only when you are faced with deadly force should you respond by using your gun. Any questions?"

"What if a felon is leaving a crime? Can I shoot?" I asked.

"Good question," he replied. "If you are confronted with a fleeing felon, it is in your best interest to hold your fire unless you are assisting a police officer who has specifically asked for your help."

The sergeant sounded a lot like Thomas. But what if I had bought a gun without taking this training class? I would have been in real trouble.

Sergeant Stires continued, "In general, never shoot at a running man unless he has committed a killing or savage crime before your very eyes. And, that crime would have to be with such ferocity that you believed that he would put the general public at extreme danger as long as he remained at large. I can tell you a tragic story about a guy who shot an innocent civilian who was running from a mugger. The mugger and the victim were struggling outside the guy's house. The victim knocked the mugger down and began to run away. Well, the guy came outside and saw the mugger on the ground and the victim running and assumed that the one running was the criminal and shot him. Luckily, he survived, but this is a good example that you should be careful if you come upon this type of situation. It is not always clear who is the good guy and who is the bad."

The sergeant's advice could not have been any more supportive of Thomas' argument. It was as if Thomas had prepped him prior to my visit.

"Next question," he said. "Would you rather wound an assailant than kill him?"

"Well, if I could make sure he was no longer a danger by just wounding him, I guess so."

"Let's clear up this misconception right away. Never, ever shoot to wound. If you draw your gun, that should be an indication that your life or the life of a loved one is threatened, period. When you draw, you should be prepared to use that gun to stop or neutralize the threat. Besides, if you are in a situation where you have to draw your gun, your blood pressure will be at an all-time high. Your nerves will be going haywire. You can't afford to aim at a small target like a knee or arm and expect to be accurate under those conditions. You need to aim for the largest target you can, the torso."

I pictured my target—the red circle on the back of his shirt.

"One final thought on this, just so you are thoroughly convinced. Though you may think wounding the assailant is more humane, it may not be. Do you realize just how much damage can be done by a non-fatal wound? We watch movie stars treating flesh wounds like scratches and they hardly limp after taking a bullet in the leg. Television and movies have given us the idea that a gunshot wound is little more than a remote-control punch. This just isn't true. A high-powered bullet through the thigh can render the leg crippled for life. A bullet in the abdomen can fatally damage the liver or kidneys. And, there is always the possibility of death from hemorrhage or shock. From a legal standpoint, if your assailant dies of the wound or related complications within a year and a day, it's the same as if he died the day of the shooting. And a crippled man can sue you much more easily than a dead man."

I thought of my case. I had chosen for my attacker to die. I hadn't really considered which option, dead or crippled, would be worse though it looked like I had picked the better one.

The sergeant continued. "So, I hope it is clear to you that a shot to wound should never be used. The very fact that you did not shoot to kill could be construed that even you did not consider the situation worthy of deadly force."

The sergeant leaned back in his chair. He crossed his arms, never taking his piercing blue eyes off of me. It looked as if he was waiting for me to absorb all of this information he was spilling forth. I had expected his $150 fee to be spent on the shooting range and learning how to use a gun. I didn't anticipate receiving information on when to use the gun and the legal ramifications of those actions, though I didn't mind. This information would certainly help me develop the case, although it was making me more concerned about being acquitted.

"Next question. When should you fire a warning shot?"

I was silent for fear I'd say the wrong thing.

"Like the shot to wound, you should never fire a warning shot."

A warning shot had never entered my mind.

"As a civilian," Sergeant Stires continued, "You have no need to fire warning shots when under attack. It will only cost you precious time and a precious bullet. If you have justification to shoot, you should shoot to kill. If deadly force is not warranted, the gun should not be drawn, period.

"Now, let's talk about escalation of force. When I was a police officer dealing with an armed man, I was required to identify myself and order the gunman to drop his weapon before I took any other action. If the gunman turned on me, then I had no choice but to shoot. I had to assume that he intended to kill me. As we discussed before, I did not aim to wound, but to stop. This was the standard procedure then and still is today."

I nodded.

"It's a good protocol for a couple of reasons. First, every shooting will undergo a thorough investigation. Any hint of impropriety, like shooting a suspect before it was absolutely necessary, could trigger a media and community uprising. Secondly, and more importantly, killing another human being can be a hard reality to live with. Most of my former squad would tell you that they couldn't sleep at night if they didn't feel one hundred percent justified in taking that life. This is why we adopted the standard procedure of giving a gunman a chance to surrender first."

The sergeant looked off into the distance giving me a break from his intense eye lock.

"And trust me, you still think about it. The taking of a human life is an emotionally devastating act. And it's not just the fact that the person you shot is gone from this world. You also have to face his family. Let me tell you that if you don't know in your heart of hearts that you had to shoot, the thought of them and their pain will haunt you for the rest of your life."

I had not even considered the loved ones. What kind of family would he have? Could he be living a double life where he seemed normal to them, even though he turned into a demon at night? Could his family be so unaware of his derangement that they would not see any bad in him? Was living in fear of him actually better than carrying the burden of taking another life and the pain I could have caused them?

The sergeant looked back at me.

"Now, do you, the private citizen, have to follow the same procedure? The answer is no. If time permits, you may give a verbal warning to the assailant. However, you, as a civilian, don't have to allow that much leeway for the sake of justifying your actions. It is possible that by the time you yell stop, your assailant will have unloaded his first bullet into you. So, the rule for you is as follows—if you have time, give a verbal warning, but not a warning or disabling shot. If the warning is ignored or cannot be done without risking your own life or those around you, the situation has escalated. It has reached the point where the degree of force that is justifiable includes the right to kill. Any questions?"

"No, it's pretty clear," I replied.

"Do you still want to learn to shoot a gun?"

"Yes."

"Okay, then. Let's go do some shooting."

He reached into his black leather bag and pulled out a one-page form, a pair of safety glasses and a headset.

"You'll need to read and sign this form and show your driver's license up front."

I read the form and signed the waiver at the bottom, collected the glasses and headset, and followed the sergeant to the practice range. We passed through two sets of heavy doors, turned right and walked to the end stall, passing a few other shooters. Even with the headset on, it was loud.

The sergeant grabbed a broom and swept away some of the empty bullet casings on the floor of our small stall. He pulled two guns, some ammunition and some paper targets out of his bag and laid them on the small wooden shelf that spanned the length of the stall.

He also pulled out a small laminated card and pointed to the first line as he read aloud. He had to shout so I could hear him.

ALWAYS keep the gun pointed in a safe direction.

"You must always assume the gun is loaded. Therefore, keep it pointed down range. When you are finished shooting, place the gun and the cartridge on the table. If it jams, let me know. Don't try to unjam it yourself."

He used his pointer finger and thumb to make the shape of a gun, like little boys do when playing cops and robbers. He turned his pointer finger to his left.

"If I clear the jam and it accidentally goes off, what have I done?"

I replied, "You've shot the guy in the stall next to you."

"Exactly. That's why I like this stall on the end. It's safer," he said.

He pointed to and read line #2.

ALWAYS keep your finger off the trigger until ready to shoot.

"When holding the gun, rest your finger on the trigger guard or along the side of the gun. You only put your finger on the trigger when you are pointing the gun down range and are ready to shoot. There could be someone in the practice area with a loud rifle that startles you and if your finger is on the trigger, you could accidentally set off the gun."

He read the last and final line.

ALWAYS keep the gun unloaded until ready to use.

"The protocol here at the practice range is to set the gun on the shelf with the cartridge out to show it is not loaded, unless you are using it."

Sergeant Stires picked up the first gun. It had a black base and a silver top. He cocked it back as he pointed it down the range to verify that it was unloaded.

"This is a Ruger P95DC. It has a double-action, which means the first shot cocks and fires the gun, so the first shot requires more pull on the trigger. Subsequent shots will take less pressure."

He grabbed the magazine with the bullets and popped it into the gun. Then he showed me how to grip the handle so that the slide wouldn't catch my thumbs. He explained how to line up the sights, making sure the two outer white dots at the handle lined up with the inner white dot at the end of the barrel. And finally, he demonstrated how to stand with my feet shoulder-length apart, arms extended, elbows locked and leaning slightly forward. He cocked the gun and handed it to me.

"Like I said, it's a double-action so the first shot takes more pull on the trigger. Just line up the sights and squeeze gently. After your first shot, keep pointing the gun forward."

I took the gun. It was heavy and solid, but I liked the feel of it.

He clipped a paper target with a bull's eye on a pulley and sent the target about twenty feet down range. I took the stance he had demonstrated, squinted my left eye as I peered down the sight. I started squeezing the trigger. Nothing happened. I squeezed a bit harder, nervously awaiting the discharge while trying to keep the sights from wavering.

B O O M !

The gun fired, pushing my arms back slightly with the recoil. I kept the gun pointing forward as instructed and we looked down range at the target. My shot hit about two o'clock inside the black circle.

"Not bad for a beginner," he said.

I fired four more shots per his instruction, each one was easier with the single action. All hit the black circular target, but missed the bull's eye. Still, I was pleased I could hit any part of the target.

"That's pretty good," he said. "You're a natural."

I practiced a few more rounds, all with similar accuracy though a few went barely outside of the black circle. Just when I was getting more comfortable cocking the gun and squeezing the trigger, he handed me the second gun.

"This is a Glock26. It doesn't have the double-action, but has more kick. Why don't you give it a try?"

I took the gun and aimed at the black circle, but my accuracy was much worse. My early confidence dissipated.

"Don't worry," he said. "This is a harder gun to shoot. That's why if you plan to buy one, you want to try out a few first."

Sergeant Stires then switched the round target to the outline of a male figure and sent it about twenty-five feet down range.

"Now, your accuracy was real good when you had time to concentrate, but that's not reality. This time, we'll leave the gun on the table. You have to grab it, aim it and fire two shots back to back. And pretend this guy is coming at you so you don't have time to waste. Cock the gun with one stroke and fire as soon as the front sight comes in line with your target. Hold the gun with both hands and aim for the torso. Again, never aim to wound or disable, but to stop him."

This exercise made me nervous. Even though it was just a drill, my heart started to beat more rapidly. I took my stance, grabbed the gun and fired twice. One shot hit the neck and the other went outside the figure.

"Pretty good," he said. "That was decent speed and the neck shot would have stopped him. But you need to aim for the torso, and you need to fire the shots in three seconds. At twenty-five feet away, he'll be on you in three seconds."

The sergeant took the gun from me and placed it back on the table. "Try again."

My heart raced more—my adrenaline was pumping. I grabbed the gun from the table and fired two shots. One hit the area of the right kidney. The other went outside the outline of the figure.

I'm not sure I could have even hit him if I had tried.

We did a few more practice rounds. I hit the target on about three shots out of four. I also figured that I would have shot more than just two bullets so maybe I could have hit him with a few more tries.

"Last exercise," the sergeant said. "Your right arm is injured so you have to shoot solely with your left hand. The gunman is holding your best friend hostage in front of him so you only have a shot at his head. You get one try with your left hand to save your friend's life."

"Seriously?" I asked in disbelief. My first lesson in self-defense had become the impossible task of saving Vicki's life, and left-handed at that.

"Pick your weapon," he said.

I took the Ruger, of course, as I had consistently shot better with it. It felt awkward in my left hand. I aimed, my hand wobbling. I took a deep breath and concentrated. It wasn't unlike playing golf. The mind controlled the shot, not the body. I squeezed the trigger gently and steadily.

B O O M !

I had taken out his right eye and saved Vicki's life.

"Wow. I'm impressed," he said. I was surprised too.

"Well, that is a good note to end on," he said, as he started packing up the guns. Once we were back in the shop, I took off the glasses and headset. My ears were ringing a little.

"So, if I wanted to buy a gun, what would be the next step?" I asked.

"I'd recommend you still shoot a few other types to see which one you like best."

"I kind of like the Ruger," I admitted. "How could I buy one like yours?"

"I see you're a lady who makes up her mind fast. You can buy one here or at any gun shop, but ..."

"Is there a background check or waiting period?" I interrupted.

He paused. "There's an instant background check through the Georgia Bureau of Investigation. It costs five dollars."

"That's it?" I had thought there would be a waiting period of some sort but that wasn't the case in Georgia.

"Yes," he confirmed.

"And do I have to register the gun with someone?"

"No. Once you pass the background check you are good to go, but do not neglect your training. It is essential to be comfortable with the gun under emergency situations and often in the dark. That skill only comes with time and practice. And, you need to continue the quick-draw drills we did to prevent a criminal from getting too close to you and taking the gun from you."

"How much is a Ruger?"

"The practice ammo is about $15 a box. The guns range from about $450 to $600 depending on the type."

I caught Sergeant Stires' overt way of pushing the lessons.

In very short order, I had picked out the gun I wanted, passed the background check, paid the clerk and was the proud owner of a new 9mm Ruger.

The concerned look on Sergeant Stires' face didn't go away until I made an appointment with him for my next lesson.

He gave me a few more instructions on how to store the gun at home, especially keeping it out of the reach of children. Before saying goodbye, he pulled out a hollow-point bullet from his bag. The difference between it and the range bullets was quite obvious. The hollow-point was a monster.

"Next time, we'll shoot a few of these so you can feel the difference. These are the kind of bullets you'll keep in the gun for protection."

I could tell he was throwing out an enticement to ensure I'd come back for more training. Perhaps he had been stood up before by new gun owners and didn't want a novice with a new gun on his conscience.

Obviously, he didn't know me.

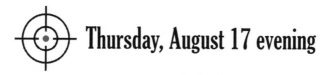 # Thursday, August 17 evening

I stored my shiny new purchase under the bed. No need to worry about children finding it. Lucy's kids were the only ones that came to the house, and they were in South Carolina.

As I made dinner, I thought about how I'd explain my impulse purchase to Chris. By the time he arrived, the smell of lasagna and garlic bread filled the house. After a second helping, he was relaxing with his wine on the couch. I started to give him a back massage.

"You made dinner and now a massage. What did you do?" he asked.

I kind of knew Chris would guess that something was up by my behavior and I wanted it that way, to soften the blow.

"Well, I do have something to tell you that you may not like."

Chris' brows lowered, but he kept his eyes fixed on me.

"What?"

"I know you don't like the idea, but I'm not happy with just the alarm, so I bought a gun today."

"You what?" Chris shouted, nearly spilling his wine as he sat upright on the couch.

"You heard me. I bought a gun."

"You just go off and buy a gun without discussing this with me, when you know I'm opposed to having a gun in the house? Laura, these are decisions that we should make as a couple. This is not how we decide things."

"Chris, you travel all the time. I still don't feel safe, and I wanted one."

"We have the alarm system. And if you really don't feel that is enough, we can get a damn dog. I'd rather live with hives than mistakenly get shot."

"I don't want a dog," I argued.

Chris countered, "You don't even know how to use a gun."

"I'm taking lessons."

"Where?"

"At the Sandy Springs Gun Club. They have an instructor there who already gave me a lesson today. I was pretty good."

"Well, I see you've already set everything in motion. What if my travel plans change and I come home early one night and forget to tell you? Are you just going to shoot me?" Chris' voice was still elevated.

"You should remember to tell me if you are coming home early."

His tone changed to slow and deliberate. "Laura, I hope you remember this conversation when you are a grieving widow because you've shot and killed me."

"Who says I'll be grieving?" I snapped, and then quickly covered my mouth with my hand. Chris was staring at me in disbelief.

"I'm sorry. I didn't mean that. You know I didn't mean that." I gathered myself. "You are gone a lot, and I need some protection for when he comes back."

"What do you mean? Why do you think he is coming back? He knows you're a fighter."

"He said he was. Remember? He said you win *for now* and not to forget him. Of course he's not done with this. He's out there somewhere plotting the right time to come back."

"Honey, I don't think he's coming back. Of course, he would say that because he lost. He didn't get to control you so he had to leave with something that still gave him power. He would have to know that we added security—it's too risky for him now. I know that is all logic and how can we assume this nut job is logical, but I really don't think he'll come back. Even the police said that. Don't you remember? And, Dr. Cole doesn't think he'll come back, either."

I replied, "We don't know that. All we know is that he is still out there, a free man. And maybe he is hunting other women, but maybe he doesn't like that I fought back. I need a gun. I'll learn how to use it. I'll be careful with it, but I need to have it in case he comes back."

Chris just shook his head.

After sitting in silence for a moment, he said, "Let me see it."

I went into the bedroom. He followed. I knelt under the bed and pulled out the unloaded Ruger and bullet cartridge.

"It's not loaded," I confirmed, doing the same check that Sergeant Stires had shown me at the range. I then handed the gun to Chris.

He instinctively knew to point it downward and away as he inspected it.

"I know you want it, but I still don't like it," he said, not taking his eyes off the gun.

"Let me take the classes. You can come with me and shoot it yourself. Then we can decide."

"Who do you think you're fooling? You won't return a pair of shoes that don't fit. I'm supposed to believe you'd return this gun?"

I didn't answer.

"I might as well buy you a membership to the NRA. How much did this thing cost anyway?"

"About five rounds of golf," I said.

"You owe me five rounds of golf."

I touched his arm. "You know, shooting it is a lot like golf," I said. "It takes concentration and muscle control. You may find you like it."

"Trust me, I won't," he scoffed.

"Why exactly are you so anti-guns anyway?"

"Laura, I spend my days in hospitals. Mind you, it's mostly in conference rooms, but we check out the equipment, too. Where do you think the majority of our CTs go? The ER. The ER where kids come in with their guts ripped open because someone stupid had a gun. You know what? Forget the rounds of golf. If you insist on keeping this gun, you're taking a trip to the ER to see the damage for yourself."

That wasn't a trade I expected to make, but unfortunately I couldn't deny that it was a fair request. Maybe he'd forget. Then again, maybe this was his best way of fighting back, to show me all the gore and blood in hopes I'd change my mind.

"Fine," I said.

"And you'd better tell Troy, too," he added, "so you don't accidentally shoot him."

He had a good point. Troy had a key to our house and knew the alarm code—he was just as likely as Chris to be mistaken for an intruder.

"I'll tell him. By the way, Troy wouldn't take me shooting unless I told you first, so I had to go without him. I'm not sure what kind of macho guy alliance you two have, but you should know he was loyal."

 Tuesday, August 22

Tuesday rolled around again and I was headed back to Barbara's office. I had gone another week without a flashback nightmare of the attack. Overall, my bad dreams were less disturbing and much less frequent.

Barbara asked me in her usual soothing voice, "So, Laura, how have you been?"

"I've been pretty good actually. I didn't have much to add to the log in the way of dreams. I guess my secluded memory island is a populated oasis now."

Barbara laughed, then asked, "No new dreams or observations?"

"Not really."

"I see."

Barbara glanced down at her notes and then asked, "Laura, I was thinking about our last session and there were a few things that you said that I didn't quite understand. These things may all be part of your work and nothing we have discussed or even should discuss, but I thought I'd ask if something might have you preoccupied?"

"What do you mean?"

"Well, I noticed that you talked about visiting the jail and the police chief, and you were thinking of buying a gun."

"Actually, I bought one last week," I replied with a hint of accomplishment. "Chris wasn't happy to say the least, and we haven't really decided how to resolve our differences. I'd like him to come to a shooting class with me and he wants me to go see gunshot victims in the ER with him. So you can see, like the rest of America, we're at a bit of an impasse on the gun issue."

"I hadn't realized you were so close to making a gun purchase," Barbara commented.

"Well, I wasn't really planning to buy one right away. I took a gun class last week and just felt like I was ready to do it. I had talked to the police chief who had given me a gun instructor's name. Actually, this all kind of came up from that conversation around self-defense that we had a while back. I wanted to know if I would have been able to claim self-defense if I had shot my attacker when he was leaving."

I paused.

Now was as good a time as any to tell Barbara about my project with Thomas.

"I also decided to talk to a criminal defense lawyer to ask the same question. I lucked out and found one in this building named Thomas Bennett."

Barbara's eyebrows rose briefly and then she cleared her throat.

"I see," she said. "Did you find the answers you were seeking?"

"Kind of. It's not really a cut and dry answer. On the surface, it appears I wouldn't have a clear case of self-defense, but I want to challenge that. I decided to write a hypothetical legal case and Mr. Bennett agreed to help me. I'm just at the beginning of my research."

I looked for Barbara's reaction, especially for any signs of disapproval. As I studied her face, I scratched my chest, revealing red bumps across my décolleté.

Barbara replied, "You seem to have a lot of passion around the legal aspects of that night. What do you think is driving that?"

"I guess it's the journalist in me. I was ignorant about the laws of self-defense, so I'm assuming the general public may be as well. I pitched it to my editor and he liked the idea of playing out the hypothetical case, with the help of a legal consultant, of course."

"Does owning a gun play into the story? Do you have to learn how to shoot for the story?"

"Oh, no. That's just for my own protection. I feel safer with it in the house."

Barbara continued, "You said the nightmares are dissipating, but is there something else still concerning you?"

"I guess I'm just more aware of the need for self-protection. But, now that I'm not having nightmares anymore, I'm doing a lot better."

I noticed Barbara looking at my chest. I didn't even realize that I was scratching it again.

"Are you okay?" Barbara asked.

"Oh, it's nothing. I've had this rash a few days now. I suppose if it stays much longer, I'll have to see a dermatologist. I thought the jail seemed clean, but who knows what kind of creepy crawlies I may have caught there." I shivered at the thought.

"And you went to the jail for your story?"

"Yes. In the hypothetical scenario, if I shot my attacker, I would have gone to jail. So I wanted to see it for myself. I'm also attending an arraignment tomorrow."

Barbara rubbed her lower lip back and forth with her pointer finger.

I guess I had dumped quite a bit on her—the legal story, the gun, the jail, but I thought she'd be happy I was getting back into my work.

She asked, "Do you think you're ready to deal with all of this information? I'm concerned it will draw you closer toward the night of the attack, instead of allowing yourself some distance to heal."

"I'll be alright," I confirmed. "It's all hypothetical anyway. And I think it will make a really interesting story. I'm hoping it will turn my terrible experience into something productive and helpful for others."

"Speaking of which, we've had two productive sessions of EMDR. Do you feel you'd like to continue down that path some more?"

"Well, I don't know when it's actually done, but now that my nightmares are gone, I think we can call it a success. You know, after I've finished the case, I might write an article on EMDR. I had never heard of it until you introduced me to it. That is, if you would be open to us collaborating in that way?"

"I suppose we could talk about that, but right now my primary concern is your well-being."

I smiled. "I appreciate that. You've been wonderful. Beyond wonderful, you've changed my mind on the value of therapy. I just don't think I'd get much out of any more EMDR work. It did what it was supposed to. My nightmares are gone."

I continued, in a sheepish tone, "I think I might be ready to go back to how my life was before."

"Meaning?"

I looked down. "Where I didn't need to come to therapy every week."

"So you'd like to conclude our sessions?"

I paused.

"Yes, I think so." I hadn't necessarily planned to end our sessions today. But, the more I talked, the more I realized that they had run their course.

Barbara didn't speak for what seemed like a long time.

"Laura, it does seem like this legal case has captured your attention, which is certainly your prerogative, but I think there's more to your healing than just stopping the nightmares."

"Oh, I hope I'm not offending you by wanting to stop our sessions. I don't mean to. I really think you've done me a world of good."

"Thank you. No, I'm not offended. The key to therapy is that we both have to want to be here. I remember our first meeting when you told me that your husband had made the appointment. I was worried about making progress with you, that you would be an unwilling client. But I was wrong. You were very open and eager to heal, which made me feel very hopeful."

"Well, you were easy to talk to."

Barbara smiled. "And I enjoyed getting to meet Chris and seeing that you have a caring partner at home."

I just nodded.

Barbara continued, "I don't know that therapy is ever done. I suppose there are always things to work on in our lives. For now, it seems that you have a lot of energy around this legal case. If there comes a time when you find there is more to talk about, we can always pick up from here."

"Okay. I'd like that. And I'll be over here for the next month or two working with Thomas Bennett, so maybe I'll see you around."

"Indeed." Barbara paused before speaking again. "Out of respect for our therapist-client relationship, I won't acknowledge you publicly, unless you initiate the interaction. It's not meant to be rude but to protect your privacy."

"Oh. It's fine if you speak to me. I'm sure Mike, the guard, has made it his business to find out that I'm seeing you anyway."

"Ah, Mr. Howard. Yes, he takes his job of knowing the comings and goings of this building quite seriously."

There was an awkward silence, one of the few times I felt awkward around her.

"Well, thanks again for everything," I said. "I'll let Alisa know to take me off the usual Tuesday afternoon schedule. I really am grateful that I met you, Barbara."

"Likewise, Laura."

With that, I left the office, making my seventh visit my last.

FROM THE DESK OF
BARBARA COLE

August 22, Visit 7

Laura Holland

Bought a gun, without discussing with her husband

Working with Thomas on hypothetical, vigilante legal case

> Why is Thomas doing a pro-bono case with my patient?
>
> Did he make the connection from my question?
>
> Does he think he's helping me? Helping her?
>
> Messy triangle

Patient

Therapist   Lawyer

Immersed in legal story

- holding on to her trauma, using it to fuel her drive, to pursue this story with Thomas, clearly not ready to let go

Rash on her chest

- not healed, manifesting in her body, transposed the mental trauma of her nightmares to physical outbreak on her body

—BAC

 # Wednesday, August 23

I awoke to my 7 a.m. alarm. I was meeting Thomas at the Fulton County Courthouse to watch bond hearings and arraignments. Originally, I was going to drive with Thomas—we had discovered that he lived in the next neighborhood over—but he needed to be at the courthouse all afternoon and I didn't plan to stay beyond the morning.

I exited at Martin Luther King Jr. Drive and found the parking garage across from the courthouse, just as Thomas had described. As I walked from my car to the garage elevators, a large black truck pulled up behind me. Instead of passing around me, it slowly followed me. I sped up my pace. Once safely at the elevator enclave, I turned back to get a better view of the driver. It was a black guy with a shaven head and a beard.

Not him.

Then I realized that he could have grown a beard, shaved his head or done any other manner of things to alter his appearance. After all, he didn't know I couldn't recognize him. A shiver went down my spine as I hurried into the open elevator and made my way to the street level. It was an unusually windy August morning. I had my hair in a bun but it started to unravel as I crossed the street. Though I had lived in Atlanta most of my life, I had never been to the courthouse. The building was a large concrete gray structure, with ornate lion statues that acted as bookends for the wide front steps. Once I passed through the glass doors, I immediately saw Thomas dressed in a charcoal suit, light blue shirt and black tie, waiting for me at security.

"Find it here okay?" he asked.

"No problem," I replied, as I tried to smooth the loose strands of my hair.

He gestured for me to go through the screening, so I handed my purse and iPad to the guard to run them through the X-ray equipment. I started to take off my heels when Thomas grabbed my arm. I instinctively jerked away.

"The security isn't so strict here," he said, seeming—or pretending—not to notice my reaction.

After we both passed through the X-ray scanner, Thomas led me to a courtroom on the fifth floor. The room had long rows of light brown wooden benches. There appeared to be a jury box on the left and the judge's bench was directly in front. The Georgia state flag and the state seal hung on the wall behind the judge's chair.

I sat next to Thomas on the bench—probably the closest we had physically been, other than him grabbing my arm. I could smell his cologne. I didn't recognize the scent but it was nice, something I would have bought for Chris.

It was just before nine o'clock.

Thomas leaned over. "The judge should be here soon."

Just then, the bailiff instructed us to turn off our cell phones and told the gentlemen to tuck in their shirts. I found that an odd request but guess it was a sign of respect, especially in a southern courtroom.

"All rise," the bailiff ordered.

An elderly black man entered the room in his majestic black robe. The fifteen or so people in the courtroom stood.

"You may be seated," the judge said. I was surprised when he started with a lecture.

"People. There is something I just don't understand. We have folks in jail for twelve months, eighteen months, even longer without discovery having been done. Do we all agree on the process here? It's not complicated. We have the accused. We have the preliminary hearing and bonds are set. If the grand jury indicts, the case is put on the calendar. We have an arraignment, exchange discovery and either go to trial or negotiate a deal. What is so complicated about that? We have a thing called the 14th amendment in this country. Every citizen is entitled to due process. I've seen everything but due process in my courtroom. Let's get it together, people. You lawyers would give an aspirin a headache!"

Wow. This guy is a character.

The bailiff called the first case. A young, black man was brought into the courtroom from the right side door. His hands were cuffed in the front and he wore a navy jumpsuit with FULTON COUNTY JAIL in bold, white letters on the back.

A probation officer explained that the defendant had been charged with cocaine possession and had been given ten years on probation. He had failed to show up at his first probation meeting, so he had been brought into custody. His lawyer tried to defend him, but the prosecutor requested the maximum sentence of two years. The judge agreed. The case was over quickly and the man in handcuffs was carted away.

I leaned over to Thomas, almost afraid to ask a question for fear of getting a personal lecture from the judge.

I whispered, "So he missed his probation meeting and is now going to jail for two years?"

"Yes. Some judges might have just given him a warning, telling him to show up next time. This guy takes the hard line. There's a lot of luck involved in who gives you a break and who doesn't."

The next case was a bond hearing. A young black kid was brought in wearing handcuffs and the same navy jumpsuit. The defense introduced the boy and stated that he was accused of armed robbery, assault and possession of a firearm. His bond had been set at $25,000, and the defense was asking for a lesser amount of $10,000.

The judge looked at the defendant who was just standing there with his head hung low.

"Son, how long did you go to school?" he bellowed.

"I'm still in school, sir," the young man replied.

"What are you studying? How to rob people!" he asked sarcastically. There was a slight chuckle across the courtroom. I laughed myself.

This guy should have his own TV show.

"Bond remains at $25,000. You'll just never learn, will you? Get him out of here."

They escorted the defendant back out of the room and called the next case.

The defendant was an older black man. He was dressed in a suit and stood by his lawyer silently as the prosecutor opened the case.

"Your Honor, this is Frank Caldwell. He is forty-eight years old and lives in Atlanta. He is charged with aggravated assault, but is accepting a plea of simple assault. Mr. Caldwell is a clerk at a convenience store. He got into a verbal altercation and is accused of hitting the victim with a baseball bat. The state is recommending a twelve month suspended sentence, a $100 fine and no contact with the victim."

The defense council spoke up. "Your Honor, if I could elaborate a little more on the circumstances. Mr. Caldwell has worked at that store for sixteen years. He gets along with the community. The victim was intoxicated and my client refused to sell him more alcohol. The victim became belligerent, demanding to be served while my client tried to reason with him. Eventually, my client used the bat for his own protection and to coax the intoxicated man out of the store. He never hit him, but merely pushed him with the bat. We've agreed to the lesser charge as my client would like to put this whole incident behind him. We have the $100 cash for the fine and would like to get this handled today, if possible."

The judge agreed to the plea. Thomas leaned over to explain.

"He got a suspended sentence as long as he stays out of trouble for the next twelve months. He won't even have probation but has to stay away from the victim."

I replied, "The *victim*? You mean the drunk guy? Mr. Caldwell seems to be the victim here. Instead of being commended for not selling alcohol to a drunk, he gets a criminal record?"

Thomas nodded. We watched a few more cases until that courtroom adjourned for lunch.

"Want to see more?" he asked.

"No, I get the gist of it."

My stomach growled.

"Do you want to grab some lunch?" I asked. I had a few more questions I wanted to ask while they were fresh on my mind.

Thomas looked at his watch. "Okay, I have time. Do you like Italian?"

"Sure."

We walked a block to Mama Mia's Pizzeria & Grill as I asked my questions.

"What was the point of the reduced sentence for Mr. Caldwell?"

"Well, they reduced the charge from aggravated assault to simple assault, which reduced the sentence from a maximum of twenty years to twelve months, and he will no longer be a convicted felon."

"But now he has a criminal record. Why wouldn't he try to fight it?"

"He could have. But, you heard his attorney. He wanted it over. He probably didn't want the hassle of a trial or the additional legal fees. Plus, there still is a risk with a jury trial."

We arrived at the restaurant and took a booth by the window. The waitress brought us two glasses of water and took our order. After she left, Thomas drew the parallels to my case.

"You know, a plea is something you could consider, as well."

"I don't think innocent people should compromise," I retorted. Caldwell's case had unnerved me.

Thomas took a sip of his water. We sat in silence for a moment.

"Okay," I said. "For argument's sake, what would we plea?"

He grinned.

"For starters, I'd contact the prosecutor's office to see if they would offer a deal. We'd want to see their attitude about going to trial. Though they may have appeared harsh at the earlier hearings, they may realize this case isn't a slam dunk to win."

"Meaning they would be afraid the jury would sympathize with me?" I asked.

"Right. The jury might be sympathetic to your story and wonder why the prosecution was spending their hard earned tax dollars chasing a woman who was not a threat to society. Plus, you never know the prosecution's situation. They could be flooded with cases and want to close this one quickly."

"What do you think they'd offer?" I asked.

"Probably involuntary manslaughter. Instead of twenty years for voluntary manslaughter, it would go down to ten years, and you could possibly get probation."

"So with probation, I wouldn't serve any more jail time but it would be on my record, just like Mr. Caldwell?"

"Right, but you'd still be a convicted felon," he confirmed. "And your sentence could range from probation to the full ten years. As you recall from the plea deal we just saw, the prosecutor would recommend a sentence so we would know in advance if they were asking for any prison time."

"So as my lawyer, you'd recommend that we negotiate a plea?"

"That's probably the best route. After all, you're not denying that you shot and killed the guy."

Just then, the waitress brought our plates. She obviously heard Thomas' last comment based on the troubled look on her face. She served our lunch quickly and left, all the while averting her eyes from looking at me.

"Nice timing," I commented. "Want to say that a little louder?"

Thomas looked completely amused. "I can counsel you about being on death row when she comes back."

"You're supposed to be defending me, not sending me to the electric chair."

"Actually, it's lethal injection. The Georgia Supreme Court ruled death by electrocution cruel and unusual punishment back in 2001."

I just rolled my eyes. There was nothing worse than an intelligent smart-ass.

I twirled my spaghetti around my fork as I thought about Thomas' advice to take a plea deal.

"So if I agreed to a plea deal and there's no jail time, what's the downside? Having a record?"

"Well, there are a few things," Thomas replied. "First, if you were ever arrested again it would show up. That would affect your ability to get a bond. It also would show up on a background check if you were applying for a job. And, as a convicted felon, you can't vote, serve in the military or own firearms."

"But if I go to trial and am acquitted, it wouldn't be on my record?"

"The arrest would show, but there would be no conviction," he confirmed.

"What if we didn't like the plea deal they offered? Do we have to take it?"

"Not at all," Thomas replied. "It's just an offer. It's ours to accept or refuse. Though I suppose a quick plea deal doesn't make for a very interesting story."

"It's more than the story. I'm not sure I would encourage anyone to take a deal, to settle, when they were not at fault. What if we move forward, without the plea?"

"Then the trial date would be set. We would exchange discovery. That's where the state shows us their evidence and vice versa. We'd interview witnesses and decide on your best course of defense."

"What do you think would be my best defense?" I asked.

"Well, as crazy as it sounds, our first approach would be that you didn't shoot the guy."

"But I've already admitted it to the police," I countered.

"True, but as your defense lawyer, I'm going to think of every possible angle. The first one is the most basic, that you didn't do it, that your admission was false. So, you ask, why confess to a crime that you didn't commit? Easy. The police are really good at coercing people to confess, and they can persuade people to admit to crimes they didn't commit. It wouldn't be the first time."

"I guess that's true. I would have been under duress."

I played out that idea in my mind.

Something feels off.

Thomas continued, "And sometimes people confess because they are protecting someone else."

"I hadn't thought of that."

"It's called the SODDIT defense, Some Other Dude Did It."

"That's a technical term?" I asked.

Thomas laughed. "No, that's my term. But you could have been protecting someone else, say your husband."

"But he was out of town, and what good would it do me to throw the blame on my own husband? Besides, won't the police have my recorded confession and a gun with my fingerprints?"

I realized what felt wrong. This defense was a lie, and what good ever came from telling a lie?

"You ever thought about going into prosecution as a second career?" Thomas asked.

"Well, I just don't think this defense makes any sense."

"Fair, but what I'm trying to show you is that, as your defense attorney, I'll look at all angles, no matter how far-fetched."

"What about temporary insanity?" I asked.

"Georgia doesn't have temporary insanity. We have what is called NGRI, Not Guilty by Reason of Insanity."

Thomas paused and reflected for a moment. "No, that won't work. I don't think we could prove you were insane. And, if the police tapes don't get thrown out, the jury will hear a lucid person talking about her attack."

"But what about the heat of the moment? Can't we show that I was so shaken by the attack that I lost my ability to reason properly, that I shot him before I really comprehended the severity of my actions?"

"Sure, we'll show that, but that's not an insanity defense. Heat of the moment has more to do with malice aforethought. It has to do with distinguishing malice murder from felony murder or voluntary manslaughter. This was not a planned murder, which is where we would argue that your actions were done in the heat of the moment, not planned and free of malice."

I was puzzled. "Then I don't really understand how anyone uses an insanity defense."

"Let me explain. To use NGRI under Georgia law, first you would have to admit to everything. You would have to say that everything happened just as the police described it. Your defense would be that you should not be held responsible for your conduct because you were so mentally ill at the time that you couldn't distinguish right from wrong. We would have to show that you were acting under some delusional compulsion. This is why the Georgia insanity law is so hard to prove. I'd have to show that you were under such a severe delusional state that your reaction was appropriate."

"But my reaction was appropriate."

"Well, here's the part you won't like. If you are found NGRI, you won't be released, but rather sent to the state mental hospital. You would stay there until the doctors determined that you were mentally ready to be discharged, if ever."

"Well they'd realize I'm not mentally ill and let me go."

"Maybe. Maybe not. In the meantime, forget the mean inmates, now you're dealing with plain ole crazy."

"So NGRI is not a win for me. I'm not going that route."

"Well, as part of your defense, I would still suggest that you be evaluated mentally, to be on the safe side, to be sure that wasn't a possible area to explore."

"Evaluate me all you want. I'm not going to a mental hospital," I said defiantly.

I looked to my right to see the waitress standing there with a pitcher to refill our iced tea glasses. The waitress didn't say a word. She poured the tea and then darted away.

"Could her timing be any worse?" I said.

Thomas laughed. "If this were real, we wouldn't be discussing it at the lunch table."

"She doesn't know that. She thinks I'm a murdering mental case."

"I bet you'd enjoy life more if you quit worrying what other people thought of you."

"I enjoy life just fine," I quipped.

He took a sip of tea, failing to hide the smug grin on his face.

"So what's left as far as my options go?" I asked. "Self-defense?"

"Looks like it. It's the only way you could be completely acquitted, but it's an uphill battle."

"Okay, let's cover that for our next meeting. I've got plenty here to keep me busy for a while."

As we finished lunch, I tried to learn more about Thomas. It was really the first time we had talked about anything other than my case. He told me a little about his undergrad at Morehouse and then going to Duke Law School. He had gone from being surrounded by fellow

African Americans at Morehouse to being a minority at Duke, which was quite a change. I asked about his family but he didn't say much other than that he had three sisters who lived here, and that his mom was just south of Atlanta in Fort Valley.

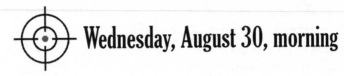

Wednesday, August 30, morning

I couldn't help but feel that I had disappointed Barbara. This was the first week I was visiting the Georgia Building without my usual Tuesday therapy visit.

As I passed Mike on my way into the building, he asked, "Been out in the sun?"

I looked at my chest.

This damn rash!

I assured him that I was fine and stopped in the lobby bathroom to douse myself with more cortisone cream.

I took the elevator to the eighth floor and put the bag of bagels and cream cheese I had brought in the kitchenette. Joanne followed me, pulled out some plates and napkins, then called Thomas to join us. We took our plates back to Thomas' office and Joanne returned to manning the front desk, bagel in hand.

We sat down in our usual spots, me in the leather chair and Thomas facing me behind his desk. I picked up from where we had left off at the restaurant.

"So last time, we were going to talk about self-defense. It seems like that's my only option."

"It's probably your best option," he replied. "So when we go to trial, it will be my job to prove that you were acting in self-defense. Our first order of business will be to prove that he actually attacked you."

"What do you mean? Isn't that obvious?"

"Well, you said there were no fingerprints found in your house that could be traced to him."

"Right, but they didn't look very hard since I wasn't raped."

"What about the forced entry? Any evidence there?"

"Troy, my neighbor, found where he had pried open the kitchen window."

Thomas asked, "Can you prove the damage to the window happened that night? How do you know the window wasn't already in that condition?"

I had never thought about anyone questioning the break-in.

Thomas continued, "What if the DA says that Perry was never in your house? What if he says this innocent guy was just outside jogging and the next thing he knew he was face down on the pavement with your bullets in his back?"

"Who is going to believe he was just out jogging at 4 a.m.?" I replied sarcastically.

"Maybe he couldn't sleep. Maybe he was training for a marathon before work. The important fact is this—if he can't be physically linked to being inside your home, it would be only your word saying that he was. What if the DA throws even more doubt into the situation? Say he concedes, for argument's sake, that you were attacked. How do you prove that the person you shot was the person who attacked you?"

"I don't follow."

Thomas explained, "You lost your view of him when you were retrieving your gun. Say Perry was out jogging and saw some other guy sprinting past him who was the real attacker. You could have shot the wrong guy. Think about that. Not only do we have to prove you shot him in self-defense, but we have to prove he was the person who attacked you."

"But he was."

"You said yourself you never got a good look at his face. In fact, all you can say is that he was about six feet tall and black. That describes thousands of men in Atlanta, including me."

Thomas stared intently at me with that last comment. I was well aware, upon every encounter with him, that he matched my attacker's description.

He continued, "The reason our country doesn't subscribe to vigilante law is for this very reason. You could have killed an innocent person. Was any DNA collected?"

"Well, no, but I suppose if I had actually killed him, they would have done more than dust for fingerprints that night. Wouldn't they have found his DNA in my bedroom? In the struggle, I'm sure he would have lost some strands of hair."

"You've been watching too much CSI," Thomas replied cynically. "I doubt they would have even looked for his DNA inside your home. For your story, you'll need to decide if you want to have proof. It would help your case if you could actually place him inside your house. It depends on if you want to portray reality or if you want a sexy forensics angle."

"I want reality," I said. "What about the bite? Couldn't we prove it came from him? Couldn't we find his DNA on my fingers?"

"They might be able to find some trace DNA, but I seriously doubt they would have bothered. They could even suggest at trial that you bit yourself to bolster your story. Were there any other signs of the attack?"

"The knife."

"Yes, but since it was your own kitchen knife, the police could say that you planted it, especially since there were no fingerprints."

I thought back to my second meeting with Thomas.

He knew about the knife from the police report. Had the report also indicated that it was my own kitchen knife? Is that how he knew?

I needed to get a copy of that report.

When I looked up, Thomas was taking a big bite of his bagel. He sank his teeth into the bread while pulling back his lips to avoid smearing them with cream cheese. I looked at the precise imprint on the cream cheese and then looked at the crescent shaped scab on my hand. I couldn't take my eyes off his mouth.

He finished chewing and continued, "Assuming we can prove that the guy you shot was the guy in your house, we now need to prove that you didn't know him. We need to trump the DA's proposition that you had a relationship with this guy."

"A relationship?"

"Of course. Don't be naïve. They'll likely suggest you weren't strangers. The DA may say, 'How do we know this wasn't her boyfriend, just because no one ever saw them out together? Of course no one would see them in public together. She was a married woman, trying to hide her inter-racial affair. Her husband was out of town. Maybe this was nothing more than a lover's quarrel or maybe he was going to expose the affair to her husband so she had to stop him?'"

"They can't get away with that!" I erupted. The combination of watching Thomas devour his bagel and talking about false lovers had me unnerved.

"Well, it's my job to preempt it. I'd subpoena his phone records to show that he never called you and I'd show your phone records to prove that you never called him. We'd need to play tough offense here, leaving no doubt that he was a stranger."

"Well I would hope so. This is bad enough without trying to ruin my reputation or my marriage."

"That brings up another point. Like it or not, we'd need to talk about your marriage. I'd need to know if there were any problems or infidelities because you know the DA will be probing there."

"Are you kidding? Chris is the love of my life. Not everyone is lucky enough to find their soul mate, but I did. In fact, he is taking me on a romantic trip this weekend."

"For your anniversary?"

I stopped in my tracks, completely stunned.

How did Thomas know it was my anniversary? I had told Joanne—we had become friends. But, I never said anything to Thomas.

My thoughts raced.

My wedding album. The one he ruined. It had my wedding date.

"How did you know that?" I demanded.

Thomas gritted his teeth, sucking a slight amount of air between them. He didn't answer but his face showed guilt.

He looked away for a moment and then finally replied.

"Look, after we first met, I did a background check on you. I know that sounds dirty, but I needed to make sure you were legit before I agreed to work with you. The report had details about your husband and your wedding date. I remember thinking that you were married on Labor Day weekend. I know now that you're the real deal, but I didn't know then, so I had to check you out."

I was still shocked. How dare he do a background check on me! And how paranoid was he to assume that I had some false pretense for meeting with him. I looked at Thomas with suspicion and disgust, which he clearly perceived.

He tried to recover. "You have to understand, as a criminal defense lawyer, I get all kinds of whack jobs coming into my office. I had to be sure that you didn't have some underlying motive or vendetta for meeting with me. I had to be sure what you were telling me was the truth."

I faltered. He sounded sincere. But there was this little nagging voice inside of me–aren't most psychopaths also charmers?

"Look, I know you're pissed at me for doing that," he said. "I'll make it up to you."

I tried to discern if his contrition was sincere. I couldn't tell. And why was he apologizing? Was he trying to ensure I didn't leave? I guess I could understand his reasoning for the background check. Plus I really needed to finish my case.

"Okay," I said coldly. "I'll let you make that breach of trust up to me. Anything else I should know about?" My stare dared him to hide anything else from me.

Thomas looked me directly in the eyes and assured me there was nothing else to share.

"I'm going to take a break," I said. "I'll be right back."

I wanted to diffuse the situation. I walked down the hallway to the ladies room, facing myself in the mirror. On the outside, with the exception of the rash, I looked the same—thin body, pale skin, long brunette hair, light blue eyes.

On the inside, however, I knew I was different. How many times now had Thomas said or done something that set me off? With the slightest trigger, he could send me into a spiraling circle of suspicion. I splashed my face with water and reached in my purse for more cortisone cream before heading back to Thomas' office.

When I returned, Thomas looked at me like nothing had happened. He apparently harbored no shame or guilt for violating my trust.

"Still friends?" he asked amused. I disliked the flippant tone in his voice.

"Barely friends," I muttered. "So where were we? Oh yes, you were trying to poke holes in my solid marriage."

"Peace," he said. "Let's assume the DA doesn't find any ammo on your marriage. He will still try to dig up past boyfriends to discredit you. What if they find an ex that says you were abusive?"

"I met Chris when I was twenty years old. I was married by twenty-two, but I guess you know that from your little report. Besides a few high school boyfriends, there's not a long list of exes. And none of them would testify against me."

"You never know who wants their fifteen minutes, even if it is to speak mistruths. It could be someone you don't even know, but we'd cross that bridge if and when we had to. Next, we would keep plugging away at Perry's character. Say we couldn't find anything before the grand jury convened, that doesn't mean we would stop searching. I'd continue to run his criminal history and, by now, we'd have his DNA to run through the CODIS database.

"What's that?"

"CODIS stands for Combined DNA Index System. It's a national, searchable DNA database established by the FBI. There is a convicted offender index which contains DNA profiles of criminals. There is also a forensic index which contains DNA obtained from crime scene evidence. With these two indexes, the center can compare the DNA from any crime scene to the offender list to see if there is a match."

I asked, "What if this was the first time they received his DNA, but he had committed other crimes?"

"We'd potentially find the match," he said. "And even if he had no criminal history, we would still get into this guy's life. We'd find out where he lived, if he was a drug user, if there were current or past girlfriends that had anything to say about him. We'd do anything we could to muddy the waters about his character. So, you'll need to think about what we find. If it were so egregious, we still might convince the DA to drop the charges, but that depends on what we learn about him."

"So assume we take the worst case scenario. Say we don't find anything incriminating about him. What else do we do to prepare my defense?"

Thomas tapped his fingers on the desk. I noticed his perfectly manicured fingernails. He didn't wear any jewelry—no wedding band.

He continued, "Like we talked about earlier, we would want to show that the whole episode occurred in the heat of the moment, over a very brief time period. Because the DA will try to show that you had time to think about what you were doing, we would want to show how quickly it all played out."

Thomas paused and then asked very slowly, "How long did it take for you to grab your can of Mace and run to the door?"

"I don't know. Maybe a minute."

"I bet it was less. Unfortunately, there's no evidence of the timing except your recollection. You may think it took a minute when, in reality, I bet it was mere seconds. To prove this, I'd call in an expert witness to testify about people's perception of time during a traumatic event. An expert will tell you that in the majority of cases, a witness has a tendency to perceive that events took longer than they did.

"Our expert would testify that your perception of time had been distorted by fear and that your reaction was actually much quicker. Furthermore, if we film what we believe to be actual time based on a reenactment, we could show it took only seconds for you to grab your gun in the bedroom and run to your porch and shoot, not minutes. Now, all of the sudden the cooling off period that the DA will try to establish will seem almost nonexistent."

"We'd actually reenact what happened?"

"Sure. I'd go to your neighborhood at night and film it. Trust me, no matter where you live, a video at night is creepy. Go outside your house at midnight. Unless you live in a really busy area, it will be quiet and eerie. And this will be a good tool to have because it will draw in the jury. We'd dim the lights and play the video in silence. We'd start inside your bedroom and film your path to the door, with a timer showing how quickly everything happened. It would bring jurors into the moment, and let's face it, jurors love TV. It would give them a taste of your heart-pounding fear."

"I like it. I like it a lot. What else would you do?" I asked.

"I think we have to address what you actually saw when you shot the gun. For example, can we prove that the lighting was bad? I'd pull the city maintenance records to see if any work had been done on the street lights, especially after the date of your attack. If we can show any lights had been repaired after that night, we can imply that you couldn't see well."

"The lights were good because I could see the red circle on the back of his shirt," I said bluntly.

Both of Thomas' palms dropped to his desk, making a loud clap.

"I'd encourage you to not even think like that. You just admitted that you could see clearly and that you deliberately aimed for his back!"

"Well they'll already have clear evidence that he was shot in the back. I'm not disputing that," I replied.

"Of course we are. We'll bring in a ballistics expert who will examine the trajectory of the bullets. We may be able to show that it looked like Perry was turning toward you. And in the dim light, how could you be sure exactly which way he was facing, right?"

Thomas pounded his desk when he emphasized dim light and right. It was clear that he couldn't coach me on what to say but could try to frame things. I wondered if that was what he did with all of his clients.

Just then, Thomas' intercom rang. It was Joanne announcing his next appointment, so we would have to stop for the day.

"I wanted to let you know that I'm out of town next week," he said. "We can set up time for the week after and continue with the defense. Will that work for you?"

I wasn't too disappointed this time. I had enough content to last for at least a week's worth of writing.

"I do have one request," I asked, thinking now would be a good time to cash in on his offer to appease me for the background check.

"Yes?"

"Would it be possible for me to set up my laptop someplace close by, like your library? I'll probably do most of my writing at home, but it would be convenient to write here occasionally if that wouldn't be a problem?"

Thomas thought for a moment.

"I've got an even better place for you. I'll see if we can let you have our open office. We call it the closet but it has a desk and is quiet."

I hadn't counted on my own office. I was thrilled about the possibility of having somewhere besides home to write.

"That'd be great," I said.

"Let me see if anyone is using that office. I'll be right back."

Thomas quickly walked out the door and returned a few minutes later. "Okay, we have a deal. Let me show you."

I followed Thomas down a wide corridor toward the office at the end of the hall. With his coat jacket off, I noticed his muscular shoulders tapering to his trim waist. I pictured a red bulls-eye on the back of his shirt as he walked.

Stop it!

I barely listened as he talked—all I could think about was his physique.

"We just need you to check in with Joanne when you come and go. If you're here and want to meet with me, Joanne has my calendar in case I'm with a client or in court, but it would be good to keep scheduling our regular weekly meetings."

"Sure," I agreed, forcing myself to shake the image of the bulls-eye.

He continued, "I assume that you'll be here about two months based on your deadline? We can talk if you need the space longer. I doubt anyone else will take it. It's quite small."

He opened the door at the end of the hall. He was right about the name—the closet. It was so small that it only had room for a greenish gray metal desk, one chair and a matching filing cabinet. There were no windows. My master bathroom was larger than this space but I didn't care. It was a place to work during the day. I opened one of the drawers. The cheap metal clanged as I rolled it back. It was empty, a good place to store my purse and files.

"This is perfect," I said. "Thanks. And I won't disturb you unless we have an appointment. Can I start writing from here today?"

"Knock yourself out," he replied. "Joanne gets here at 8 a.m. so the front door will be locked before then, but you can stay as late as you like."

"Great," I replied.

He smiled and asked, "Friends?"

I looked back at him, trying to suppress a smile. "Friendly acquaintances."

He gave a slight bow as if saying, as you wish, and left for his next appointment.

September

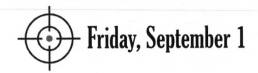 **Friday, September 1**

It was Labor Day weekend and we were going away for our ninth wedding anniversary. Chris had told me to pack a suitcase but wouldn't tell me where we were going.

"Well, are we flying or driving?" I asked.

"Driving."

"That helps. At least I'll know the weather."

Early September in Georgia would still be warm and even if we weren't staying in Georgia, I couldn't imagine that we would drive more than a few hours; otherwise Chris would have flown.

"And bring comfortable shoes," he added.

"Bathing suit?" I asked.

"Skinny dipping is preferred," he said with a grin.

I rolled my eyes at him and threw a bathing suit into my suitcase.

"Give me a hint. What direction are we headed?" I asked.

North would mean mountains. Anything else would likely be the Atlantic Ocean or Gulf of Mexico.

"No hints."

I had no choice but to over pack, not knowing what to expect. We loaded the suitcases into Chris' Infiniti and drove northwest on Interstate 75.

"Aren't you going to use your GPS?" I asked.

He just looked at me and smiled—he wasn't giving his secret away this early in the trip. I figured he was taking me to Chattanooga or Nashville. Maybe he had tickets to the Grand Ole' Opry? But when he turned north onto Highway 575, I figured it out.

"You're taking me to Ellijay!" I guessed.

Ellijay was a quaint mountain town that we had visited once for a friend's wedding. I had always talked about going back for a weekend because the place was so relaxing. We stopped in the small town square and Chris went into a country store that advertised cabin rentals. He came back with a key and a map. He then reached into his backpack and pulled out a blindfold.

"Since you're making it impossible to surprise you, at least you have to be surprised by the cabin." He handed me the blindfold.

"Wearing this will make me carsick," I protested.

"Okay. You have a choice. Wear it now or wear it tonight." He had a devilish smile.

"Fine. I'll wear it tonight," I said, grinning, and threw the blindfold back at him. He looked surprised—and pleased.

We drove out of the small town and up a narrow road that turned off onto a dirt pathway. After about six miles of wilderness, we passed through an overgrown area into a clearing. I saw a light brown one-story log cabin with a huge porch and matching wooden rocking chairs. Off to the side was a heart-shaped hot tub and a small fire pit with two reclining chairs.

"It's beautiful," I exclaimed.

As we unloaded the car, I noticed that Chris had packed a huge cooler. It wasn't like we were going to run to a local restaurant this far from civilization. I paused outside the car and breathed in the fresh mountain air. The sun was just starting to set and the frogs were making that low-pitched xylophone noise that is so distinctively summer. It was a peaceful place, so why wasn't I at peace? The calm and solitude felt too remote. This was the kind of place where dead bodies wouldn't be found for days.

I shook off that thought and scoped out the cabin while Chris stocked the kitchen and started making dinner. Later that evening, we sat in front of the fire in the reclining chairs. The night sky was full of stars and there were all kinds of sounds from nature—crickets, an owl, something rustling in the bushes—a raccoon, Chris speculated.

The next morning, Chris cooked my favorite: fresh blueberry waffles, made on the waffle maker he had brought all the way from Atlanta. After breakfast, we put on hiking gear and drove to a nearby path on Springer Mountain. We hiked about five miles, which took us to the most southern point of the Appalachian Trail.

"Let's take a photo here," Chris said. "Next year for our anniversary, we'll fly to Maine and take a photo at the other end and say we hiked the whole thing!"

"Cute," I replied.

As I looked out over the view, I realized that I was standing on my mountain top. The start of the trail was an open clearing on bare, grey rock. In the distance, I could see the peaks of other smaller mountains and below them was nothing but a vast forest of trees. The air was clean with a slight breeze. Chris couldn't have possibly known that he had brought me to my imaginary peaceful spot. That was the best gift I could have ever asked for. I just looked at him and smiled.

After the long hike, we stopped in town to have an early dinner. We were dirty and sweaty but didn't care, and the townspeople didn't seem to care either. As we ate garlic bread and waited for the pasta to arrive, Chris told me about our anniversary plans, which would be the next day.

"So tomorrow, I want to give you your present."

"I thought this trip was my present?" I replied.

"It is, but there is one more thing."

Chris knew that surprises always made me curious and eager.

"Okay, give me three hints," I asked.

"Alright. It's bigger than a bread box," he teased.

"You think that's not useful, but it is," I laughed. "Now I know it's not jewelry."

"True."

"What else?" I asked.

"Well, it can be reused over and over without ever running out."

"Okay, so it's not a new car," I said.

"You don't need a new car," he protested. He was right; my Audi was only two years old.

"I know. Give me a better hint," I begged.

"You'll find out soon enough tomorrow."

"Will you give it to me first thing?" I asked impatiently.

"You already have it."

"Oh, it's your undying love for me," I said. "Bigger than a bread box and will never run out."

Chris laughed. "Excellent guess, my dear, but it's actually something tangible."

I fake pouted. I would just have to wait.

He, on the other hand, wouldn't receive his gift tomorrow. When I found out that Chris was taking me away for the weekend, I asked Troy to accompany me to buy a flat screen TV—the same TV that Chris had planned to purchase before the attack, the one that he denied himself to buy the alarm system. Troy and I plotted to have it installed while we were away for the weekend. I couldn't wait to see the look on his face when he walked in the house on Monday after the trip.

"Well now, you are making me feel bad," I complained.

"Why?"

"Because I don't have a present for you for tomorrow." I liked making him think that he wasn't getting anything. It would make the TV more of a surprise. I'd have to find a time to slip away and call Troy to be sure everything went well with the installation.

"Don't worry about that. We can both share in your present."

Saturday, September 2

I woke up before Chris and made breakfast for a change. After we ate, he suggested we take a drive so we climbed into his car and went further up the deserted road past our cabin. He turned into a driveway but was forced to stop as the driveway had a locked metal gate blocking the entrance. A "No Trespassing" sign was posted on top of the gate.

"Come on. Let's look around," he said.

"Are you crazy? This is private property and we're in North Georgia. Let's go back. You promised my present first thing."

"I don't think anyone is around. Come on," he nudged.

With that, Chris jumped out of the car, ducked under the metal gate and walked further up the drive out of sight. He was gone before I even had time to get irritated. I sat in the car for a moment—surely he would come back when he saw I wasn't going to trespass with him.

I waited. And waited some more, my agitation growing. I yelled out the window to him.

"Chris, come on. Let's go back."

No reply.

The trees stood motionless. There was no breeze, just stillness. I looked for any signs of motion—envisioning a predator sneaking around in the woods. Was he hidden behind a bush? Did he see I was alone? Had he followed us to this mountain retreat?

I shifted over to the driver's seat and reached for the ignition.

Chris had taken the keys.

Was it safer to lock the doors and hide or to find Chris and make him leave? Taking a deep breath, I got out of the car and dashed under the gate to find my husband.

I walked into a large open lot. There was no building, just empty land with a clearing in the center where the trees had been removed. Though it was daylight, it was creepy. It was too quiet, too remote. And, Chris was nowhere to be found.

I started to panic again.

Where is he?

"Chris," I called. It was part yell, part whisper.

No answer.

What if that rustling we had heard last night wasn't an animal? What if it was someone? What if he had done something to Chris?

Just then, I heard someone walking behind me, the leaves crunched under his steps. Panic surged through me like an ice-cold electric current. My mind told my body to run but I couldn't move a muscle.

He bear-hugged me with such force that I couldn't move my arms. Instinctively, I lifted my right leg and kicked him in the shin with all my might.

"Fuck!" he yelled.

I whipped around to see Chris on the ground, gripping his ankle in pain.

"What the fuck did you do that for?" he yelled.

"Why did you attack me?" I burst into tears. "Why would you scare me like that?"

"Jesus Christ," he shouted. "I was trying to surprise you."

Chris reached into his jeans pocket with his left hand, all the while keeping pressure on his shin with his right hand. He handed me a piece of paper. I bent down to take it and unfolded it to see a property deed in the names of Laura and Chris Holland, notarized by Linda Strickland.

"I bought the land so we can build a cabin here," he said. "That is your present."

I was speechless, still looking at the paper. I should appreciate the gift, but how could he have been so thoughtless in how he tried to surprise me? Just because I had let him use the blindfold last night in bed didn't mean I wanted to be abandoned in the woods. And I couldn't help but notice that his secretary had notarized the paperwork. She knew about my surprise before I did. That irritated me.

When I didn't reply, he downplayed the gift. "Hey, if you don't like it, I can always sell it. Linda got me a really good deal on the land—she could probably help me find another buyer."

"You're completely missing the point," I sneered.

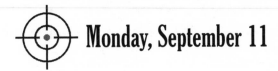 Monday, September 11

Though it had been over a decade since the attack of September 11, the whole country was in a somber mood. There was a light drizzle outside and the sky was gray, appropriate for the day. I watched some of the memorials on TV, feeling so sad for the families who were reliving their loss.

I thought back to that life-changing day. I had been working from my apartment with CNN running in the background. The extra commotion had drawn me to the TV in time to see the replay of the first plane flying straight into the tower against a placid blue backdrop. I had called Chris immediately and he turned on the news at work. Together, in disbelief, we witnessed the second plane crash into the second tower. The world would never feel quite the same.

The phone rang that afternoon around 2:00 p.m. I saw a local number that I didn't recognize. I almost didn't answer it, assuming another telemarketer, but something told me to pay attention.

It was the health clinic with my AIDS test results—I had gone there on Sept 7, the three month mark.

My heart pounded. I held my breath.

Please let it be negative, Lord, please, please, please.

After verifying my social security number, the woman from the clinic explained, "I'm calling with the results of an HIV test you took last Thursday."

"Yes?" I asked eagerly and at the same time not wanting to know. This was it. My fears could potentially become reality. Not knowing had been horrible. Now, I preferred to continue the uncertainty, at least it provided room for hope.

"Mrs. Holland, the results were negative. You do not have any signs of infection with the virus at this time."

"Thank you," I said, my voice cracking. I managed to say goodbye before I completely burst into tears. I fell to the couch and buried my head in a pillow. I was okay. It was over. My attack was finally over. I picked up my cell phone and called Chris.

"Hi. What's up?" he asked.

"I just got the test results back," I said, still crying.

"Oh my God! How? How from just a bite? They told me it was next to impossible!"

"Oh no, honey, it was negative. I'm okay!" I blurted.

"Then why are you crying?"

"Because I'm happy," I said.

"Damn it, Laura! When are you going to learn how to tell me things? You're crying. You should have told me immediately that the test results were negative."

"But I am telling you."

"Yeah, after giving me heart failure! Delivery. Timing. They mean everything in the way people communicate effectively. I know that from sales. You should know that from journalism. You should practice that with me!"

"Fine. Then you practice it with me and quit yelling at me and come home."

There was silence on the other end of the phone.

In a much calmer voice, he said, "You're right. I'll be right there."

I showered, freshly shaved my legs and sprayed his favorite perfume, Amirage, on the back of my neck. I put on my Victoria's Secret pink lace teddy given to me last Valentine's Day. I waited impatiently for Chris to arrive home, and finally heard his Infiniti pull up outside.

I walked to the front window and pulled back the drapes to look for him. I thought I had heard his car, but all I saw was an older grey car parked across the street. The passenger side was facing my house so I couldn't see if anyone was inside.

Just then, I saw Chris' car turn the corner and pull into our driveway. At the same time, the other car drove off.

I pulled the drapes in front of me, worried that the person in the gray car had seen me standing there in my teddy. As Chris walked up the steps, I cracked opened the door. I thought he would be pleased to see how I was dressed but he had a troubled look on his face. He reached over my shoulder to the alarm and punched in the code out of habit.

"What's wrong?" I asked.

"Nothing."

The look didn't go away.

"What?" I asked again.

He just shook his head, walked over to the window, pulled back the drapes and looked outside. The car was gone. Without facing me, he mumbled, "I thought I recognized him."

"Who?" The guy in the gray car?"

He nodded.

"Who was it?"

"I'm not sure. He looked like Linda's husband," he replied.

I pictured Linda and then thought of her two blonde boys. I had never met her husband—they were already estranged when she started working for Chris.

"Why would he be at our house?" I asked.

Then a thought occurred to me.

"Is he the natural father of those boys? I mean, he isn't black, is he?"

Chris shook his head. "No, he's white. White trash. Besides, if he were coming after anyone, it would be me, not you."

"What! Oh my God. We can't both be in danger."

A chill came over my body. My knees felt like they were going to give way.

"We need to move," I said. "We can't stay here."

"Calm down," he replied. "He's not coming after me. I just meant that you don't need to worry. I'm not even sure that was him."

My face must have shown that I wasn't convinced.

"Look, I've only seen him once at the office—he was harassing Linda. When I stepped in, he slunk away like a coward."

He pulled me closer and rubbed his hands up and down my arms, trying to wipe away the goose bumps.

"Can we find out?" I asked. "Maybe we should hire a PI and have him followed."

"Look, I'm sorry I said anything. Besides, I think he drives a truck. You know what it is? All of your suspicions are rubbing off on me. Now I'm the one who's acting paranoid."

I just stared at him.

"And we're not moving," he said as he pulled me toward the bedroom.

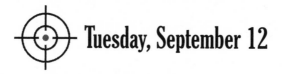 # Tuesday, September 12

"Laura, this is Barbara Cole. Alisa said that you had called earlier."

"Barbara! Yes. Thanks for calling me back," I said. "I wanted to share the good news. I'm not HIV-positive. The test results came back yesterday. I'm so relieved and wanted you to know."

"Oh, that's really good to hear, Laura. I'm very happy for you. And how is everything else going?"

"Oh, very well. Thomas has taken me to court to see a hearing and we're working on my defense for my story. At this rate, I should be finished in less than two months."

"You seem to have a lot of energy around this work," said Barbara.

"I do. It's fascinating. I'm turning what was a bad experience into something educational."

"And your rash? Has it gotten better?"

"For the most part. It still comes and goes."

Barbara paused. Then spoke.

"Well, thank you for letting me know about the test results. If you ever feel like you need to talk more, we can always set up another appointment."

"Thank you, Barbara. I appreciate it. I'll send you a copy of the story when it's done. That is, if you like."

"It would certainly give me a diversion from my typical reading."

Another pause.

"Is there anything else?" she asked.

I hadn't realized it before, but I missed Barbara. I had looked forward to our Tuesday meetings each week. I enjoyed having someone who was there just for me.

Now, it felt like a friend who had moved away and the distance was already starting to chip away at the once close relationship. It made me sad, but at the same time, I had the sense that Barbara was not completely out of my life.

"No, I guess not," I replied.

Another pause.

"Well my door is always open if you need it, and thanks for sharing your good news, Laura."

"Sure. I wanted you to know."

"Goodbye, then."

"Goodbye."

I hung up the phone. Why had sharing the joy of my negative HIV test left me feeling so empty?

 # Wednesday, September 13

Because Thomas had been out of town the prior week, I took advantage of using my closet office to document our discussion of my defense. I had captured his approach of first proving I was attacked by a stranger to reenacting the scene with a timed video.

I walked into his office for our meeting.

"So how was your time away?" I asked.

"Uneventful," he replied, not elaborating so I didn't pry.

I handed him a printed copy of the defense chapter I had written. "You don't have to read it right now, but when you have a chance. I want to make sure I haven't left anything out."

He held the document in his palm as if weighing it on a scale. "Looks like you are making good progress."

"Yes, I've captured how you would defend me, but what do you think the prosecution is going to do? And how would you counter it?"

Thomas leaned back in his chair, placing his hands behind his head with elbows pointing outward. This was a classic body posture portraying confidence, sometimes over-confidence in my experience. Somehow he seemed cockier after his week away.

Thomas jumped right back into the story without skipping a beat.

"The prosecution is going to focus on the fact that Perry was retreating. If you testify, no doubt the DA is going to ask you under oath what was going through your mind when you grabbed your gun, ran after him, and pulled the trigger."

"Well, once I realized he was actually leaving, I knew I had to stop him."

"Why?" Thomas asked.

"So he wouldn't get away."

Thomas shook his head while lowering his arms to the desk. He leaned forward slightly. "There is a term called good faith. It means that, throughout the incident, you avoided using any more force than you had to. If it can be proven that even though you were free of malice at the start, you decided somewhere during the struggle to retaliate with undue force, you've just lost your claim of self-defense."

"Is wanting to stop him retaliation?" I asked.

Thomas countered, "More importantly, is wanting to stop him the same as defending yourself?

I did not have a good answer to his question. All I had was my truth.

He continued, "Moreover, when does self-defense end and revenge begin?"

"Revenge? I acted on instinct. There was no logic going through my mind that distinguished self-defense from retaliation. It wasn't like that."

Thomas just looked at me. I tried to find words to get us on track. Even though it had only been a little over a week, it was as if we were having to get acquainted again.

"So, as my lawyer, what would you do?"

"To win self-defense, we would have to show that you continued to be afraid of this guy, afraid of immediate bodily injury or death. It's the middle of the night, you're alone, you've been startled from sleep and terrorized. Maybe, when you shot the gun, you thought he was running to get a weapon and coming right back to harm you. Though that last argument leaves the door open for the prosecution."

"How?"

"In the time it took you to grab your gun, you could have grabbed the phone and called 911. Why didn't you do that?"

"He had taken our home phone off the hook."

"When did you learn he had done that?" asked Thomas.

"When I came back in the house and tried to call Troy," I replied.

"Voila. The DA would rejoice over that, especially if he unveiled this tidbit of information on the stand, before we thought about it. Hypothetically, you would have already shot the poor bastard. It wasn't like you were prevented from making a phone call. You didn't even try."

I tried another approach. "Well, the gun was closer than the phone."

Thomas clarified, "You mean the Mace. Tell me about that. Where would the gun have been?"

I thought of my bedroom and where I now stored my Ruger. "Under my bed."

"And where were you exactly?"

"On the floor next to the bed."

"How far away was the gun?"

"It would have been right next to me." I extended my arm showing the distance.

"So it wasn't like you had to deliberately go to another room and find it. It was right there as you got up. And was it already loaded?"

"Yes, loaded, under the bed with the clip in."

"You don't have any kids around, do you?"

"No."

"Good, because we'd need to emphasize that you're a responsible gun owner. Then we can show it was just an extension of your arm to grab it as you ran from your bedroom. Now, where was your home phone?"

"We have one in the kitchen and one in the office. He had taken the kitchen phone off the hook."

"No phones in the bedroom?"

"Right," I confirmed.

"And your cell phone, where was it?"

"In the office."

"That helps. Your closest means of protection was the weapon, not the phone. We'd show that in the video or with a diagram of the house, though there's no point in stressing how he disabled the phone. At the point in time you shot him, you didn't know that."

Thomas paused, then asked, "When you shot him, did you know he had a knife?"

I shook my head. I hadn't known about the knife until the police arrived and searched my bedroom.

"Are you certain? You never felt it or saw it while he was in your bedroom?" Thomas asked again.

"No, why?"

"There is a term called disparity of force. Basically, if you knew your attacker had a knife, then you're more justified to counterattack with your own weapon. His use of a knife opens the door to your use of a gun, if you will. But if you didn't know about the knife, it's just like the phone being off the hook. It doesn't help us."

I just shrugged my shoulders.

Thomas continued, "Now sometimes disparity is considered equal if you have a weapon and your attacker doesn't—if he's physically stronger than you. The courts might consider the use of a gun justified, at least during the attack, to equalize the force since he was physically more dominant. The tricky part here revolves around his departure. If the immediate danger ended, where's the need for self-defense? And the DA will argue that you had a moment of time to cool off before you reacted."

"Define a moment," I asked. "Are we talking seconds here?"

"It could be. I'll need to look up the specific jury instructions on the cooling-off period—that's certainly a distinction we better understand. I'm meeting with another lawyer in the office today. Let me ask him how he interprets that part of the law, if that's okay with you."

"That's fine," I replied. This was the first time I had seen Thomas admit to asking for help.

"So you guys help each other out?" I asked.

"Sometimes. I'm sitting second chair with Andy Hayes for a murder case in two weeks."

"A murder case?" I repeated enthusiastically. "Can I watch?"

"The courtroom is open to the public," he replied, which really didn't answer my question.

"I mean would you or Andy mind? I don't want to crash your courtroom if that would make you uncomfortable."

Thomas just chuckled.

 # Wednesday, September 27

I had only been called to jury duty once in my life and it had been years earlier. I barely remembered it, except that I was excused early on. Because I had such little personal experience to draw upon, I would basically need to start from scratch learning about jury selection.

I arrived at my borrowed office early that Wednesday afternoon to proofread and wait for Thomas. Just before 3 p.m., I grabbed two cold water bottles from the kitchenette, which I had stocked. The other lawyers in the office, including Andy, knew who I was and that I was working with Thomas. Originally, I think they were indifferent to my presence, but now appreciated the Dasani water, Cokes and bagels that appeared in the kitchenette on the days I was there. I walked over to Thomas' office and saw that his door was open.

"Ready for me?" I asked as I peered in the doorway.

"Always," he said. His tone was almost a little too intimate.

Thomas folded his laptop down and turned toward me. He was dressed in grey pinstriped pants and a coral buttoned-down shirt. His coat and tie were hanging on the wooden stand by the door, ready if he had to make an appearance in court. Though I was no slouch at looking stylish, he routinely outdid me.

I handed him a bottled water, careful to not let the condensation drip on his perfectly creased sleeve.

His fingers brushed against mine as he took the water—I instinctively jerked away. *Was that deliberate?*

I brushed the thought away, sat down across the desk from him and opened my iPad. I thought about asking how trial preparation with Andy was going, but since it was already late in the day, I wanted to get right to the business of jury selection.

"So, can you give me an overview so I'll know what to expect tomorrow?"

"Sure. Jury selection is literally the beginning of the trial. As the defendant, you'd be there for the jury selection so we should probably talk about how I would prepare you. Because you would be coming from jail, you'd need your husband to make sure you had clothes for trial. You'd want to wear dark colors and be conservative. Soft hair and make-up. Little to no accessories and no designer stuff."

Thomas pointed to my red lips, sparkling diamond earrings and Pandora bracelet as he made his comments about not looking flashy, as if singling out my flaws.

He continued, "As the defendant, it's okay to be sad or nervous, but I'd want you to act serious and demure. No laughing, even if it's nervous laughter. Watch your body language. Sit up straight, be attentive. You can glance at the jury but don't stare at them or make them uncomfortable. I'd advise you to take notes of who seems to smile at you and who seems hostile."

"Would I have any say-so in who I liked?" I asked.

"Sure. There will be breaks during the panels where you could give input. In reality, most of my clients don't have anything to add. At this point, they're so scared they aren't thinking clearly. For your case, because it would be a murder trial, I'd have co-counsel helping me with jury selection like I'm doing for Andy tomorrow. And if you could afford it, we could consider hiring a jury consultant."

"How much would that cost?"

"The really good ones can be over $10,000."

"Wow, that's pricey."

"It is, and I suppose you never really know if it makes a difference," Thomas said. "About sixty people will shuffle in and the first fourteen will be asked to sit in the jury box—that's the first panel. The rest will sit in the benches in the courtroom. Some will probably be acting like this is a tremendous drudgery—those will be the ones I'll look for first."

"Why?" I asked.

"There is a common falsehood that people don't want to be on jury duty. If it's a civil case, that's probably true. But for a criminal case like this, a murder trial, it would be interesting. So one of the first things I look for are the people acting like they don't want to be on the jury because then I know they are liars."

I couldn't think of anything to say to that. Thomas was so skeptical. I tended to give people the benefit of the doubt, until they proved me wrong. Thomas, on the other hand, seemed to look for the dark side in people first.

He continued, "Those people, the ones trying to appear overly disinterested, are my first red flag. We just want the everyday people who are there to follow the process. So, while I'm watching them, the judge will go over the basic, statutory questions. For example, he'll ask if any of them are related by blood or marriage to you. If so, they will be dismissed for cause."

"Do they dismiss anyone in law enforcement?" I asked.

"We will, but not at this point. That comes later. Then, all sixty are asked to take an oath, swearing to answer the questions truthfully. After the oath, the judge will read the litany of charges against you, most of which the jury pool will not fully understand."

I thought of my case. I hadn't understood the difference between malice murder and felony murder.

"Then the DA is allowed to ask his general questions. The jurors will be asked to raise their hand if they reply affirmatively. For example, he may ask if anyone has ever served on a jury before. If they have, they will raise their hand and both he and I will record their jury number. When he's finished, I will have an opportunity to ask my general questions, basically filling in anything the DA left out that I want to know."

"What kinds of questions will you ask?"

"It depends on what the DA has left out. He'll probably ask if anyone has ever been a victim of a violent crime and if anyone has ever been prosecuted or had a family member prosecuted. And, to your earlier question, he'll ask if anyone has law enforcement experience. You get the drill. Any time that a juror raises his or her hand, we'll take note because we may want to follow-up."

"How much will you know about the jurors before the trial?"

"Good question. I will have a form with each potential juror's number, name and some pertinent information like their marital status and number of kids. Not to sound prejudiced, but I have codes for them that I add to the form, like 'O' for old."

I frowned at the abbreviation. "Would we prefer someone who is older for my trial?" I asked.

"Yes, especially if the person was an older, white male with female children. He would likely think about this incident happening to his own daughter and be very protective of you."

"So, on the contrary, we wouldn't want a young, black male?"

"Right, with the caveat that a young, black male will identify with me, which isn't a bad thing. But, given the choice, I'd take the father first."

"It's almost like jury de-selection."

"Exactly. Jury selection is really a misnomer because it's more about getting rid of the worst jurors than finding the best ones. Here in Georgia, we have what is called equal strikes, which means both the prosecution and the defense are allocated nine strikes each to eliminate potential jurors."

"So, of the sixty people who come into the court room, eighteen will be dismissed by using strikes?" I asked.

"Right."

"That leaves a pool of forty-two people, but you only need twelve. Why do they start with so many?"

"Don't forget about the two alternates, which means we need fourteen jurors. But, there is another way to eliminate someone from the jury panel—*striking for cause.*"

"So we just try to strike all the young, black men? Is that allowed?" I asked.

Thomas chuckled slightly and leaned back in his chair.

"No. It's not that easy. A lawyer can use a strike for any legal, legitimate reason, but I couldn't strike a juror based on race. But, striking for cause is something different. The judge can strike a juror who somehow has a relationship to the case. Law enforcement officers can be struck for cause. Or, if I can show an inherent conflict of interest, I can request the judge strike someone.

"Oddly enough, most strikes for cause come from the potential jurors themselves, when they express an opinion about the guilt or innocence of the defendant. Sometimes you'll get a juror who says the defendant just looks guilty. I love it when they start confessing their true feelings because as soon as one starts being honest, it usually triggers the others to start talking. And we'd much rather cleanse the jury pool of these people for cause versus using a precious strike."

I asked, "So after you've determined who to strike for cause, do those people get dismissed?"

"No, we keep track of them, but they aren't actually dismissed until the end of selection. And, only the judge can strike for cause. I can only make recommendations."

"I see."

"Next, we start asking individual questions, person by person. Again, the DA goes first and, as the defense, I'll ask my individual questions after him."

"What kinds of questions do you ask?"

"My usual spiel goes something like this, 'Good morning. I'm Thomas Bennett, a criminal defense lawyer here in DeKalb County. I grew up in Georgia and live here in the community. I'm single, have three older sisters, who have all made it their mission that I don't remain single, and like to write music in my spare time. I tell you this because I'm about to ask you quite a few personal questions and don't mean for our dialogue to feel one-sided or intrusive.'"

This was my first glimpse into Thomas' personal life.

"You see, I'll do everything I can to be personable to the jury pool," Thomas continued. "And because the DA has gone first and usually forgets to introduce himself in a likeable way, I instantly seem more friendly," Thomas grinned. "It is an age-old tactic, but it works the majority of the time and tends to infuriate the DA."

"So they have to answer these individual questions in front of everyone else? How personal do you get?" I asked.

"It can become pretty personal, though I tell them that if they aren't comfortable replying out loud, to let me know and we can discuss it in private in front of the judge's bench. It's another trick to appear friendly because the DA will forget to say this, too.

"As far as what I would ask, I'd follow up with anyone who had raised his or her hand about being a victim of a crime. I'd want to know more details about the crime and how they felt it was handled. If anyone said they had an alarm system, I'd want to know about their fear of crime. I would also follow up with anyone who said they were a gun owner. Here, I would ask what kind of gun and if it was used for hunting, self-protection, or both. You'd be surprised at how many people in Georgia are armed. This is a gun-happy state."

I thought of the Ruger under my bed. I was now contributing to the gun-happiness of the state. It also reminded me that I had another class with Sergeant Stires next week and would try to talk Chris into going. So far, my husband hadn't insisted that I return the gun, but I knew the debate wasn't over. In fact, in an effort to remind me of his concern, Chris had doubled both of our life insurance policies.

I turned my attention back to Thomas. "For the gun owners, we want them in the jury pool, right?"

"It depends," he said. "If the DA tries to argue that you had time to cool off and that your actions to retrieve, load, aim and shoot your gun indicate vengeance, gun owners may not help us. They will be more familiar with the time it takes to load and aim a gun. That said, gun owners may be more sympathetic to your case, especially if they own a gun for self-protection. This is where the questioning becomes so critical, to get a glimpse into each person's perspective."

I countered, "But the more you like someone, the more the DA will try to strike that person, right?"

"True, but it's still important to find out as much as we can. I'd rather he strike someone we want than to be surprised later because we weren't thorough. One of my favorite questions used to be to ask what bumper stickers people had on their cars. Most judges won't let you ask that anymore. It's a shame. 'Recycle America' versus 'NRA' can tell you a lot."

I nodded in agreement. "So who will the DA want on their jury?"

"Basically anyone we don't want. They will like anyone who is buddies with the DA, like an ex-cop. They'll look for particular personality types, such as a tax collector or maybe someone with a military background. These people would not be good jurors for us because they will believe in the law and would likely feel that your shooting was vigilantism. The DA might also want a real liberal person because of the race issue. It's almost reverse racism where a liberal might overreact to a white person shooting a black person."

It was a little surprising how casually Thomas talked about race, like he wasn't part of any ethnic group.

"That reminds me," he continued. "We haven't really talked about who will be at the DA's table. The lead DA will certainly be a senior prosecutor. If they are smart, and they are, they'll have a few assistants, one black to counter me and one female that they'll use to question you. Do you plan to testify in your story?"

"Yes. I know we all have the right to the Fifth Amendment, but I've always felt that people who weren't willing to talk have something to hide. I'd want to tell my side of the story."

"Okay. We'll need to practice your testimony, especially the tricks the DA will use to fluster you. Let's do that once this trial with Andy is over. Oh, and does the jury find out you're a journalist?"

"Sure, why not?"

"Because jurors hate journalists."

"As much as lawyers?" I quipped back.

"Probably more," he retorted without missing a beat.

Without speaking, Thomas stood up from his chair, walked around his desk and headed toward me.

What is he doing?

Instinctively, I rolled the leather chair backward but he kept advancing. His hawk-like stare pierced through me—he looked cold, almost inhuman. I felt a strange flash of déjà vu, where I saw myself pinned on my bedroom floor struggling with him on top of me. The feeling had come out of nowhere and lasted only seconds, but it was so visceral that it lingered.

Thomas passed by my chair, which I had moved out of his way, and approached his bookshelf. He pulled out a binder of newspaper articles, thumbed through a stack of them and found one that he handed to me. The defendant, a righteous journalist, had inflamed the jury and lost the case.

I was still reeling from the image of him pinning me to the floor. I couldn't discern what had just happened.

Is this some sort of flashback memory?

Thomas strolled back to his chair and continued his lecture. "One last item on potential jurors I didn't mention earlier. Believe it or not, sometimes I look for the troublemakers. If it is going to be a tough case to win, sometimes I'll pick jurors who I know will be disharmonious in hopes of a hung jury."

I couldn't respond. My mind was elsewhere.

"A hung jury would require the case to be retried. And, if the DA can't win after two tries, he usually drops the charges. The downside of a second trial, of course, is that the state usually does a better job. Whatever mistakes they made before tend to get fixed."

My déjà vu feeling was fading, like a dream that goes fuzzy and disappears moments after waking. I looked down at my iPad, averting eye contact with Thomas and tried to make sense of what just happened.

It's rational to be afraid of him. He reminds you of him—it's reasonable he would scare you. But why did this weird feeling come out of nowhere? And why was it so real?

Thomas continued his explanation.

"After we question the first panel of fourteen, that group is sent to the benches and the next fourteen are brought to the jury box and questioned. We repeat the process, which takes a good part of the day. Then, the DA and I will review anyone that should be excused for cause and confirm the removal of those jurors with the judge. At the end of the day, we'll go through the selection process. It's a silent procedure where the clerk passes a clipboard with the numbers of the remaining jurors between me and the prosecution. In order, we each will either accept or strike the juror. So if the prosecutor accepts someone, that person is on the jury unless I strike him or her."

I had only caught the tail end of what Thomas was saying. Trying to feign engagement, I asked, "This selection is done person by person?"

"Yes, it's like a tennis match between the DA and the defense, and we do this process quietly while the folks sit and wonder what the hell is going on. We are usually out of strikes by the third panel. Of course, we'll be stuck with some jurors we don't want, but it's a situation where we use our nine strikes for the worst ones."

I listened numbly. I didn't sense that I was in danger any longer—not like that first day when I asked Joanne to come back with coffee. Still, there was a pit in my stomach.

"Now here's an interesting tidbit," said Thomas. "When the trial is over and if we debrief with the jury on the case, do you know the first thing they tend to ask?

I didn't answer.

"They want to know why we picked them for the jury! They don't realize that it wasn't that we chose them, as much as that they were the least worst. Of course, I don't tell them that. I'm not going to be a jerk. You never know when they'll be back in the jury pool. But, it never ceases to amaze me, the defendant may have just lost his or her whole life and, instead of asking about the sentencing or what will happen to this poor bastard on trial, they just selfishly want to know how they were picked!"

I stared at him. I had seen his arrogant side before, but had never seen him act so disdainful.

"Anyway, it will be good for you to see the real deal tomorrow," he said.

I nodded. "What time should I get there?"

"Around nine, and if the judge asks who you are, don't tell him you're a journalist. Just say you are interested in the jury selection process. Legally, any citizen has a right to be there."

My discomfort grew. Thomas was asking me to withhold the truth and he didn't seem to have any ill conscience about doing so.

I needed to leave. I needed to talk to Barbara.

Leaving Thomas' office was a relief. Thankfully, Barbara's office was only two flights up. I took the stairs to get there as quickly as possible.

I pushed open the heavy stairwell door. When I was just shy of the ninth floor, I heard the metal door one floor below slam shut. It echoed down the hollow stairwell.

Though I had never taken the stairs before, I thought it was odd that someone would be just behind me. I took a step, my heels tapped loudly on the concrete floor. The person one floor below took a step. I took another step, this time trying to quiet the heel of my shoe. The person below followed with a single step. I tried to discern if he was going up or down the stairs. I couldn't tell and I wasn't going to wait to find out.

Instead, I picked up my pace running up the stairs, gripping my computer bag and purse close to my body. As if synchronized, he picked up the pace.

By the time I reached the 10th floor I was out of breath. I grabbed the metal door handle and jerked it back. It didn't budge. The door to the stairs was locked. I was trapped. The feet below me continued to mount.

Wednesday, September 27 afternoon

BEEP. BEEP. BEEP.

Chris' cell phone was busy.

I hit redial.

BEEP. BEEP. BEEP.

Busy again.

Redial.

I looked down the stairs. I couldn't see anyone yet.

Finally, I heard my husband's voice on the phone, "Hey, I was just ..."

"YOU HAVE TO COME OPEN THE DOOR!" I screamed. "The door's locked. Come open it now! Hurry, please!"

"Slow down. Where are you?" he asked.

I listened. The feet were retreating down the stairs. Did my call scare him off? He didn't know that Chris wasn't in this building. For all he knew, the person I was talking to was just down the hall, about to rescue me.

I continued in a panicked whisper, just in case he was still within ear shot, "At the Georgia Building. Stuck in the stairwell. 10th floor. Hurry. I'm trapped."

In an even lower whisper, I cried, "Someone's here. Someone's following me. Hurry!"

"Okay, calm down," he said. "Can you try another door?"

"CHRIS!" I wailed louder again. "COME GET ME!"

"Okay, okay. I'm right here. Stay on the line with me. I'll get you out."

"Are you coming?" I cried.

"I'm at my office. I'll call for help," he replied.

The line was quiet for a moment, then I heard my husband talking on his other line.

"Hi Alisa, this is Chris Holland. My wife, Laura Holland, is a patient of Dr. Cole's. This is an odd request I know, but she is trapped inside the stairwell on the 10th floor of your building. She's panicking. Could you do me a huge favor and go get her? I'll be right there. Can you just take her back to your office until I arrive?"

I heard a click. Had we been disconnected? Then I heard Chris' voice again.

"Laura, honey, Alisa is coming to get you. I'm going to stay on the line until she gets there, okay?"

I grabbed the door handle again with my right hand, tugging it with all my might. It wouldn't budge. I started banging on the door with my fist. I could hear Chris on the phone telling me to calm down, but where was he? He wasn't coming for me.

Just then, I heard a loud metal release. The door opened and there stood Alisa. She picked up my things, put her arm around my waist, and escorted me back to Barbara's waiting room.

Chris arrived fifteen minutes later. I was hunched on the couch with a blanket wrapped around me. My hands encircled a mug of hot chamomile tea. Streaks of black mascara ran down both of my cheeks.

Chris sat next to me, picking up a Kleenex from the coffee table to wipe my face.

"What happened?" he asked.

"I had just met with Thomas and needed to see Barbara," I said. "So I took the stairs. Someone was right behind me, following me."

"Are you sure?"

"Absolutely. He moved when I moved. When I started to run, he chased me up the stairwell."

"Did you get a look at him?" Chris asked.

"No. I think my call to you scared him off."

Chris frowned, then asked, "Are you sure he wasn't going the other way? Down the stairs? I mean if someone was intending to do you harm, I don't think a mere phone call would have scared him away."

"But there was someone following me. He took a step when I took a step. And who would enter the stairwell right after me unless he was following me?"

Chris looked toward the closed door across the waiting room.

"Are you going to see Barbara?" he asked.

"Yes, she's with a patient right now but Alisa said she would fit me in."

"Do you want me to wait for you?"

"No. I want you to come. I need to tell you both what happened with Thomas today."

Chris' brows furrowed.

We waited in silence for a while before Barbara's door opened. Seeing the familiar flowing skirt, blazer and spectacles dangling from a silver chain brought me instant comfort. We entered her office, sat on the couch just like our first visit and I revealed everything—from how

I first found Thomas by seeing him with Barbara, to the weird déjà vu I had just experienced in his office to being followed in the stairwell.

"Oh my," was all Barbara could muster.

"Look," said Chris. "You obviously know Thomas. Is there anything we should be worried about here? I mean, about his character. I've always wondered why he would help Laura for free. What's in it for him?"

Barbara looked at Chris, then me, then back at Chris. It seemed as if her eyes wanted to talk but her mouth wouldn't open. Instead, she replied, "I think we need to focus this conversation on Laura. This legal story is not helping her heal. I know you want to educate people, but it's forcing your mind to actively think about the night of your attack instead of distancing yourself from it."

I replied, "Barbara, I had a flashback of Thomas on top of me. Is that real? Am I remembering more from that night that maybe I had suppressed before?"

Barbara looked out the window. Her face was troubled.

Chris interjected, "He's not a patient, is he? Is there something wrong with him?"

"You know I can't reply to a question like that," she said.

There was a moment of silence.

Barbara continued, "But this is not about Thomas. This is about Laura. I'd strongly advise that she stop pursuing this story."

Barbara's greyish-blue eyes were steely. Her voice was more stern than I had ever heard before.

I asked again. "I just want to know why I had that image of him. If it's just my mind playing tricks on me, I can deal with it."

Chris placed his palms square on my shoulders turning me toward him.

"If Thomas is scaring you, why don't you just find someone else to work with?"

"I can't," I replied. "We have jury selection tomorrow."

"It's not worth it, Laura. You're not being rational. Working with him is making you paranoid."

I snapped back, "You don't believe I was followed?"

Chris replied, "Maybe you were. Maybe it was Thomas checking out where you were going. Either way, I don't like it, Laura. I don't know any lawyer who would give so much free time to a total stranger.

There's a motive here we don't see. I don't trust him."

I countered, "He's getting a byline. It's great press for him. Isn't that reason enough?"

Barbara watched us without interrupting.

I wrapped my hands around Chris' biceps—his hands were still locked on my shoulders forming a bridge between us. "That image was so real."

"I don't know, maybe you're tired. You've been staying up late to write, you know. And the only time I get déjà vu is when I haven't had much sleep. I think my brain skips and makes me think I'm experiencing something from before, but I'm really not."

Chris looked at Barbara and asked, "What do you think?"

"About...?" she asked.

"About the image of Thomas that Laura saw? And her feeling like she had seen it before? Could this be remnants of her EMDR? Or maybe she's just having déjà vu from being tired?"

Barbara didn't reply right away.

"It wouldn't have to do with the EMDR. I suppose it could be visual disconnect," she said.

"What's that?" I asked.

"When one hemisphere of the brain starts processing information faster than the other hemisphere, it is called visual disconnect. The delayed information reaching the other hemisphere is perceived as a memory instead of a real-time event, but ..."

I interrupted, "So, if that's the case, my mind is just playing tricks on me."

Barbara shook her head. "Laura, I know you're looking for a tidy answer—a simple cause and effect. But you know as well as I do that not everything in life comes with simple answers. I know you are attached to this story, but I have to say it again. As long as you hold on to this, you are not letting yourself heal, and it could get worse."

"I'll go to bed early if that's what you think caused the déjà vu."

Alisa lightly tapped on the door and peered in. "Dr. Cole, I'm sorry to interrupt but your next appointment is here."

Barbara pressed her lips together and looked at her watch. "I'm sorry but I don't have more time today. Laura, can we schedule another session?"

"I think you should," added Chris.

I didn't reply.

"Are you okay to drive home?" he asked.

"I'm fine."

Chris glanced at Barbara. Their eyes met. There was an unspoken exchange that they didn't think I noticed.

"Why don't I drive you home just to be safe?" he suggested.

Thursday, September 28 early morning

I heard leaves crunching outside.

Is that a squirrel? No. Too heavy to be a squirrel.

I looked at the clock in our home office.

6:30 a.m.

I'd been up writing in the office since 4 a.m. I had bought some sleeping pills—my own because Chris' made me feel funny. I was also going to bed early to avert another déjà vu, but that only made me wake up early.

I quietly stood from my chair and carefully pulled back a sliver of the curtain. I couldn't see anything—it was still dark outside. The sound was coming from the front corner of the house.

I tiptoed to the master bedroom and heard the shower running.

"Chris, get dressed," I whispered through the glass door. "I think someone is outside."

"What?" he replied.

"Hurry up. Get dressed," I repeated.

I walked quickly to the bed, knelt down and grabbed my Ruger. I popped in the clip and turned off the safety.

Still dressed in my sweats and slippers, I tiptoed toward the front door, peering outside again from behind the curtains.

A shadow moved across the front porch and to the side of the house.

Something inside me snapped. I was not going to live in fear any longer.

This game is over. You can follow me in the stairwell. You can prowl around my house. It's time I put an end to it.

I disarmed the home alarm and slowly opened the front door, extending my arms with the gun pointing toward the direction of the shadow.

He was just beyond the front corner of the house, out of eyesight, but I could hear him.

"Who's there?" I demanded.

No answer.

"Show yourself!" I yelled louder as I walked closer to the noise. I should have been more afraid or at least waited until Chris could go outside with me. Why I had such bravery or foolishness, I'm not sure.

I stood just as Sergeant Stires had taught me, legs shoulder width apart, arms fully extended, eyes looking through the sight of the gun.

A figure walked around the corner of the house.

"Don't move or I'll blow your head off."

"What the fuck!" he shouted.

"What the hell are you doing?" I demanded.

"I'm here to pick up Chris. Put that fucking thing down."

"Why didn't you come to the door? Why are you snooping around out here?"

Dan looked over his shoulder and pointed.

"I thought I saw someone at the edge of the house. I came to take a look."

"Who did you see?"

"I can't say for sure. It was just a glimpse. I think he ran off when I pulled up."

Is he for real? He's acting guilty. I don't believe him.

"Where's Chris?" Dan asked.

I glared at him. "Which way did he run? I don't see anyone."

"Maybe there wasn't anyone. Maybe it was just a dog."

He thinks I'm just going to brush this off?

"What's going on out here?" Chris shouted. He was standing at the front door, barefoot and shirtless with his hair dripping wet.

"Dan *thinks* he saw someone," I replied, pointing to the side of the house.

Chris ran past Dan to the edge of the porch and looked around. He stared into the darkness.

"Where? Who'd you see?" Chris asked.

"I don't know. I just saw a movement. It looked like a person," replied Dan, with more conviction now than he had shown with me.

"What was he wearing?" asked Chris.

"It was dark. I don't know."

Chris stepped off the porch and walked around the side of the house as if looking for some kind of sign, some clue to reveal who was there but found nothing.

"Chris, you're going to catch a cold. Let's go inside," I yelled after him. I had dropped my stance and now held the gun to my side.

Chris came back, looked at me, then the gun, then frowned.

We all walked inside and stood in the kitchen. Dan stood slightly behind Chris as if using him as a shield from me.

Chris suggested, "Why don't you work from my office today, Laura?" He then pointed to my gun. "And put that away."

"No. I have jury selection with Thomas."

He walked over to me and took the gun. He popped out the clip and cleared the chamber with more ease than you'd expect from a novice.

I could read his mind. *"What if you had just shot Dan by mistake?"*

I was actually surprised by his constraint.

"I've got to get dressed," said Chris. With that, he walked back into the bedroom, gun in hand.

Dan and I spent an uncomfortable moment of silence together in the kitchen. Chris was our only connection and when he wasn't around, we had nothing to say.

I finally broke the silence.

"Do you two have a meeting or something?"

"No, why?"

"Well, why are you here?"

"Chris said he left his car downtown and needed a ride to work."

I remembered that my husband had indeed driven us home in my car from the impromptu therapy session.

More silence.

 **Thursday, September 28 morning**

"I know it's early, but can you come over?" I asked. I hadn't called Troy in a while.

"Sure. What's up?" His voice sounded eager to hear from me.

"I'll tell you when you get here."

Troy was at our front door a few minutes later in wrinkled blue jeans and a wool sweater. His hair had been combed but still had that "just-woken-up" look. I poured him a cup of coffee and we sat at the kitchen table. He seemed pleased that I had called, given the distance I had put between us after his drunken confession.

I spoke. "I used to think it was a random attack, but now I'm starting to wonder."

"What do you mean?" he asked. Troy poured more cream into his coffee until it turned light brown.

"Well, I've been thinking more about that night and things that have happened since then. I haven't told anyone else this, not even Chris, but I'm beginning to wonder if it wasn't random. What if it wasn't a failed rape, but a failed murder? What if someone wants me out of the picture?"

"What are you talking about?"

"Well, it's no secret that Dan and I don't get along. Maybe because I see him for what he is—a leech off of Chris. And, he's never accepted that I replaced him as Chris' best friend. What if he wanted me out of the picture?"

"What? You actually think he set up the attack?" I could see the disbelief in Troy's face.

"I don't know. He was acting really weird today. He came over to pick up Chris but was snooping around outside our house. He *said* he saw someone, but I think he made it up."

"Where was he?"

"At the side of the house. Not your side, the other one."

"There's nothing there except your air conditioning units. And how would anyone get past the back fence?"

"Let's go look," I suggested.

I was still in my sweats and slippers but didn't care. We walked from the front porch to the side of the house and looked around. Indeed, there was nothing there of interest except the air units. The ground was cold and dry—no sign of any footprints.

I noticed a pink rectangular piece of paper on the ground and picked it up.

"How did this get here?" I said out loud.

"What is it?" he asked.

I read the pink ticket. "It's a parking stub from the Georgia Building."

"Is it yours?" he asked.

"It could be. I park there all the time, but how did it get here?"

"Today's garbage day. Maybe it blew out of your trash."

I pointed to the garage. Chris had forgotten to roll out the cans.

"Call me Nancy Drew, but how would this ticket get from there to the side of our house?"

Thursday, September 28 late morning

Troy watched TV while I got showered and dressed. With the scare Dan had given me and the mystery of the parking ticket, I appreciated having the company. I left him still guarding the house as I drove to the DeKalb County courthouse.

To get to the courtroom, I had to pass through a gauntlet of jurors sitting on wooden benches on both sides of the narrow hallway. As they watched me pass—their eyes felt heavy. I tugged on the lapel of my black jacket clasping it tighter over my tan blouse. My heels echoed as I walked, drawing more attention to me.

Hold your head high, walk fast and pretend you know what you're doing.

I opened the door to the courtroom where a guard allowed me to enter. I tried to be inconspicuous, slipping into the back row of the wooden benches. Thomas and Andy were already sitting at the defense table with a man between them. I could only see the defendant's back and the cornrows of his long, dark hair.

I remembered Andy from the office. He was a middle aged, tall, wiry guy with classic Irish features—red hair, freckles and light green eyes. Andy was doing most of the talking as the judge, an older white gentleman with a permanent scowl, listened.

The judge instructed the bailiff to bring in the jury and the people who had been waiting in the hallway shuffled in. The judge introduced himself and asked the lawyers to do the same. When Andy introduced the defendant, he turned around to face the jurors. I studied his profile—it wasn't him.

Thomas saw me sitting in the back row and gave a quick nod acknowledging my presence. Looking at these two men standing side by side, the defendant and Thomas, I couldn't help but notice that Thomas looked more hardened than the guy on trial.

The judge read the indictment which sounded about the same as the list I had in my case—malice murder, felony murder, aggravated assault, aggravated battery, attempt to commit a felony, commission of a crime with a firearm and there were five others that I didn't quite catch. Andy indicated a plea of not guilty on all accounts.

As Thomas had described, the potential jurors were asked to take an oath to provide truthful answers. They were then asked by the judge if they had a bias against or were related to the accused.

The room was deathly silent.

The judge asked if anyone had a hardship or conflict that would prevent them from serving. Thirteen of them raised their hands and the judge listened to their excuses one by one. Though Thomas had said he would look for anyone feigning disinterest, these people really seemed like they didn't want to be there. The excuses ranged from funerals to business trips to daycare issues. The judge listened but didn't let a single person go, not even the crying woman that said she needed to go bury her father.

Next, the DA started asking his general questions, instructing the jurors to raise their hands if the answer was yes. He wanted to know if anyone ...

... knew one or more of the lawyers on the case?

... ever had a bad experience with the DA's office?

... ever was accused or convicted of a crime?

... owned a gun?

... ever had a home invasion?

... was a supervisor or manager?

I wrote the word "supervisor?" on my notepad. A few of the jurors were watching me as I took notes.

Then, Andy stood up, introduced himself again, but added a friendly tidbit about his wife and two children.

Much more likeable than the DA.

Andy proceeded with his questions.

He asked if anyone ...

... knew the witnesses that he listed?

... was a member of the armed forces?

... had been to law school?

... had friends or relatives in law enforcement?

... had trouble viewing autopsy pictures?

... knew anyone who had died from a gunshot wound?

... or owned a gun?

The judge chimed in, "Do any of you have those guns on you now?"

There were laughs in the courtroom as the judge briefly smiled at his successful attempt at humor in an otherwise dull process. His face returned to the scowl.

Andy continued, "Does anyone think that the mere fact my client was arrested makes him guilty?"

"Objection," the DA shouted.

"Objection sustained," said the judge.

Andy continued, "Does anyone disagree with the principle that a person is innocent until proven guilty?"

"Objection," the DA shouted again.

"Sustained," the judge confirmed and glared at Andy.

Andy tried a third time, "Does anyone believe the defendant has to testify to prove his innocence?"

"Objection!"

From out of the audience, one of the jurors blurted out, "Just let it go, man!"

I could see it was a young, black guy, second row on the end.

"Who said that?" demanded the judge. "Don't do it again or you'll be in contempt of court!"

Thomas and Andy were scanning the crowd trying to ascertain who had spoken out of turn. Thomas looked directly at me. I knew his silent question—did I know who it was? I nodded my head once and texted "second row on end" to Thomas. Maybe I was a jury consultant after all.

The judge sustained the last objection and decided to take a break—an eleven-minute break, to be precise. He gave instructions for the jury to not discuss the case, to stay on the fifth floor and to be back in exactly eleven minutes. As soon as the jury had left the room, Thomas walked briskly over to me.

"You're sure it was him?"

"Positive."

I noticed this particular juror when he first walked in, long before he had spoken out of turn. When he walked past me, I instinctively recoiled—his pants were sagging halfway down his hips, looking more like a defendant than a juror.

"Okay. Thanks," said Thomas, obviously pleased that he had the identity of the trouble maker.

"Do you have time for a quick question?" I asked.

Thomas gave a hurried nod.

"Why did the DA ask if anyone was a supervisor?"

"To see who is likely to become the foreman. Someone who is a supervisor or manager is more apt to take charge. So, we pay extra attention to those people as they may become the spokesperson for the other jurors."

"And what exactly is he charged with—murder?"

"Appears to be a drug deal gone bad. It's not clear who actually shot the gun. There were other people involved who haven't been caught yet."

"How can he afford you?"

"Only child, raised by his aunt; she's probably spending her life's savings for him."

Just then, Andy called Thomas to rejoin him. They had business with the judge and DA before the jurors returned. Thomas leaned over to Andy and whispered something.

"Your Honor," Andy said. "We need to strike the juror who spoke out."

The judge replied, "How do you know who it was?"

Andy pointed to me. "Your Honor, we have a witness in the back of the courtroom."

The judge peered over at me and then looked back at Andy.

"Mr. Hayes," he said. "You may strike that juror for cause. Bailiff, bring them back in, please." I wondered briefly if the juror had spoken out of turn on purpose to get cut.

The jury shuffled back in and the DA began asking individual questions to each person, followed by Andy asking his personal questions. I noted items that I wanted Thomas to clarify later. For example, when the police officer stated his profession, the DA stopped asking questions. I also noticed that neither the DA, nor Andy asked the grieving woman any questions. It was becoming clear who was getting struck for cause.

The questioning went all the way to lunch, when the judge announced a one-hour break. I chased after Thomas and Andy, following them to a small conference room in the courthouse. To my dismay, they weren't planning to eat, but started playing jury poker. They discussed, at a lightning pace, who they wanted in or out, tossing unflattering descriptions of the jurors around so quickly that I couldn't keep up. In the end, Andy and Thomas listed eleven people who would be struck for cause and tallied their nine defense strikes, with labels like prosecutor-wanna-be, military-girl and cop-wife.

After the rapid-fire jury striking concluded, Andy excused himself. I sat in front of Thomas, hungry and baffled as to how they had so quickly made the strikes.

"Questions?" he asked.

I looked at my notes. "The cop got dismissed for cause?"

"Yes. By law, he can't serve."

"So why even give him a jury summons?"

"I know. It's silly," he confirmed.

"Why do you care if someone has taken legal courses?" I asked.

"The only thing worse than a real lawyer on the jury is a self-proclaimed lawyer, someone who thinks he knows the law from a few classes when he doesn't really know anything. He could try to influence the other jurors with fancy talk."

"Oh."

I looked at my notes again. I was out of questions and drained from the long morning with no food. But, I didn't want to waste precious time with Thomas.

"So, of all the jurors you saw today, who would we want for my trial?"

"Well, I would have asked additional questions that we didn't ask here. I'd want to know if anyone had dealt with domestic abuse or rape. For the women, I'd want to find out who lived alone."

"You can ask that?"

"Not directly, but I have their marital status. If they're divorced with grown kids, you can assume they live alone. Or if they are married, I can ask what the husband does for a living. Say he's a Delta pilot or a salesman, she's going to be home alone a lot."

Chris was in sales. I was home alone a lot.

Andy came back into the conference room and summoned Thomas to return to the courtroom. Just as Thomas had described, they began the silent process of selecting the jurors. The people who had caught my attention, whether good for the prosecution or the defense, had all been dismissed.

The judge gave everyone another eleven-minute break and Thomas walked over to me in the back of the courtroom.

"So now we start the trial. Do you want to stay?"

"No, thanks. I want to get this on paper while it's fresh in my mind."

"You satisfied with the jury?" I asked.

"Well, they nixed our good ones and we nixed theirs, so it's even."

"Yeah, that occurred to me."

He replied. "I sometimes wonder if we just took the first fourteen people to show up in the morning, if we'd have any different outcomes. Although I suppose you wouldn't want to test that theory when it was your life on the line."

"Probably not. This was useful—lets me see that I wouldn't get the jury I wanted."

"Thanks for helping us clear out the troublemaker," he replied.

I smiled and left the courtroom, feeling fortunate that I could come and go as I wanted. That drug-dealing defendant had no such choice.

October

 **Thursday, October 5**

Thomas and Andy were not in the office the following week. They were still at the courthouse defending their client so I used the time to write my jury selection chapters. For breaks, I would chat with Joanne at the front desk.

I liked Joanne; she was a class act, professional and discreet. Her short, bobbed hair was always in place and her clothes were stylish, yet conservative. She catered to the eight lawyers in the office like they were CEOs of Fortune 100 companies, going out of her way to update their calendars and highlight urgent emails.

From my loaner office, I sent a text message to Thomas: "r we on for fri? hows trial going?"

Thomas texted back, "He got life. OK for Friday."

It hadn't occurred to me that Thomas and Andy would lose.

The next afternoon, Thomas was dressed casually for the first time. He wore pressed khaki Dockers and a dark green V-neck sweater with a crisp white collared shirt.

"Sorry to hear about the verdict," I said, as I sat down across from him.

"Yeah," Thomas replied without emotion.

We sat quietly for a moment until it got uncomfortable.

"So, we've selected the jury," I said. "Now it's time for me to testify, right?"

"Eager to vindicate yourself, eh?" he asked, with a bitter inflection. Apparently he was in a bad mood.

"Would you call me first?" I asked, trying to ignore his mood.

"Would you struggle?"

Of course I'd fight back. He knows I struggled.

"Why do you ask?"

"It depends," he said.

More silence.

He put his elbows on his desk, pressed his palms together as if praying and then tilted his hands forward, pointing at me.

"If I thought you would struggle, I'd call you first so the other witnesses, especially the experts, could follow-up. But if I thought you'd be a strong witness, I'd call you last."

Oh, he meant would I struggle on the witness stand.

Thomas looked over at the picture on his desk and then back at me.

"Before we get into the testimony, let me explain some of the rules," he said. "You see, there are different rules for the defense versus the prosecution. On direct examination, I'm not allowed to ask leading questions. I have to ask open-ended questions, which makes it difficult to control the testimony. You are likely to over explain or add details that aren't relevant rather than just answering the question. So, the first thing I tell my clients when preparing for testimony is to listen to my question and answer only my question.

He continued. "The DA, on the other hand, is going to pepper you with leading questions. 'You said this, didn't you? You did that, didn't you?' And he'll ask the same questions over and over to try to fluster you, so you'll appear inconsistent. The other thing I'd coach you on is that you'll have to check your attitude at the door. You'll feel righteous indignation that you are even in this situation, having to defend yourself. You'll see yourself as a victim and are likely to come off as pissy, for lack of a better term. If the jury catches your vibe, you are going to turn them off. What you want is for the jury to empathize with you and like you so much that they feel the righteous indignation for you."

After spending so much time in jail awaiting trial, I didn't think "pissy" would describe me; I would be weak and broken if anything.

"Now, on to your testimony," he said. "For starters, we need the jury to understand who you are. So before I ask about that night in June, I'll ask where you grew up and where you work. I'll ask you to tell me about your marriage hoping that the husband questions will make you tearful and the jury sympathetic.

"I'd also hold back some questions and not practice them because your pain has to be real, not rehearsed. Most people in the courtroom, even when they are on trial for their life, will default to being polite and impersonal, so I'm going to have to shock you out of polite to show your pain."

"Like what?" I asked.

"I'd ask how your husband feels about what happened to you? It may be easier for you to show pain if you are talking about how this ordeal has impacted him."

"That's good. What else would you ask?"

"Well, I need to know your answers to these questions to know what to ask next."

I stopped typing and looked up at Thomas. I wasn't going to actually answer his questions about my marriage. I planned to write my answers in private. Sharing personal information real-time was completely out of the question.

"I don't need to go over the answers," I protested. "I can do that later. I just need to know the questions you'd ask."

Thomas shook his head. "That won't work. In reality, we'd practice your answers to avoid me getting surprised in court."

"You can just pretend I'll behave just as you expect on the stand."

"Humor me," he said, still persisting. "Two questions. Let's see if you answer them as I expect."

He was making me uncomfortable, but I decided to prove him wrong.

"Alright. Two questions. Then we move on," I said firmly.

Thomas grinned. He quickly posed the first question before I could change my mind.

"Tell me about the best day in your marriage?" he asked.

I thought back to the Ellijay trip. With the exception of Chris scaring me in the woods, it was a fun weekend. It wasn't the best time of my marriage, but it was the most recent good time and tame enough to share with Thomas.

"Well, I told you that Chris was taking me on an anniversary trip." I said. "He surprised me with a plot of land so we can build a cabin."

"Is that what you would tell me on the witness stand?" he asked.

"Well no, because if I had been in jail, I wouldn't have gone on an anniversary trip. But that's not what you asked."

"Tell me what you would have said on the stand."

I thought some more.

"It's cliché, but it was our wedding day."

"Well, if you were on the stand, you'd want to elaborate. You'd talk about the butterflies in your stomach and how excited you were in your Cinderella white lace dress looking at your handsome husband-to-be. We'd need you to get all dreamy-eyed to evoke the jury's emotions."

How did he know the style of my wedding dress?

"I'm not a good actress. I can't role-play like this," I said.

Thomas ignored my protest and continued. "Okay. Question two. Tell me about the worst day in your marriage?"

I thought back to my most recent argument with Chris about the gun. It wasn't our worst day, but it was our most recent fight.

"Chris and I got in a fight when I bought a gun," I said bluntly.

"That's a terrible answer!" Thomas exclaimed.

"Why?"

"Because you want the jury tied to your emotions. You just erased all sympathy they felt for you and filled their minds with the image of a pissed-off vigilante."

I frowned and begrudgingly replied, "I suppose the worst day would be talking to my husband behind the glass barrier in the jail."

"Better," he replied, "but you'd still need to elaborate. Look, I'll give you just the questions if you want, but if you want to be efficient with our time, we should just run through it now."

I didn't like it, but I was beginning to understand that I would actually have to role play with Thomas.

"Okay, fine," I said.

"It gets worse," he replied. "Then, I'd ask you if you ever had an affair."

"Of course not! I've already told you that."

"We're running through what I'd ask you on the stand. We'd need to establish you had a solid marriage and there was no cheating going on. Has your husband ever cheated on you?"

"No!"

"Are you sure?" he asked.

I glared at Thomas.

He murmured, "They're always so sure. Anyway, let's talk about that night. Tell me exactly what happened."

I remember the sound of my bedroom door crashing open. In an instant, I was jolted from a deep sleep to sitting upright in bed.

I remember looking toward the source of the noise. In the darkness, I saw a black silhouette in the doorway.

I remember wondering if it was Chris, returning early from his trip?

I squinted as I studied the outline of the body. Approximately six feet tall. Wide shoulders tapering down to a slender waist. The silhouette could have been Chris, but I knew it wasn't—this figure radiated a sinister vibe that I could feel from across the room.

All I could think to myself was that a stranger was in my bedroom. This was real! This was really happening to me! I had no choice but to deal with the situation. He could not be wished away.

I instinctively screamed as he charged at me. I screamed even louder, with all my vigor, promising myself not to stop until he was gone. He pounced on top of me and threw me from the bed to the floor.

I remember feeling pinned on my back against the hardwood surface with him panting on top of me. His acrid smell permeated the air as he yanked my cotton T-shirt above my waist exposing my bare body.

I remember thinking of my sister, Lucy. She knew self-defense and had taught a workshop to all of her freshman students in college, including me.

Like a panicked, cornered animal, I began to fight back. I tried to knee him in the crotch, but he had my legs spread and pinned outside of his. With the weight of his body on top of me, I couldn't move my legs at all.

I remembered Lucy saying, "Pretend to caress his hair at the temples and then dig his eyes out with your thumbnail."

At the time, I couldn't imagine doing that to anyone, not even a rapist. Now I had no qualms about gouging his eyeballs out of their sockets. I pulled my left hand from my side and went straight for his right eye, fingernail first, with a hooked thumb. He reacted quickly, latching on to my ring and pinky fingers with his teeth. He bit into my flesh and shook his head violently like a wild dog devouring its prey.

I remember seeing the diamond of my engagement ring sparkle in the dim light as he thrashed his head. This was the only time I caught a glimpse of his dark face, with my fingers in his mouth. He did not seem human—but like a rabid beast attacking me in the night.

I jerked my hand from his teeth ripping my knuckles. I needed to find some means of defense. With my free hand, I fumbled overhead and found the leg of my nightstand. I yanked it forward. The lamp that rested on it tilted and crashed on his back.

He let out a low, guttural growl. With one, swift twist of his shoulders, he tossed the lamp.

I think I was still screaming.

I looked through the bedroom doorway where the only meager light shone from the outside street lamp slightly illuminating the den.

I remember screaming even louder hoping Troy might hear me. He snarled and pressed his palm over my mouth to quiet me, but I grabbed his wrist with my bloody hand and shoved it away with more ease than I expected.

My voice was the only defense I had left.

He, too, must have been surprised by my tenacity or adrenaline because he did not try to quiet me again. Instead, he spoke to me for the first time.

In a hurried whisper he said, "If you shut up, I'll leave."

I was dumbfounded. He was willing to leave?

By speaking, this beast had become human, actually showing signs of weakness as he tried to negotiate rather than enforce my silence.

I remember thinking that he must be crazy if he thinks I'll stop screaming. Now I felt I had some power over the situation. I screamed even louder.

Finally, in an eerie, rushed voice he said, "You win for now, but don't you forget Sweet Sam."

With that, he jumped up and bolted from the bedroom, through the den and out the front door.

I was stunned.

Was he actually leaving? Had I struggled that hard? Was he afraid the neighbors had heard my screams? Were my screams even loud enough? I couldn't tell.

With his weight off of me, I sat upright, pressing my palms against the floor for support. I pulled my T-shirt down to my thighs smearing blood from my left ring finger on the white cotton.

I remember looking at my extended legs and feeling like they were tree trunks. For a moment I felt immobilized. There was something shiny next to the broken lamp but I couldn't tell what it was in the darkness.

All of the sudden, I realized he was getting away.

I swiveled around and faced the nightstand. I opened the top drawer and fumbled around the back of it until I felt a long, cold metal cylinder. There it was—my twelve-year-old can of Mace. And, as if on autopilot, I stood up, jumped over the broken lamp, rounded the edge of the bed and found myself running through the den to the front door.

I stood on the porch—barefoot, bloodied, tangled hair—screaming with what was left of my voice.

I could see him running away down the street. As he passed under a street lamp, I saw his dark pants and a white T-shirt with a large, red circle in the middle.

I kept screaming, hoping the neighbors would awaken and catch him.

Instead, I watched as he disappeared into the darkness.

 # Friday, October 6 late afternoon

"Well?" Thomas demanded.

"What?" I asked.

I had been far away.

"You're on the stand. I've asked you to tell me what happened that night."

I let out a brief sigh. It was inevitable. I'd have to relive that night in detail in Thomas' office.

I started slowly. "I was home alone because Chris was out of town."

"Stop," said Thomas. "Tell the story in present tense. You want the jury to feel like they are right there with you. Tell what you see, what you smell, what you feel. Is it dark out? Is it hot? What do you hear? Do you hear the sound of crickets? Do you hear traffic noise? Do you hear nothing but his breathing? Start again."

"Fine. I am home alone because Chris is on a trip."

I stressed the present-tense verb as if I was punching Thomas with each word.

"It isn't unusual because he travels a lot. I am getting ready for bed and have this eerie feeling that I'm being watched, so I change clothes in the bathroom."

"Stop. Where did you leave the clothes you changed out of?"

"In the bathroom. Why?"

"So when I cross-examine the cop, before you've ever even testified, I'll ask if he found women's clothes in your bathroom. He won't understand the significance, but by confirming he did, he will corroborate your testimony. He's just bolstered the validity of your account. That's why we practice, so I know the details to ask of the prosecution's witnesses. What happens next, in present tense?"

I thought back to that night. "Well, because I feel so eerie, I bolt the little latch on the bedroom door before getting into bed, which is something I don't normally do."

"Stop," Thomas said again, in a controlled voice. "You never informed me about a bedroom latch when I asked for signs of forced entry? You only talked about the kitchen window being pried open. Did the police note the broken latch on your bedroom door?"

I was getting irritated with how he kept ordering me to stop after nearly every sentence. "I don't think they even looked."

"Perfect. Any negligence on their part bolsters your testimony. Picture me cross-examining the cop, 'Officer, did you examine the bedroom door for pry marks, or to see if there was a latch that had been broken?'"

Thomas raised his voice to mock the officer's reply, "Well, we didn't need to. The guy was dead in the street."

He then continued in his normal tone, "So you never bothered to document the inside of the house? You didn't feel that was necessary?"

In his high voice again, "No we didn't."

"When I'm closing I'd say, my client even told the police that she latched her bedroom door, but because they didn't investigate it, didn't even take a photograph, there was no evidence. What would the state's case have been, if they had just taken the time to look at that doorway and seen the broken latch? Perhaps they wouldn't have jumped to the assumption of a lover's quarrel and realized she had actually been attacked!"

I nodded. Thomas could be a jerk, but he was a clever jerk.

He continued, "And trust me, the jury will take note of the detective's sloppiness and hold it against him. Okay, what happens next?"

"I go to sleep. Then, all of the sudden, I awake to the sound of my bedroom door crashing open."

Thomas interrupted, "Let's talk about going to sleep. What's your typical routine?"

I let out a nervous laugh. "Are you kidding? Why in the world do you care about that?"

"Say you take a medication at night, like Ambien. I'd want to know if your response or perception could have been altered by any medications," Thomas explained.

I conceded the question was fair but felt it was far too detailed for what we were trying to accomplish.

"Are you a good sleeper?" he asked. "How long does it take you to fall asleep?"

"I don't know. Maybe ten or fifteen minutes," I replied, questioning again the relevance.

"Do you watch TV before going to bed?"

"No."

"Do you have any lights that you leave on?

"Not back then," I replied, wondering if I would ever be able to sleep in complete darkness again.

Why was he so interested in every detail of my sleep preparation? Was it an appropriate way to plan my defense strategy? He seemed, at the very least, vicariously involved in the feelings and sensations that consumed me that night.

"Where do you sleep on the bed?" he asked.

"What does that matter?" I protested.

He ignored me and fired his next question. "What about your covers. Do you use just sheets or do you have a bedspread or comforter?"

"This is absurd. Why does any of this matter?"

"Because if you testify that you sleep with just the sheets and the crime scene photos show a big, down comforter, that's an inconsistency we don't want to have to explain. We want all the little details to support your version of the events."

"I'm not going to write this much detail. Can we move on?"

"So what happens next?" he asked, unfazed by my comment.

"Like I said, I'm asleep and hear the sound of my door crashing open."

"What does your body feel like? What does your brain say when you hear that noise?"

"I was startled."

"Present tense," he corrected. "Merely startled or out of your mind terrified? What is your first thought?"

Thomas' voice was getting louder, as if he was trying to force the emotion out of me.

"I don't know," I said. "I look to the source of the noise and see a silhouette in the doorway. I think it's Chris, but realize it isn't."

"Why?"

"Because I feel this evil coming from him."

"Physically, how do you feel?" he asked, even louder.

"Terrified," I said flatly, purposely using his earlier description.

"What does it feel like to be terrified? Are you calm like you are sitting here now, or is your heart pounding out of your chest?"

"Isn't that leading?" I said, trying to regain some control over the conversation.

"Yes, which is why we practice. I can't ask you that when you testify. You have to already know to say it. If you're this guarded with just me, imagine how you'd be in a courtroom."

"I get it, Thomas. I know how to describe what happened to me."

"What you don't get is that the DA is going to gloss over this whole part of the story. He will focus solely on the shooting. We'll have just one chance to make an attack that lasted minutes seem like it lasted all night, so it will stick with the jury. That's why I would go through, in exacting detail and step-by-step, what happened in your bedroom. Can you handle that or do you want to quit?"

"I can handle it," I said coldly.

"So, you see his silhouette, then what happens?"

"I scream. The next thing I remember, I'm on the floor."

"Where?" he asked.

"Next to the bed."

"Are you sitting up? On your stomach? On your back?"

"He has me pinned on my back." I was trying to remain detached but Thomas was frightening me, getting physically closer with each question.

"When you say pinned, what does that mean? Describe how your arms and legs are positioned."

I took a deep breath. "His knees have my thighs pressed open where I can't move them and he is gripping my wrists with his hands."

Thomas pointed his finger in my face with enthusiasm. "That's the first good description you've given. That's something the jury can picture. Where is your face? Can you smell his breath?"

"My face is inches from his. He smells...nauseating."

"Describe the smell."

"It's a musky overpowering smell, like ink mixed with strong cologne."

"What are you thinking?"

"I'm thinking I have to fight back," I replied.

"Go on."

"I remember some self-defense moves that my sister taught me and try them. I try to kick him in the crotch but I can't because my legs are pinned. Then I try to dig out his eyes with my thumb, but he catches my fingers in his mouth and bites me."

"Which fingers? When someone is telling the truth, they are able to be very detailed. Lies are always vague. The more detailed you are, the better."

I pointed to my scarred ring and pinky fingers on my left hand.

"Good, the more you demonstrate, the better," he said.

Why is he getting so excited hearing this?

Thomas asked, "Did the police do DNA scrapings? If you tried to gouge his eye out, you're going to have his DNA under your fingernails."

"I was going to say they found his DNA from the bite wound, but you said that wasn't realistic."

"Yes, right. We'll use that omission just like the latch, to show the negligence on the part of the detectives. Then what happens?"

"I keep screaming and he covers my mouth with his hand. I grab his hand and pull it off my mouth so I can keep screaming."

"Wait, you just said he is biting your hand. How are you able to use it to uncover your mouth?"

"He is using his left hand to cover my mouth, which frees up my right one. I use my right hand to pull his hand off my mouth."

"Show me," Thomas demanded.

He stood up, swiftly walked around his desk and knelt in front of me so we were at eye level. His piercing dark eyes were inches from mine, making what was a difficult testimony now unbearable. Instinctively, I tilted my head to the right to avoid a dead-on stare.

Thomas suddenly grabbed both of my wrists with his hands and jerked them shoulder high. I froze for a second in shock, then forcefully snatched my hands free.

"That's enough!" I shouted.

Thomas chuckled and backed off. "I'd want you to show me in court. All of these right-hand, left-hand descriptions are confusing. It's better for the jurors to just see what happened."

He stood up, casually walked back to his chair and sat down.

"Next, the prosecutor would question you. Shall we review that?"

"No. Not today," I said.

I needed to get out of there.

"Sure," he replied nonchalantly.

I swiveled the chair so it faced the door and stumbled slightly as I got up. I was trying so hard to act composed that I was more clumsy than normal, like when you concentrate to walk a straight line, you can't help but wobble.

 # Monday, October 9

I pushed open the door to the ladies room on the tenth floor of the Georgia Building, just down the hall from Barbara's office. As I stepped into the stall and slid the metal latch, I thought back to the flimsy latch that I had secured the night of my attack. Somehow, I had known I was in danger before ever going to sleep that night.

As I started to unbutton my pants, I heard the bathroom door open and slam shut.

I listened, expecting to hear the high-pitched click of women's heels on tile. Instead I heard slow, heavy steps. They walked to what sounded like the end stall. I heard the stall door open, but instead of walking in and closing the door, the footsteps walked to the next stall. Again, I heard the door swing back on its hinges, knock into the side barrier and bounce back. The footsteps proceeded to the next stall—now three down from me.

I gasped.

Who is in here and is he searching for me?

I quietly sat down on the toilet seat and lifted my feet to the rim. In case he was looking under the stalls, he wouldn't see me.

Straining forward, I carefully pulled my phone from the side pocket of my purse, turned it to silent mode and texted Barbara.

"need help bathroom 10 floor"

I tried to quiet my breathing, to not make a sound, but feared my inhales and exhales were too loud. I gripped the phone in my right hand and covered my mouth with my left.

He had advanced—only two stalls away now. What would happen when he tried to open my locked door?

"hurry" I texted.

My heart was pounding uncontrollably. Would he be bold enough to come after me in broad daylight, in a busy office building?

I stared at my phone. No reply. I started to dial 9-1-1. It was my only option left.

Just then, I heard the bathroom door open and Barbara's voice call out.

"Laura? Are you in here?"

"Barbara!" I screamed and rushed out of the stall.

There stood Barbara and a young, sandy-haired man in janitor's coveralls holding a broom.

"Thank God!" I cried as I ran to her.

"Come dear, let's go to my office. She faced the janitor. "You really should post a sign outside," she admonished.

Barbara put her arm around my shoulder and guided me to her office through the back entry.

"I think I'm losing my mind," I cried. "I was so afraid. How can I be so paranoid?"

"Well, he should have made his presence known. I'm going to speak to the building management."

"I get spooked so easily. He spooked me. Thomas spooked me. I don't know what's real anymore."

"Thomas spooked you?" She eyed me sharply. I sat down on the couch and she opened the door to the waiting room, letting Alisa know that I was already there.

I looked down as she walked to the chair diagonal from me.

"Well, I know you don't approve of me working with Thomas…"

Barbara pressed her lips together but didn't speak.

"Last Friday, we were practicing my testimony and it got weird."

"How so?" she asked.

"I don't know. It's like he's enjoying it—maybe too much. Chris keeps saying it's odd for him to help me when all he is getting is a byline. Why do you think he is helping me?"

"Why do you think Thomas is helping you?"

I smiled slightly. "I should have known you wouldn't answer. I mean I know you are friends with him."

"Why do you think he's helping you?" Barbara asked again.

"At first, I thought it was for the publicity."

"Assume, for argument's sake, it wasn't. What else would motivate him?"

I thought for a while.

"It's hard to say. He's not an easy person to read. One minute he's too busy for me, like when he had trial, and the next he seems way too interested in how I felt that night. I can't really say for sure why he is spending all this time with me, but it feels like there is more to it than what meets the eye—like I'm missing something."

Barbara sat still without speaking.

I continued, "I mean everything has crossed my mind from the good to the … not so good."

"What's the good?" she asked.

"Maybe he's just a generous person, giving of his time when he has it."

"And if not that?"

I looked down, admitting for the first time out loud what I had wondered myself. "Maybe he's attracted to me. He's asked about my marriage more than once and challenged if Chris has been faithful."

"And if not that?"

"Maybe he gets his jollies hearing about a woman about to get raped."

Barbara blurted, "What if he is not reliving that night for you, but for himself?"

"What do you mean?"

Barbara shook her head.

"Reliving that night for himself?" I asked. "I don't get it."

Barbara stood up and walked over to her desk. Her back was facing me. Without turning around, she said, "Having this conversation is inappropriate."

"I know it's tricky—the fact that you are friends with him. And it wasn't right of me to hide it from you, that I approached Thomas because I saw you with him."

Barbara turned around and looked at me. She didn't speak but I was eager to hear what she would say next.

Finally, she said, "I think it might be best if I refer you to one of my colleagues."

"What?" I was in shock.

"I won't charge you for today's session," she said.

"I don't understand." I was still in disbelief.

Am I getting fired by my therapist?

She replied, "I'm only trying to do what's best for everyone."

Barbara nodded once as if she was giving herself a final confirmation that she had chosen the right course of action.

With that, she walked over to me, held out her hand and escorted me to the door.

 # Wednesday, October 11

As I walked into the Georgia Building, I thought of my last conversation with Barbara. None of it made sense but I had to believe she wouldn't allow me to work with a man that she knew to be dangerous.

I was deliberately reserved as I entered Thomas' office. He wasn't apologetic for how he had treated me the prior week but was softer in his tone and demeanor. Thomas pulled back some aluminum foil from a plate on his desk revealing molasses cookies.

"I was in Fort Valley over the weekend," he said. "Want to try one of my mom's cookies?"

That apparently was the best peace offering he could muster.

"Thanks," I said icily. I was not going to let him off the hook. "I'd like to go over the questions the prosecution would ask me," I said, brisk and firm. "I don't need to pretend I'm on the stand anymore. I'm not using that much detail."

"Okay, but we didn't really finish your testimony last time."

I asked skeptically, "What did we miss?"

"Well, I'd at least ask you what happened up to the police arriving."

"Alright. We can cover that, but I'm not going to role play," I said again firmly.

"No problem. I'll just walk it through and you tell me if I've got it right. So, in court, I'll ask you to show me how you were held." He paused but didn't move. "Like before."

I glared at him. If anything, he seemed amused by my tenacity. It was as if he had predicted how I would behave upon returning and was pleased that I was living up to his expectations. Even with his new gentleness, it still felt like he was pulling my strings.

He continued, "You won't like it, but I'll probably ask you to scream for the jury just like you did that night. It would make you so uncomfortable that you would probably cry and make some of the jurors cry, too. The DA may ask why none of your neighbors heard your screams. We'd preempt that with photos of your house to show that your neighbors' houses aren't really close to yours."

How does he know that?

"I'd ask you how you felt as you screamed. I'd ask if your attacker ever talked to you. And I'd ask how you felt when he started to leave."

Thomas was going too quickly. I was willing to clarify some of his questions—but I didn't want to role play. I blurted out, "I was in shock that he was actually leaving. I knew I was going to keep screaming until he left or killed me, but I didn't think he was really going to leave."

Thomas looked surprised.

He repeated cautiously, "You didn't think he was really going to leave? So, what did you do next?"

"I ran after him."

"Okay," he said slowly. "How long did it take to run to the doorway. Here is where you'd say it took seconds. I'd ask you what you saw and you'd say you saw him. I'd stop you there, before you could ever say he was *running away*. I'd ask, 'So, you saw him. He hadn't left yet. He wasn't gone. Was he?' And you would say no."

I nodded, relieved that Thomas was playing out both sides.

He continued, "Now the defense is going to object because this is leading, but I won't care. The jury will have heard your answer. I'll harp on how quickly everything happened and that the whole time you were still in fear for your life. Once you shot the gun, what happened?"

"I ran in the house to call my neighbor, Troy."

"Why didn't you call 911 first? The DA will be sure to go after you for that."

"Because Troy was closer. He could get there faster than anyone else."

"That's a good answer. It shows you still felt like you needed protection."

Thomas continued, "You know, I'd probably call Troy right after you to testify about your demeanor. We'd have him describe you as frantic, pale as a ghost, shaking and talking a hundred miles a minute. This would help to counter the 'cooling off period' argument from the prosecution. Then we'd talk about how the police showed up and handcuffed you and wouldn't listen to you. Finally, I'd ask my closing question, 'Did they ever understand what happened to you?' And we'd end with your testimony saying, 'No, not until now have I even been able to explain.' And we let the jury feel the outrage of how you have been treated."

I nodded. I was glad I had come back.

"Okay. Now we go to the cross-exam," he said. "First, know that a savvy DA will ask you how many times you met with your lawyer to practice your testimony."

"What should I say?" I asked.

"You have to tell the truth. That's why I don't practice too much with my clients. Ideally, we go over your testimony no more than twice. Like I said before, we don't want you to look too rehearsed."

"Okay."

"And I deliberately stayed away from asking you about the shooting because I wouldn't want to give any insights to the DA. You see, one of the cardinal rules of cross-examination is to ask only questions where you already know the answer. So if I haven't elicited anything on direct about the shooting, it puts the DA in an uncomfortable position."

"I see."

"Another technique the DA will use on cross is to ask you to repeat what you said when I was questioning you. Anyone, even someone telling the truth, can't repeat the same story exactly the same way. He'll try to uncover inconsistencies. The DA will also go out of sequence, so I'd prepare you to expect that. It's a trick to disrupt the logical order of events that you have in your mind."

I nodded as I typed, not looking up from my keyboard.

"People tend to think cross exam is like what they see on TV, that Perry Mason moment when he asks five or six questions and by the seventh question, the accused just breaks down and confesses."

I stopped typing and looked up. "I've never thought that was realistic."

"It's not. In cross, 90 percent of the time the DA will appear to be asking seemingly harmless questions. He'll ask little bits of information and you'll be wondering why he's even bothering with those questions. It's like what I explained I'd do with the cop and the location of your clothes. Both of us will use these little bits of information to tie together our story."

"Will he have me walk through the whole thing like you did?" I asked.

"No. He'll just ask about specific parts, always in the context of clarifying. And each time, all you will be able to say is yes or no."

"I don't get to explain anything?"

"No. Surviving a skilled cross-exam is not about explaining. It's about staying calm, no matter what. No matter how bad your words get twisted and turned, no matter how bad the DA is making you look to the jury, you have to stay calm and collected. Just stick to 'yes', 'no' or 'I don't remember.'"

"But what if the DA leaves the jury with the wrong impression?" I asked.

"You'd wait for me to redirect, when I'm back in control. The DA is going to try to portray you as an NRA enthusiast hungry for a fight. In redirect, I'd ask about your husband traveling and your need to feel safe at home. I'll portray you as a woman in need of self-defense, not a trigger-happy vigilante. Bottom line is that any explanations should be done when I'm the one asking, not the DA."

"Okay, I understand."

"And the DA is going to bait you. If he can get the tiniest bit of aggression to show in you, he will have succeeded. It contaminates the jury feeling sorry for you."

"What will he bait me with?" I asked.

"Maybe the 911 call. He'll say, 'Your testimony is that you were scared for your life, correct?' You'll say, 'Yes.' Then he'll say, 'Yet, you didn't think to call the police?'"

"I did call the police."

Thomas corrected, "Your neighbor called the police."

"He was calling for me. It's not like I tried to stop him."

"The DA will say, 'Instead of calling the police, instead of staying inside and locking your door, you deliberately ran after him, didn't you?'"

"No," I replied. "Can't I say that's twisting what happened?"

"You'll just sound peevish. Let the jury conclude he is twisting your words."

I shook my head. "What if they don't?"

"I'd redirect if we needed damage control."

I wasn't comforted by that answer.

Thomas continued, "He may investigate your background and find out where you bought the gun or learned to shoot. He'll check how many times you've been to the range or taken shooting lessons. No matter what the number, he'll find a way to make it sound nefarious."

"I've been to the range several times with my instructor. But it's the responsible thing to do," I defended myself.

"The DA would say you are practicing to be accurate, to be sure that when you shoot someone, you kill them."

I shook my head again. It was amazing how fast Thomas could come up with the counter argument.

"He can twist every single thing I say."

"Yep. If you practice shooting too much, you are blood thirsty. If you say you don't practice, then he can say it's pretty remarkable that you were able to mow this guy down so easily. In essence, he'll make it look like you're lying. Or worse, he'll pull the records of your visits to the range only after you testify that you don't practice. Then he'll have caught you in a blatant lie."

"Will he ask me what I was thinking when I shot the gun?"

"He might say, 'You were thinking you were going to get him, right?'"

"I'll say no."

"Didn't your instructor tell you that if you draw your gun, your intention must always be to kill?"

"How did you know that?"

"Guns 101, that's basic. If you have admitted to taking classes, the DA will know that you've been told that."

I was perplexed. "Yes, but in gun class, it's a controlled environment. This happened so fast I didn't have time to think."

Thomas smiled. "That's the best answer you can give. If you keep your answers short, keep your composure and don't ever contradict your self-defense argument, the DA will lose you as a witness. That's the best you can hope for.

"One last point," he continued. "And it's the most critical of all. You have to believe this guy was just about to come back at you. That it wasn't over. If you suggest in any way that you knew he was retreating, you destroy your self-defense argument. That will be all the DA talks about in closing. He'll say, 'We're sorry for her. We feel terrible for her. It's so sad this happened to her, but no one gets to kill someone in the street because they are mad.' "

I nodded. This indeed was the tricky part. I typed in my iPad, "Have to believe—this isn't over."

Thomas looked at the clock as he stood up. "You have enough for today?"

"Yes, this is good." I paused. "I did have one question for you."

I thought back to the conversation with Barbara that ended my therapy, about Thomas' motive for helping me.

"Yes?" he asked.

Standing above me, he looked so imposing.

"Never mind."

Wednesday, October 18

Another week had passed. I was back at Thomas' office.

"Okay, let's hear your best closing argument," I challenged.

"Actually, the DA goes first. Then I go. Then, he has the final shot, no pun intended," he chuckled.

"He gets to go twice?" I asked.

"Afraid so. He gets the first and last word."

"That's so unfair."

"That's the judicial system. For me, it's a double-edged sword because I want to have a strong closing, but I also know the DA can try to refute anything I say. And even though the jury is instructed that closing arguments are not evidence, most jurors don't know how to distinguish the difference."

"Of course they don't. Everything the lawyers say is going to affect them. And the DA gets to have the last word. That's not good."

Thomas just nodded.

I asked, "So if the DA gets to go first, what do you think he'll say?"

"It will go something like this, 'I'm going to come back and speak with you in more detail, but the bottom line is that we can feel terribly sorry for this lady. We can believe that she was attacked by this would-be rapist. In fact, let's take her version of the story as the truth, that this man broke in, intending to do her the worst kind of harm. We still don't allow people to take the law into their own hands. Our society doesn't allow an individual to chase another person down the street and shoot them in cold blood. That is why we have the criminal justice system. And no matter how you feel about her, no matter how sorry you might feel for her, you have to keep that in mind because you are the protectors of our legal system. It is your job as jurors to uphold this system so that we do not have mayhem.'

"Then he'll sit down and it's my turn. So I'll stand up and face the jury and say something like this, 'He's right. It is your job to uphold our system of justice, but this is absolutely not a case of someone taking the law into her own hands. Folks, what we have here is a difference of opinion about the scenario. We all agree this man broke in. We all agree he intended to rape her. We all agree that she was lying there on the floor with her legs spread apart by this man. And we all agree that what she did was get up, get the gun and shoot her attacker. But what we don't agree on is the why. Let's look at what really happened. She was so terrified, so scared. She did not take the law into her own hands, but rather stopped the attack. And as far as she was concerned, it was not over. He was coming back for more. She isn't a vigilante. She isn't someone who calculated or contrived a way to track this man down and kill him. No. She simply reacted, a gut animal instinct to protect herself from the most frightening crime a woman can imagine."

I stopped typing and let the recorder on my iPad pick up every word.

He continued, "And look at the facts. She begged the police to investigate her case. She pleaded with them when she was locked in those cold, steel handcuffs with the stench of that man still on her. Her small, shaking voice was stifled by the police who refused to listen. Did they take pictures of her bedroom to see the tangled sheets? No. How about the broken latch on her bedroom door, a critical piece of evidence totally ignored because they decided right from the beginning this was a vigilante case. Did they care about the fact that she was almost raped? No. No one cared about what she went through. Look at this woman. She is not a cold calculating murderer. She's not a bloodthirsty killer. This is not one of those cases. And it's your job as jurors to make sure that you send a clear message that there is an irrefutable distinction between vigilantism and self-defense."

"That's really good," I said. "Can't you say something like, 'Put yourself in her shoes' to make them think about what they would have done?"

"I'm not allowed to do that, but I could say something like, 'Imagine how she felt standing in the doorway, her heart pounding, knowing any second he was coming back.'"

"That was really compelling. So when the DA gets his final word, what will he say?"

"He'll probably try to undermine me in a fake, friendly way. He'll say something like, 'I've known Thomas Bennett for years. He's a great lawyer who is trying to do the best for his client, but he's just got it wrong this time. I know he feels awfully sorry for her, like we all do. It's a tragic, unfortunate situation. But at the end of the day, we cannot forget that a human life was needlessly taken.'"

"Now, if he was able to rattle you on the stand, he may be more aggressive, saying something like, 'You saw that little hint of temper, didn't you? This wasn't some poor, terrified girl. She was pissed. She was not about to let him get away with it. She hunted him down like any other predator and she took care of business. And maybe a little part of you applauds what she did, but that is not how our justice system works.'"

I shook my head. "No. I'm not going to let the DA rattle me. Then what would he do?"

"Then I think he would play up the fact that Perry was retreating and you were no longer in danger. He'll say, 'Our victim was found dead in the street, shot in the back, not in the front, not in the side, not in the leg or knee, but in the back. She used deadly force to kill him. And he wasn't just a few feet away. He wasn't even a few yards away. He was in the middle of the street, completely off of her property.'"

He'll say, 'She could have stayed inside her house, locked the door and called the police. But she didn't. Ladies and gentlemen, no one can murder another human being in cold blood just because she's afraid. We have the police. If we stop trusting law enforcement to do that job for us, society will break down. That's why vigilantism is perhaps the hardest crime to prosecute, but the most important one, because the minute we start letting people get away with murdering others, we've unleashed anarchy.'"

I squirmed in my chair. "It's awfully damaging that the DA gets the last word."

"There's more," he said. "He might decide to throw in a bit of doubt that you're telling the complete truth. He'll say something like, 'Who's to say this is actually what happened? All we have is her story because we don't have anyone to tell the other side. Unfortunately, he's dead.' And then he'll cue the grieving family to start crying."

"Yuck. You're just as good at playing the DA as you are defending me."

Thomas smiled. "It's not an easy case, that's for sure."

"So why are you doing it?"

I blurted out the question without thinking.

For the first time since I'd known him, Thomas looked genuinely surprised.

He didn't answer right away.

Finally, in a slow, calculated tone, he asked, "Do you know the story of Pinocchio?"

"Yes," I replied, thinking how, as a kid, I used to hold my fingers to the tip of my noise and pretend it was growing to imply Lucy was lying.

"Let's just say it's for Pinocchio."

He paused and then jumped right back into the trial. "Finally, the judge will give the jury some basic instructions and send them off to deliberate while we wait."

That's bizarre. What's this about Pinocchio? He can't drop a weird bomb like that and expect me not to question him.

Then again, I knew Thomas well enough to read the sign that he had already moved on. I'd have to wait and pick the right time to learn anything more.

"How long do you think it would take for them to decide?" I asked. At the same time, I typed 'Pinocchio' in my iPad with a question mark.

"It depends. Say they come back in less than an hour. That's usually a good sign for us. It probably means it was unanimous and not guilty. Or it could take days, especially if they are debating murder versus manslaughter or if there is a split jury."

"So what are the possible outcomes and what do you think would happen?"

"That's the million-dollar question, isn't it?" Thomas leaned back in his chair and rested his hands behind his head.

"Yes it is." I leaned forward. "What's the million-dollar answer?"

Thursday, October 19

I had been writing all day from my closet office to capture the testimony and closing arguments. I considered the four outcomes—mistrial, guilty of voluntary manslaughter, guilty of murder, and not guilty—and decided to wait on the final verdict until I talked to Thomas again. Maybe he could provide the odds for each ending.

Around 7:00 p.m., I packed up my computer and peered into Thomas' office on my way out.

"Hey, I'm calling it quits for today," I said.

Thomas glanced at the clock. "Wow, it's getting late."

"Yes, time for both of us to get a life."

"Actually, I've got one tonight. You'd probably be surprised if you knew just what."

"Really? Am I supposed to guess?" I asked.

"Sure, why not, but I don't think you will."

"Hmmm," I said. "Well I guess that means it's not something as ordinary as a dinner date?"

I instantly realized that I had allowed myself to get too personal. We had never talked about Thomas' private life, though he opened the door by asking me to guess. In fact, in the two and a half months we had been working together, Thomas had never mentioned a girlfriend or even dating anyone.

"No, not that ordinary," he replied.

I recovered by having my next guess be something preposterous, and impersonal. "Okay, then you're going bungee jumping off the top of the Peachtree Plaza Hotel?"

Thomas laughed. "No, not that daring."

"Okay. I give up. What?"

Thomas hesitated. "I'm performing. I sing at a local club."

"Really! You're right. I would never have guessed that in a million years. What kind of music do you sing?"

"Mostly pop and rock, kind of Seal meets U2, plus I've written a few songs myself."

"You're moonlighting as a singer?"

I was amused to finally know something about Thomas outside of work, especially because he knew so much about me.

"Not really. I know the owner at Eddie's Attic. After the main show, he sometimes asks me to sing a few songs. Usually it's impromptu, but he asked me last week to show up tonight. Trammell Starks is playing and he thinks the crowd will stay awhile if they keep the entertainment going."

"I didn't know you had such diverse talent. Not me. I couldn't sing if my life depended on it."

"Come now. I'm sure you could," he replied.

I stiffened instinctively.

If his tone had been joking, I probably would have brushed off that comment. But, there was something ominous in the way he said it, like he knew what I sounded like when I was screaming for my life.

I tried to downplay my feelings.

"You'll have to let me hear you sometime," I said, with as much nonchalance as I could muster, though the hair on the back of my neck was still on end.

"Actually, you can come tonight. I have a couple of extra tickets to the show. Invite your husband, if you like."

Sounds like fun, but how strange that he doesn't already have a date for tonight, especially since he's known about this gig for a while.

My curiosity could not be denied. I definitely wanted to hear and see this side of Thomas Bennett.

"Okay. Let me call Chris and see if he can make it."

Chris was not enthusiastic about a night out. He had an early flight the next day but I begged him. I rushed home to change into jeans and a tank top and we were at the club by 9:00 p.m.

Trammell Starks was still playing. The stage was in the back left corner with small round tables in front of it. To the right, dozens of people gathered around a gigantic U-shaped wooden bar. The only lighting came from small white bulbs, hanging like tinsel from the ceiling and walls. There were over a hundred people crowded into the single room. All the tables were full, but Thomas had one in front of the stage with two open chairs. As I introduced Chris to Thomas, I could tell the two men were sizing each other up.

In between sets, we made small talk about Chris' work and their tastes in wine and music. During the sets, the crowd was hushed, listening intently to the music. Thomas was sipping hot tea and Chris was nursing a glass of wine. As a result, I was enjoying a great bottle of

Gevrey-Chambertin pretty much by myself. Not long after 10:00 p.m., Thomas excused himself and headed to the side of the stage. Eddie, the owner, greeted the crowd and introduced Thomas. Several people in the audience clapped as if they had seen him perform before.

Thomas stepped on stage with quite a presence. He wore black pants and a gray pullover shirt. The top hugged his body and showed off his broad chest and muscular arms. A black shiny belt wrapped around his slim waist. He looked larger than life. As he walked to the microphone, the light bounced off of his body creating a dark silhouette. I shuddered and took another sip of wine.

"Thanks, Eddie" he said. "For starters, I'd like to share a song that I just finished, called *Let Me Breathe*."

The music started out slow and soulful and then picked up the pace. The beat was instantly addictive. Thomas' voice was smooth, strong and compelling. It was like a combination of Seal, Lenny Kravitz and Stevie Wonder, all in one. Some of the crowd were already on their feet clapping in rhythm to the music. I was shocked to see this side of him. He was so incredibly talented. It felt like I knew someone famous.

I couldn't figure out why he would spend one minute practicing law with a voice like that. The next song was even more upbeat and those who weren't already on their feet were up now. He could have been, actually should have been, the main attraction. After three more songs, he thanked the crowd and told them that he was taking a short break. The waitress brought another cup of hot tea to our table, and Thomas arrived shortly thereafter.

"That was incredible!" I said with genuine enthusiasm. "You have an awesome voice."

"Thanks," he said.

"You should make a CD. I'm not kidding. It would sell." My enthusiasm was not dissipating anytime soon, and the alcohol was making me even more animated.

"I've been thinking about it," he said.

"Forget the legal work. You should be a singer," I gushed.

Thomas grinned.

I realized that I was hogging all the wine to myself. "Do you want a glass of wine? It's almost as smooth as your voice."

I was an outspoken drunk. The self-censoring stopped after a few glasses.

"Oh, no thanks," he said. "I only drink hot tea when I'm singing and I have another set to go."

"Where did you learn to sing like that?" I asked. "You should turn professional. I mean, you're really talented."

Thomas smiled appreciatively. "I've been singing since I was four years old. My mother played the church organ, and I was in the choir along with my four older sisters."

"What about your father?" I asked.

Thomas hesitated. "My dad passed away a few days before I was born."

He turned his attention toward Chris, who was twirling the stem of his wine glass.

"I hope you are enjoying the show?"

I could tell from his fidgeting that Chris was ready to leave—he had an early flight to Miami and it was already 11:00 p.m.

Chris, however, replied with his normal diplomacy. "It's great. It was really cool of you to invite us. And Laura is right, you have a fantastic voice. I'm afraid we can't stay for the next set, though. I've got a 7:00 a.m. flight, but we'll certainly plan to come back and see you again."

I looked angrily at Chris. I didn't appreciate that he was deciding we were leaving. I was enjoying myself and we were Thomas' guests. How would it look if the two people who were at his table got up and left before he finished? I couldn't believe Chris was being so rude.

"Chris, honey," I said. "You can sleep on the plane. I'd like to stay for the next set."

Chris didn't reply but gave me a sharp look. He wasn't going to have a fight in front of Thomas, and he wasn't going to try to reason with me.

Thomas stepped in. "I can drive her home, if you like. I don't think you guys live too far from me, anyway."

"That's kind of you, Thomas, but I think we need to leave."

"We can stay a bit longer," I insisted. My husband just looked away and exhaled deeply. "You can go if you want, Chris, but I want to stay."

"You've been drinking," he replied. "How will you get home?"

"I've only had a few glasses of wine. I'm perfectly fine."

"Really, it's no problem for me to take her," Thomas interjected. "My next set isn't as long—we'll be out of here by midnight."

Chris stared at me. I could tell he wasn't going to leave me with Thomas, but would make me pay for forcing him to stay.

To my surprise, he agreed. "Okay then. Well, thanks again for the show and good meeting you."

The men shook hands and Chris kissed my forehead. He threw a hundred dollar bill on the table, thanked Thomas again and ignored me as he left the bar.

Soon after, Thomas got up for his second set. It was just as fabulous as the first. Chris had been the only person in the crowd to leave early. It was just before midnight when Thomas finished singing. On the way out, he briefly introduced me to Eddie and we stopped a few times so he could thank the fans who approached him.

In the parking lot, Thomas opened the car door for me and I clumsily plopped into the passenger's seat. For a Mercedes, the seat wasn't very comfortable until I realized that I was sitting on his black winter gloves and scarf. I pulled them from underneath me and handed them to Thomas. He turned on the seat warmer to take away some of the October chill. I rested my head back, shut my eyes and felt the car spinning from my last glass of wine.

Before I knew it, Thomas stopped in front of my one-story ranch that faced the golf course. I opened my eyes when I felt the car stop.

"Do you need some help to the door?" Thomas offered.

"No, I'm okay." I clumsily pulled myself out of the car and leaned forward through the window to say goodbye.

"Thanks for the show and for driving me home, Thomas. You're a man of many talents."

Thomas replied with a coy grin, "Only scratching the surface."

Even in my inebriated state, something about his words and tone sent a chill down my spine. It was the same troubling innuendo as before, like he wasn't saying exactly what he meant.

This is insane. Who is this guy? A smart lawyer, a great singer, a psychopath or all three?

I rushed inside the house to find Chris asleep on the couch. The door opening woke him. He staggered sleepily over to the alarm to turn it off.

"Why are you on the couch?" I asked.

"I thought you'd forget the alarm. As drunk as you were, I'm surprised you remembered how to get home."

He didn't try to hide his sarcasm.

I thought for a second. I had not given directions to Thomas. I had never even given him my address.

How does he know where I live?

 # Friday, October 20

On Friday morning, I met Vicki for our Pilates class. We placed our mats at the front of the classroom and began stretching before the instructor arrived. I told Vicki about my night out at Eddie's and Thomas' singing. I told her how Chris had rudely left and how Thomas drove to my house without asking for an address or directions.

"Are you going to ask him how he knew the way to your house?" Vicki asked, as she bent her head to her knees in a long stretch.

"Yes. I just need to figure out how to do it casually, without sounding like I'm accusing him of something. Any ideas?"

"That's a tough one. Let me think about it."

As we moved into the next stretch, I froze, my eyes locked on a woman who had just arrived wearing long black tights and a white T-shirt. On the front of the shirt was a small, red circle on the top left. The reflection in the mirror displayed the back of the shirt—a large, red bull's eye. I grabbed Vicki's arm.

"That's the shirt," I hissed. "That's the shirt he was wearing the night of the attack. I recognize the big red circle on the back. That was the huge bull's eye I've been picturing that I had shot."

Vicki glanced furtively over at the woman.

"That's a Target T-shirt," she said. "They gave away thousands of them over the summer, I think for Memorial Day. Kevin has one."

"Are you kidding me! That's his shirt. That proves he lives in the area and got one during the give-away."

"I guess. But lots of people have them and they probably gave them out across the country," she said.

I thought again about how Thomas drove me home without asking the address.

"I wonder if Thomas has one?" I said out loud.

"Well, he might," said Vicki. "You said he lives close to you and he probably shops at Target."

"Yes, but if he does, that's more proof. We need to find out."

"What's this 'we' stuff?" asked Vicki.

My mind was already plotting—I had a plan.

 Tuesday, October 24

When I arrived at the Georgia Building, I placed my purse in my metal desk and walked over to Thomas' office. I took a deep breath.

He's been pretending. Well so can I.

"Hey. Thanks again for inviting us to Eddie's," I said as I entered his office. "We had a great time. You'll have to let me know when you're playing again."

"Sure, it won't be for a while, but I'll let you know. I hope Chris wasn't too upset with us for keeping him out late."

"Oh, no. He was just sorry he couldn't stay longer. Speaking of being sorry, I apologize for snoozing on the way home. I guess I had too much to drink, since you two weren't helping me with that bottle of wine. I'm glad Chris gave you directions to our house before he left."

The bait is tossed. Will he take it?

Thomas shot me an odd look, but didn't say anything.

Of course Chris had never given him directions. And, even though we lived in the same area, Thomas shouldn't have known the exact location of my home. Unless he had been there before.

Thomas started to talk about the testimony of the other witnesses, leaving me without a conclusion on how he found my house. It was time to put my plan into action. I had already gotten his address from Joanne on the pretext of sending him a "thank you" gift. Now, I just needed to find out if he had an alarm.

"Thomas, I may have to cut out of our meeting early this morning," I said. "I'm waiting for a call from ADT, our alarm company. They are supposed to meet me at the house, but you know how they schedule things. It could be any time between 8:00 a.m. and noon."

"Okay," said Thomas, not asking anything further.

I stifled my disappointment. I had hoped that he would ask about the alarm.

I continued, "But if I have to leave, maybe we can schedule some more time later this week? I hate to do this, but it has taken them so long to confirm an appointment that I don't want to miss them."

"I'm sure we can find some time," he said.

"Great." I kept my tone casual. "Do you use ADT? Do you like them...or would you recommend someone else?"

"Oh, I don't need an alarm. I have DJ."

"DJ?" I asked.

"My dog. She barks at anything that moves."

Oh great! That's worse than an alarm.

"I didn't know you had a dog," I replied casually. "What kind is she?"

"A black lab."

I wasn't going to be deterred by a dog. Now, I just needed to find out when Thomas would be away.

"Labs are nice. Can you meet any other day?"

"Let's see," Thomas glanced at his calendar on his computer. "I could meet tomorrow or Friday. Thursday's out."

"You can't do Thursday?" I asked with interest.

"I have to go to Fort Valley."

"Fort Valley? Is everything okay with your mom?" I asked.

"Yeah, just some minor surgery."

Bingo. I have a date.

"If you have to be out of town, I could watch DJ for you. I love dogs." Another lie—I preferred cats.

"Thanks, but my sister will come by and let her out."

I tried to regroup. "Okay," I said. "Let's get back to the other witnesses. Maybe we can finish this part before ADT even calls."

We worked uninterrupted for the next two hours, but my mind was racing. Thomas didn't have an alarm and would be gone Thursday. Now I just had to maneuver around the dog and the sister who might show up.

I was distracted as he described his cross-examination of the police detective and the coroner. I was too consumed with planning the perfect break-in. It was time his true motivations were exposed. He wasn't interested in helping me. He was reveling in what he had done to me. Spending time with me was his sick memento of that night.

 # Thursday, October 26

On Thursday afternoon, it was time to execute the plan. I drove to Thomas' house with Vicki reluctantly sitting in the passenger seat.

I had plugged his address into my GPS. Indeed, he did not live far away. I parked a few doors down from his house, opened the trunk, put my purse in it and motioned to Vicki to do the same.

We had our hair pulled back in ponytails and were wearing dark jogging outfits like two women going out for a neighborhood run.

"Why are we putting our things in the trunk?" Vicki asked.

"Because I'm not locking the door, in case we have to leave fast."

"Oh Lord," sighed Vicki.

Then, I handed her a Tupperware filled with turkey meat.

"What's this?" she asked.

"Bribery for the dog."

"You didn't tell me he had a dog!" Vicki yelled. "Laura, we can't do this."

"Shhh. Don't act suspicious. And take this." I handed Vicki an empty lockbox.

"What's this for?" she asked.

"You're a realtor. If anyone catches us in the house, you can say you were showing it to me."

"It's not on the market," she replied.

"Quiet listing."

She just shook her head.

I started to walk toward the house. Vicki hadn't moved away from the trunk of the car yet.

"Are you coming?" I asked in a hushed voice.

"You're not really going to do this?" she asked. "Even if you find the T-shirt, what will that tell you? That he shopped at Target on the free T-shirt day like hundreds of other people?"

"It's another piece of evidence," I said. "Like all the other pieces that are adding up."

"This is beyond crazy. Can't you see that? You're overly obsessed with this guy. It's not healthy, Laura."

I turned away from Vicki and starting walking to Thomas' house. It was a red brick, two-story colonial. There were no fences, so I had easy access to the backyard and quickly slipped around the side of the house. I walked up the stairs on the back deck. Vicki eventually followed me.

"Where's the lockbox?" I asked.

"In the car."

"That's our alibi. Go get it."

"I came with you to see where he lived. That's enough."

I pulled two pairs of latex gloves from my pocket and handed one pair to her.

"Here, put these on."

I tried to open the back door. It was locked.

"You expected to just walk in?" Vicki asked dryly.

"You never know. It was worth a try."

"What if the dog is vicious?"

"It's a Labrador. They're nice dogs. She'll be barking because she's happy to see us. Let's try the back windows."

I stepped down from the deck and squeezed behind the shrubs, determined to find a means to get inside. I tried to open one of the windows, but it was locked. I moved over to the next window and tried it. To my surprise, it budged. I pushed it up, opening enough space to slide through.

"Give me a boost."

"Oh my God. We're already trespassing. If you go inside, that's breaking and entering."

"We'll be out before you know it. Are you gonna help me or not?"

Vicki squeezed between the shrubs next to me, cupped her hands under my foot to provide a spring board and I pulled myself into Thomas' house.

Thunderous barking filled my ears. DJ had arrived.

"Quick, give me the turkey," I said. Vicki grabbed the Tupperware from the deck and handed it up to me. I opened the lid and placed it on the floor for the dog.

"There. There. Nice puppy. Good DJ," I coaxed.

I reached for Vicki to pull her inside but she just stood there in the bushes.

"Fine. Stay there," I said and started to walk away.

"Okay. Okay. Lord help us."

Vicki extended her arms and I pulled her through the window into the family room. There was a black leather couch with a glass coffee table trimmed in sliver. On the coffee table was a men's magazine addressed to Thomas, a confirmation we were in the right house. There were matching silver lamps and a black, blue and white geometric rug on the hardwood floor. Everything about the décor was very modern and simple—except for one thing.

There was a collection of timeworn, wooden puppets sitting on the bookshelf. I did a double-take and walked toward them. On the top shelf, there sat Pinocchio, Jiminy Cricket and Geppetto.

He never explained Pinocchio.

"What are you doing?" demanded Vicki.

"Nothing. Let's find the bedroom. Keep a watch out for his sister. She might come by to let out the dog."

"Are you kidding!" Vicki shouted. "You're going to put us in jail for real! We need to leave before we get caught. You and I are not criminals and should not be breaking into someone's house."

"We'll just be a minute." I glanced over at DJ who was happily eating the turkey.

I walked from the family room down a short hallway, past a half bath to a small bedroom. It had a futon, large hand weights, an exercise bike and a TV mounted on the wall.

"Not here," I said, as I walked back to Vicki. She hadn't taken a step from the family room.

We backtracked to the staircase and went upstairs. On the second floor, we passed a laundry room and then found the master bedroom. There was a king-sized bed with a dark burgundy spread and a cherry wood headboard. Funky African art was on the walls and stacks of books piled on the nightstand and desk. I went over to the cherry wood dresser and opened the top drawer. There were rows of white sports socks and dark dress socks and a plate of loose change between them, all very neat. I opened the second drawer while Vicki nervously peered out the window toward the street. There were white T-shirts and white underwear. I opened the third drawer and saw gym shorts and colored T-shirts. I rifled through them. A Duke T-shirt. A Braves jersey. A shirt from the Buckhead Athletic Club. Then my hands fell on a plain white T-shirt; the word "TARGET" was splashed in small red print on the left side. I pulled out the shirt and flipped it around. I stared at the red bull's eye.

Suddenly Vicki sprang back from the window. "A car is coming!"

My heart jumped. Thomas wasn't due back until late evening. Maybe it was the sister. We couldn't tell her this was a quiet showing—she would know better.

Vicki's face showed sheer panic. I ran over to the window. The car cruised down the street, passing my parked car.

That was close.

"We have to leave," she insisted.

"Here's the shirt," I said, holding it up. "I found it!"

"Oh my God, that's not proof. Now put it back and let's go."

"I knew he would have it. And it was only four deep, which means he wears it a lot."

I neatly refolded the T-shirt on the bed and put it back in its fourth-place position. I shut the drawer and looked around. The master bath was just off the bedroom so I headed for it.

"What are you doing?" she hissed.

"There must be other evidence. Let's see what else is here."

DJ appeared in the bedroom doorway, but she wasn't barking. Rather she had an expectant look as if she was asking, "Is there more meat?"

Once in the bathroom, I saw a gray marble sink in front of a large mirror topped with square silver lights. On the counter was a dark blue cup, holding a toothbrush and toothpaste. Next to the cup was an electric shaver laying on its side, with the cord plugged into the wall. On the left side of the counter were several bottles of cologne. I picked the black bottle and smelled it. It was Armani Code. I recognized the fragrance; it was what Thomas wore every day. I put it down and picked up a second bottle. Dolce & Gabbana. I didn't recognize it. I picked up a third clear bottle with a silver cap. It was Burberry. I held it to my nose. Instantly, I became nauseous.

It was the sickening odor from the night of my attack. I hadn't been able to see well that night, but my sense of smell was heightened. There was no doubt in my mind that it was the same revolting scent.

"Oh my God!"

Vicki came running into the bathroom.

"What is it?" she asked, panicked.

"This is what I smelled that night—that nauseating inky smell. This is it," I said shaking the bottle. "There's the shirt, and now the cologne. It has to be him."

"You can't just draw that conclusion. This is crazy. I can't believe I agreed to do this with you. We have to go."

I shoved the bottle under her nose. "Smell it," I insisted. "It's the smell from that night."

Vicki grabbed the bottle.

"You have a guy who got a free T-shirt along with hundreds of other people, who owns a trendy cologne. Besides, *you* approached *him*. If you are that convinced, why don't you just stay away from him?"

"I know. I know. Chris says the same thing. But at what point does all this circumstantial evidence become overwhelming? At some point, he is going to let something slip, something that can't be rationalized away."

"I don't know, but can we get out of here. Now?"

"I'm not done."

I really wanted to look around some more. I was positive remnants of my wedding album were in this house.

Vicki grabbed my arm and started pulling me toward the door. I would have been better off doing this by myself but it was too late now. We slipped down the stairs, grabbed the empty Tupperware and climbed back out the window. I slowly closed it, and we raced back to the car.

"Now what do you do?" Vicki whispered as we pulled away. Even though we were safe in the car, she was nearly hyperventilating.

"I ask about his cologne. He only seems to wear the one, the Armani. Why not the others?"

"Did you put them back exactly the same way? I mean, would he be able to tell if they had been moved?"

"Shit!" I exclaimed. "I didn't think about it. Do you think he is that precise?"

"Look at how he folded his T-shirts," she replied. "What if he notices the bottles are not facing the right way or something, and then you start asking about his cologne? I just don't think it's a good idea."

I thought I had been such a good sleuth. I pulled back my hair, wore gloves, diverted DJ and refolded the T-shirt so precisely. But, in the excitement of discovering the cologne, I had totally forgotten about placing it back in the exact same position.

 Tuesday, October 31

On Halloween, the day when demons come out, I was determined to find out what demons were inside of Thomas. I had given up the idea of asking about the cologne. Everything in his house was so neat and orderly; I worried he would notice if a slight detail was out of place. Plus, I couldn't think of a clever way to ask why he had three bottles, but used only one. I had spent the weekend pondering other ways to find proof to incriminate him.

My fear of him was less pronounced than my drive to catch him. The fact that we were meeting in daylight, surrounded by other people may have contributed to my bravery.

Chris, on the other hand, was livid when I told him what I had done. He insisted I stop working with Thomas, even though he didn't think there was a remote chance this lawyer could be my attacker. He said he didn't think it was healthy for me to be around a guy who made me paranoid and irrational. Chris had also insisted that I tell Barbara about the break in—I hadn't told him that she ended our therapy sessions.

But I was determined to make sense of all the circumstantial evidence against Thomas. In fact, I had thought of the perfect plan to test Thomas, once and for all.

"Trick or treat," I said.

Thomas invited me to sit down, and I walked over to my usual brown leather chair. I breathed in his cologne, smelling the Armani that he always wore, knowing there were two others he neglected. I looked at his perfectly pressed beige shirt, knowing he wore a neatly folded white T-shirt underneath. I noticed his clean, smooth face, knowing he used an electric razor to shave it. He knew a lot about me, but I had my own secrets.

I began.

"I was thinking about what you said regarding self-defense—that I would have to prove that I still felt in danger," I said. "What if he threatened me when he was leaving?"

Thomas eyed me cautiously. "What kind of threat?" he asked, staring intently.

"What if he said he was coming back?"

"Well, certainly, that would help your case," he spoke in a measured tone. "But I thought you wanted to play this out the way it really happened?"

I paused, and took a breath. Thomas seemed to be thinking quickly on his feet. Maybe it was his way of covering because he hadn't flinched when I brought up the threat. It was almost as if he expected it. I pressed on.

"No, that is how it happened. He did threaten me before he left."

I watched to see if there was any note of recognition in his face. He played it cool, just staring back at me.

"Why haven't you told me this sooner?" he asked.

"I don't know. It's not something I'm comfortable sharing."

Thomas' voice grew harsher. "You know I expect this from my real clients. There's hardly a case where I don't get surprised by something. Even when I ask multiple times, 'Have you told me absolutely everything?' They invariably haven't. But for you, why on earth wouldn't you share everything? Hell, at this point, your hypothetical jury is already deliberating."

I pushed back. "But it makes a difference?"

"Of course it makes a difference."

I took a deep breath. "Right before he left, he said, 'This isn't over. Don't you forget Sweet Sam.'"

I looked for any sign of recognition in Thomas' eyes. As planned, I had baited him by saying the wrong phrase. If Thomas ever said 'You win for now' instead of 'This isn't over,' I would have concrete proof.

"He told you his name?" Thomas asked suspiciously.

I hadn't expected that question. He caught me off guard which made me start to quiver inside but I kept a strong, external front.

"Yes," I replied.

He squinted at me. "But when we first met, you let me invent a name for him. That's why we used Perry. Why did you let me fabricate a name if you already knew his real name?"

I thought quickly, "I told you. I wasn't comfortable talking about it."

"I see," he said. His voice was guarded.

I couldn't read him, though I had the distinct impression he didn't believe me.

Then he asked, "Are you sure that is exactly what he said?"

I swallowed hard.

"Yes, I'm sure," I lied. "Why do you ask?"

"What did he say, again?" Thomas asked.

I repeated the wrong phrase. "This isn't over. Don't you forget Sweet Sam."

Thomas wrote the phrase down on his notepad as I said it. I wondered if he was doing that to avoid a misstep. His behavior was odd. Panic was starting to build in me, like the first day we met, when I couldn't stand to be alone with him. My heart started to beat faster and my throat tightened. I breathed deeply, trying to keep my composure. I couldn't abort the mission now.

"That's a critical piece to have omitted," he stated, tilting his head and eyeing me skeptically.

"I guess it is." I avoided his eyes.

Thomas sat motionless in his chair, sizing me up. Suddenly, his demeanor changed. When he spoke, he sounded softer, almost pleasant. "What Perry, who we will now call Sam, said could be very useful for your defense, depending on how you interpreted it."

He paused and then continued. "Maybe he was abandoning the confrontation but planned to come back in the future. Maybe he never planned to come back but wanted to leave you afraid. Neither of these helps your self-defense argument because you would no longer be in immediate danger. But, and this is a crucial difference, if you interpreted his words to mean that he was continuing the fight, you have a much better justification for self-defense. If you thought ..."

Thomas looked down at his notepad to read the phrase verbatim.

"...'This isn't over' meant that he was continuing the assault, you can claim that you were still in immediate fear for your life. Do you understand the difference?"

All I could do was nod. This wasn't playing out like I had hoped at all. Thomas was deep in the legalese of what was said, but he had never slipped on the wording.

Give it time. He's probably being very careful. After all, he asked you to repeat the phrase twice and he is reading his notes each time he references the threat.

Thomas continued, "So if you go back and edit your story to include this little nugget of information, you'd better be clear on what your position will be. One way doesn't help you at all. It even bolsters the state's case that he was retreating. But, if you thought his words meant he was continuing or escalating the aggression, you have just helped yourself a great deal.

"And," Thomas continued. "If you tell me that you didn't perceive his words to be an immediate threat, I would not allow you to testify. The prosecution would eat you alive over something like that."

I wasn't getting anywhere. I conceded, "Maybe we just leave it out then."

"What else aren't you telling me?"

"Nothing. That was it."

I could tell he didn't believe me.

"Well, what did you believe?" he demanded. "That he was continuing the assault?"

I stared at him, unable to answer.

"Think about it," he said. "This is important. It could be the most powerful part of my closing argument. 'This isn't over' is an avowal of continuation. It negates any cooling off period on your part."

Thomas paused and thought for a moment. His expression changed as if a revealing, yet perplexing, idea occurred to him.

"...but it doesn't make sense. Why would he then say, 'Don't you forget Sweet Sam' right afterward? The second part doesn't jive with the intent of the first part. The second part implies that he is stopping for now, but wants you to remember him for later."

I froze. Thomas was too clever. He had just dissected every part of that phrase, revealing the inconsistency that came with my lie. I was used to thinking on my feet but had no answer for what he had just discovered. I forced myself to keep my cool, although it was getting harder by the second.

"I'm not sure I interpret it that way," I said as I struggled to remain composed.

"You could always leave out the second part. Hypothetically, Sam's dead, so it's not like he is going to correct what you say." Thomas chuckled.

My whole body tensed up. Ironically, I was the one who felt trapped. "Let's stop for now," I said. "I'm not sure I want to include this anymore anyway."

Thomas tilted his head, looking at me with piercing dark eyes. I felt naked. I was off my game and knew that he noticed it. Though I suspected Thomas, I had no concrete proof and it didn't look like I ever would. My plan had backfired with Thomas questioning the inconsistency of my fake phrase.

All I could think about was getting away and never seeing him again.

November

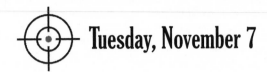

Tuesday, November 7

I stood at the kitchen counter, chopping a carrot with a sharp knife. Each slice made a harsh, striking sound against the cutting board. I was pleased that it didn't bother me. I reached for a tomato. Something about the thin layer of skin and the tender flesh underneath made me squeamish about slicing it. I forced myself to continue cutting as my mind drifted.

I thought back to an earlier conversation with Chris when he assured me that I was safe, that my fear was getting the best of me. Chris said he would never let me work with Thomas if he thought there was any danger. He assured me that even though some of the circumstantial evidence was disturbing, there was no way that Thomas could be my attacker. In a city of five and a half million people, the odds of me walking into my attacker's office were beyond infinitesimal.

I considered hiring a private investigator to follow Thomas. A professional would be able to discover far more about him than my amateur sleuthing. I hadn't decided if I would take that step, but there was one thing I knew for sure—I was in over my head trying to catch him by myself. Either I would just have to accept Chris' certainty that I was suspecting the wrong guy, or I would have to leave the detective work to someone else.

I took a deep breath as I tossed the tomato wedges into the salad bowl. As I reached for the salad dressing, the energy around me changed. I could feel that I wasn't alone—someone was watching me.

I instinctively looked toward the front window and gasped.

Standing there on my porch, taking up the full length of the window were Thomas and DJ. Thomas was wearing a black leather jacket and gloves with a dark winter scarf wrapped around his neck.

An image of that scarf wrapped around my wrists, binding them so I couldn't move, flashed in my mind. His black gloves would leave no trace of fingerprints.

Thomas gave a slight wave as he tugged on DJ's leash.

Oh my God. What is he doing here?

Thomas pointed toward the front door and walked out of view.

What do I do? I can't hide. He knows I'm here. I can't let him in. There's no one else here.

I glanced out the kitchen window. Troy's truck was not in the driveway.

Think. Think.

I slowly walked toward the front door, immobilized, unable to open it. I noticed the alarm, turned on as usual because I was home alone. I slowly opened the door without turning it off, knowing it would blare in forty seconds.

"What are you doing here?" I asked.

DJ stepped forward and licked my hand.

With one strong jerk of the leash, he pulled his dog back.

"That's funny," said Thomas. "She never does that to strangers."

"I was cooking," I improvised. "Must be the food."

In my other hand, I held the cutting knife, gripping it firmly.

Thomas looked at his dog, then at me, then brushed it off.

He began, "I was thinking more about what Sam said that night."

"How do you know where I live?" I glanced at the alarm. The light was blinking.

Any moment now.

Thomas pulled his iPhone out of his jacket pocket and turned the display toward me. It showed a map from his house to mine.

"I've been here before, remember?" he replied. "How do you think I found the way from Eddie's when you were asleep?"

"How do you have my address?" I didn't even attempt to hide the accusation in my voice.

"You gave it to Joanne."

I thought about that—he was right. Joanne had taken my contact information after our first meeting.

"I thought Chris gave you directions from Eddie's that night?" I asked. I had offered that false explanation, which he had readily accepted.

"I don't remember that," he replied. "Anyway, wouldn't you have told the police what he said that night?"

"What?" I asked.

"If you told the police what he said, then I'd put the cop at the scene on the stand to corroborate your statement. When the cop tells the jury what you told him, you'd have proof beyond just your word that Sam was escalating the fight."

The high pitched squeal of the alarm made both of us jump.

Do I turn it off or not?

DJ starting barking and Thomas pulled her away from the door. The noise was deafening—I couldn't think.

I reached over for the alarm and punched in the code.

"I need to go. ATS is going to call."

"I can wait. We need to talk about what he said."

Why is he pressing this?

"We just need to finish the witness testimony," I said flatly. My voice was lifeless, like I had just been beaten up. The roller coaster between suspicion and trust was completely draining.

"I understand," he said, "But don't you think this part is more important? If the police can corroborate the verbal threat, that's huge. It's the smoking gun we've been looking for. I think it would take your odds of being acquitted to over fifty percent."

"Thomas, I'm up against a deadline. I've written everything except the witness testimony, so there's really no point in revisiting anything else."

Thomas started to speak, to try to persuade me one last time, but I cut him off.

"I'm not going to use it. There's no time to make those kinds of edits now."

"When's your deadline?" Thomas asked.

"End of November."

"Don't you want to take the next few weeks to incorporate all of this new information into your story? It buys you a real chance at a not guilty verdict."

I shook my head.

"Let's get through the witness testimony first, and then I'll see what I can do," I lied. "By the way, I'm going to be in Chicago with Chris next week. Can we cover that part by phone?"

Thomas agreed, but there was something begrudging in his tone. With nothing more to discuss, he said goodbye and tugged on DJ's leash as they walked away. DJ looked back at me with sad puppy eyes.

Friday, November 24

Chris had a medical trade show in Chicago every year at Thanksgiving so I decided to go with him. Instead of staying at a hotel, Chris' college roommate and best man, Mark, had offered his apartment near the University of Chicago. Mark was going to graduate school in the Windy City, but was in Alabama with his family for the holiday.

I shopped on Michigan Avenue while Chris was at the show. I later joined him and his sales colleagues for dinner. However, I quickly felt like the oddball as they talked shop most of the evening. At least another show was over and we could now enjoy the weekend, even though it was a blustery 34 degrees outside.

I awoke early Saturday morning. The clock showed 6:30 a.m. Chris was still sound asleep. I scooted to the top of the bed and pried open a slit in the venetian blinds. From the twenty-first floor, I could see the south side of Chicago and the frozen edge of Lake Michigan. There was a slight movement across the lake as the icy waves slowly glided to shore. The trees below were barren and a few loose papers blew down the street. I carefully climbed out of bed, trying not to disturb Chris and walked to the kitchen. When I opened the refrigerator, there sat a bottle of ketchup, some pickles and a case of beer. I opened the freezer, hoping to at least find a can of orange juice but instead found a single bag of frozen peas.

I had seen a grocery store just a few blocks away. So I bundled up, took the key and headed outside. Not far from Mark's building, a homeless man was sleeping in a cardboard box.

Clutching my purse, I walked briskly to the small market and back. I felt safe—the streets were quiet and my sixth sense had not triggered once since we had landed.

When I opened the apartment door, I saw Chris standing at the window in his boxer shorts, scanning the city below with a pair of Mark's binoculars. He whipped around when he heard me.

"Where the hell have you been?" he snapped.

My enthusiasm about surprising him with breakfast waned as I felt his anger. "I bought us breakfast. Why are you up so early?"

"So you just leave the apartment without telling me? You just disappear? Didn't it occur to you that I'd be worried? Jesus, Laura, what were you thinking?"

"I just walked to the store a few blocks away. I thought you'd still be asleep. I was going to surprise you with breakfast in bed."

"I called you. Why didn't you answer?"

I pulled my phone from my purse—I had turned off the ringer the night before. Five missed calls.

"Don't you realize this is the south side of Chicago? It's not safe for you to go out alone. I've been scanning the streets for fifteen minutes looking for you," he said, shaking the binoculars at me. "You should have told me where you were going!"

"Okay, okay. I'm sorry. I didn't mean to worry you, but it's broad daylight. I was perfectly safe."

"Laura, just because we are seven hundred miles away doesn't mean that there aren't other dangerous people out there. You need to use your head. One breakfast isn't worth risking your life."

I could feel myself getting angry.

"Look here, I use my head every day and get by just fine, thank you. It's a wonder I survived those first twenty years of my life without you."

"So now you think you can take unwise risks? I think you're taking the opposite extreme. Now you want to prove you can do anything. Since you survived one incident, now you think you can survive anything and you're being reckless, like breaking in to Thomas' house. It's like you're daring anyone to mess with you."

"You're overreacting. I just went to the grocery store. You're the only man I know who would complain about being served breakfast in bed!"

Chris' face was tired.

"You're still stressed over the show and you're taking it out on me. My going out was not dangerous at all. I can't believe you got so worried. You need to relax and stop being so overprotective."

"You don't get it, do you?" Chris asked.

"Get what?"

"Get how thoughtless it was for you to go out without telling me. I go out of my way to make sure you're safe. I've delayed trips. I've changed plans..."

I interrupted. "I haven't asked you to change your plans for me. That was your choice. And maybe it has worked for the last six months, but you can't keep altering your schedule to protect me for the rest of our lives. Chris, I'm getting back to normal. You can't keep worrying about me."

"What, now I'm not allowed to think about you?"

"No, you're not allowed to try to fly home early. You're not allowed to ask Troy to stay with me. You're not allowed to call home more than once to see if I'm okay. You're not allowed to do anything differently than you would have before last June!"

Chris didn't answer.

December

Thursday, December 7 morning

Between the trip to Chicago and a few more weeks of shopping at home, I had all of my Christmas presents bought, wrapped and under the tree. My best present, the one to myself, had arrived earlier that week. It was the marked-up manuscript from my editor. Now, all I had to do was review the final copy with Thomas and I was finished. My editor was already shopping the story to different networks for a TV movie.

Chris' cell phone rang. It was 6:00 a.m. I was still half asleep as I listened to his conversation.

"Hey Dan, what's up?" he murmured. He turned away from me in bed and whispered, but I could still hear him and Dan's muffled voice on the other end but couldn't tell what he was saying.

"Why?" he hissed. "Have you guys pissed off one of my pending sales? What hospital?"

A muffled reply.

"Damn! We're counting on that order for fourth quarter. We can't afford to lose this one."

Chris paused and listened some more.

"I can't go out of town today." His voice lowered even more. "It's been six months to the day since the… well, you know. Her therapist said anniversaries might be hard."

Chris paused again. "Alright, as long as we're back tonight."

He hung up and rose slowly from the bed. I sat up pulling the covers around me to stay warm.

"Are you going somewhere?" I asked.

"Afraid so. Dan just called. Service screwed up a repair and now we have an angry customer. It just so happens that it is the same customer that is about to sink a pile of money into an order, or I should say was going to."

"Where?"

"Valdosta."

"You're staying overnight?" I asked.

"No. I'm flying down with Dan this morning. He'll be here in about an hour. We'll wrap this up this afternoon and catch the evening flight back."

"I see."

The fact that this trip came up so suddenly made me feel unsettled. I thought about asking him to be sure to come home that night, but in light of my independence speech in Chicago, I was too proud to say anything.

"Okay, well eat some onions for me."

"The onions are in Vidalia, my dear, not Valdosta."

"Oh, so what's in Valdosta?"

"Let's see, pecans, high school football, Valdosta State University and an angry South Georgia Medical staff. That's about it. I guess I can't ask if you want to come with me?"

"No, I can't go, and no, you can't ask. We're going back to pre-June, remember? Besides, I'm meeting Thomas for our celebration dinner tonight. I'll be fine."

"Dinner with Thomas?" he asked surprised. "You're over your suspicions?"

I nodded and took a deep breath.

"I got my proof. When we were in Chicago, I called Thomas' office—we still had to finish the witness testimony. Joanne answered. It was an odd request, I'll admit, but I asked her if there was anything on Thomas' calendar on the night of my attack. Turns out, he was out of town that whole week."

"What about the other things, like the T-shirt and the cologne?"

"I called Target. They gave away thousands of T-shirts that day. It's not like it was a one of a kind. And I don't know any more about the cologne. Maybe it was a similar smell but I can't be sure it was the exact same. Everything else was circumstantial, like you've always said."

Chris walked over to me and brushed the hair back from my forehead. It was clear that he had never believed that Thomas could be my attacker, but I had to come to that conclusion on my own.

I continued, "I guess the past few weeks of not seeing him regularly have given me more perspective."

"I'm glad," he agreed. Chris gave me a hug and went to the bathroom to take a shower. Not long after, Dan honked his horn outside. Chris kissed me goodbye. He was almost out the door when he turned around, walked back to me and gave me another hug.

"I should be home before you've even finished your dinner. By the way, what are you celebrating?" he asked.

"The case. It's done."

I put on a brave smile as I watched my husband drive off in Dan's Jeep. I immediately reset the home alarm and walked to the bathroom to get ready for the day. I had finally gotten to the point where I was able to take a shower without staring at the bathroom door. I could even close my eyes when I rinsed my hair. It was progress.

Once dressed, I didn't feel like staying at home. I decided to deliver Joanne's Christmas present in person, instead of giving it to Thomas at dinner. Plus I could surprise Thomas at the office with the final manuscript.

It had been nearly a month since I had seen him. When I had called to arrange delivery of the final copy for his review, Thomas suggested we have a celebration dinner and I could bring the copy with me.

It was amazing how much my perspective had changed in just a month.

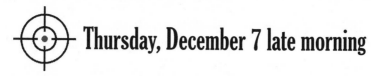 # Thursday, December 7 late morning

I drove to the Georgia Building with my manuscript and Joanne's gift in hand. When I arrived around 10:30 a.m., Thomas was standing in front of Joanne's reception desk, about to escort a client to his office.

"Hey, stranger," he said. "Did I forget a meeting today? I thought you were giving me the final copy at dinner?"

"No, you're right. I just thought I'd drop it by early, plus I have a little something for Joanne." I glanced down at a package wrapped in silver with a green ribbon.

"Can you stick around until I'm done?" he asked, looking at his watch.

"Sure. Can I still use my office?"

"It's all yours."

Joanne opened her present, a new lapel pin, and we caught up briefly. I then walked down the hall to my tiny office to proofread the story until Thomas was free. I stepped into the familiar small room, which I assume hadn't been used since I left. Being back there already felt different, like the whole experience was fading into my past. I sat down, took the manuscript from its brown envelope and began reading. At 11:15, my cell phone rang. It was Vicki.

"Hey, how about lunch?" she asked.

"I'm downtown," I replied, thinking Vicki was at home, which was at least thirty minutes away.

"Oh, even better. I just finished a closing at the attorney's office. How about we go to Davio's? My treat."

"Your treat? What's the occasion?" Then I thought for a minute. "Did Chris put you up to this?"

"What do you mean?" There was a slight falter in Vicki's voice—I could tell she wasn't being truthful.

"He went out of town abruptly this morning. I thought maybe he had already begun sending in the entourage to keep me company."

Vicki replied, "Can I take the fifth? Besides, who cares when we have a generous benefactor picking up our lunch tab?"

"Benefactor? Your attorney?" I asked.

"No, your generous benefactor who you are not supposed to know about called me to make sure you had company today. He's paying for lunch, so let's live it up."

I was miffed. "Chris is still treating me like a child. He doesn't have to bribe my friends to keep me occupied. We already had a blow out about this in Chicago, and he's still doing it."

"Let's see," said Vicki. "Chris is paying for us to go enjoy lunch and you're upset. When was the last time Kevin ever gave you money to take me out? Never. Stop complaining and let's go treat ourselves on him. I'll be there in five minutes. Can you meet me out front so I don't have to park?"

"Alright." I grabbed my cell phone and dashed out to meet Vicki. As I passed Thomas' office, I noticed the door was still shut.

I asked Joanne to relay the message that I was out for lunch but would be back later.

At the restaurant, Vicki and I celebrated the completion of my manuscript. I started with a lump crab cake followed by the seared Atlantic salmon with truffle parmigiano fries. We even splurged on a bottle of wine and split a chocolate cake for dessert, though we couldn't finish half of what we ordered.

When I returned an hour later, Thomas' office door was open, but he wasn't there.

I asked, "Joanne, did Thomas leave?"

"Oh, I think he just stepped out for lunch. Do you want me to call him?" she offered.

"Oh, no. I'll see him this evening anyway. I'll just leave the manuscript on his desk and catch up with him at dinner."

I went back to my office, took the bound copy of my story and slid it back into the envelope. I walked over to Thomas' desk to leave the envelope for him when I noticed a file folder with my name on it lying on the corner.

It was the same folder he had pulled out to show me the police report of my attack.

At one point, I had planned to get a copy of that report. I had planned to check if it detailed whether or not the kitchen knife was mine. Back when I still suspected him, Thomas had known that fact and I wanted to see if he had indeed read it from the report.

I couldn't resist the temptation. I opened the folder and pulled out the police report from the night of my attack. As I scanned the write-up, I found the section on the first page where the policeman had indicated that the knife was from my house. I looked up and let out a deep exhale. Once again, I felt silly for having suspicions of Thomas that weren't warranted.

Maybe you can let it go once and for all now.

I was putting the report back in the open file folder when I noticed a page with Thomas' handwritten notes. Something on the page caught my attention so I picked it up to examine it more closely.

Thomas had written the real phrase, the phrase that only Sam knew, but he had drawn a line through the first part, "You win for now."

Below it, he had written the fictional phrase that I had shared with him and underlined the first part, "This isn't over."

~~You win for now,~~ but don't you forget sweet Sam
<u>This isn't over</u>, but don't you forget sweet Sam

I gasped. My body started to tremble.

Thomas knew the real phrase.

He knows I've altered the wording to catch him. He's created a cheat sheet so he'll never slip up. He's been so clever, never saying the real phrase.

I racked my brain. Hadn't Joanne said he was out of town the night of my attack? Of course he would tell Joanne he was out of town. He couldn't prowl all night and be in the office the next morning.

I quickly stuffed the handwritten page, the evidence, into the envelope along with the manuscript and tucked it under my arm. I hurried out of the room, returning to my office to gather my things. I had to leave before he returned. I opened the desk drawer to retrieve my purse. It was gone.

I tried not to panic, retracing my day to be sure I had left it there. I always put my purse in the right desk drawer. I remembered that I was talking to my sister on my cell phone that morning when I came to the office and my hands were full with Joanne's gift and the manuscript. But was I carrying my purse? Had I ever put it in the drawer that morning? I thought I had, but I couldn't remember. I checked the other drawers—nothing.

Maybe I left it in the car?

I hastily left the office, retracing my steps back to the parking garage to see if I had left my purse in the car.

In the parking garage, my white Audi was in its place. I always parked in the same area. It was locked, but there was no purse inside. It had to be locked from the outside so I must have had my purse and keys with me in the morning.

I rushed back up to the office, checking the cabinets behind the desk—still nothing. I ran to Joanne's desk.

"Joanne, my purse is gone. I think I left it in my desk when I went to lunch and now it's gone."

"It's gone?" Joanne repeated.

"Yes. Did you see anyone in my office while I was out?"

"I'm sorry, Laura, I went to lunch just after you. I was only out for thirty minutes, though. Do you want me to ask around to see if anyone saw anything?"

"Yes, please."

I ran back to my office and looked around one more time. I took a mental inventory of my purse's contents to recall what was now lost. Wallet, checkbook, credit cards, and most importantly, keys. I ransacked the office again and then rushed back to Joanne's desk.

"Any luck?" I asked.

"No, I'm afraid not. No one saw anything. Where did you leave it?"

"In my desk drawer."

Purse or not, I had to leave before Thomas came back. I'd have Joanne call a cab. Wait—I didn't have any money for a cab, and without my keys, I didn't have a way to get into my house. One thought stopped me cold: what if Thomas had my keys and was already in my house?

"Do you want me to call the guard downstairs?" Joanne offered.

The last thing I wanted right now was to deal with Mike Howard, but at least he could look for my purse.

"Okay," I agreed.

Joanne picked up the phone and called down to the lobby.

"Mr. Howard, would you mind coming up to Mr. Bennett's office? We need to report a missing purse."

Joanne listened for a moment and then clarified, "No, not Mr. Barnette, Mr. Bennett. Thomas S. Bennett on the eighth floor."

Joanne paused and listened again. "Oh, all right. I'll do that. Thank you."

She hung up the phone and looked at me. "He can't leave his post, but I can go down there if you like."

I barely listened to Joanne's update. Something else had caught my attention.

"What does the 'S' stand for?" I asked. The words came out of my mouth before I even consciously knew why.

Joanne lowered her voice to prevent anyone else from hearing. She whispered, "It's Thomas Samuel Bennett. He absolutely hates to be called Samuel, though, so please don't mention it."

I froze. "Oh my God," I breathed.

"What's wrong?" Joanne asked.

I was clutching my cell phone—the only belonging I had left. I quickly called Vicki, but it went to voicemail.

"Vicki, it's Laura. You have to come back to the office where you dropped me off. Come back here no matter what. Hurry, please. Call me."

I then texted, "COME BACK URGENT."

Oblivious to Joanne, I rushed back to my office, sat at my desk and put my head in my hands. I had to figure out what to do. I had suspected Thomas off and on all along. I had ignored my sixth sense. I had ignored the clues and had eventually grown to trust him. Now I had real proof—the phrase and his name. Thomas was Sam. All this time, I had been working with my attacker. Now, he had certainly taken my purse and he had the keys to my house.

I would give Vicki one minute to call back. Otherwise, I would walk the few blocks to Chris' office and have Linda help me. I stared at my phone, praying for Vicki to call.

All of the sudden, I had a weird feeling that I was being watched. I had felt this way many times before, including the night of my attack, but never so intense.

I looked to the doorway and saw a figure standing there. He startled me to the point that I jumped back in my chair.

I looked at the man. He was tan with sandy hair and stubble at his jawline. He wore blue jeans, a plaid long sleeve shirt and he was holding my purse in his hand.

"Yes?" I asked. My hand was still pressed against my chest from the scare he had given me. I could feel my heart pounding.

"I think this is yours," he said, holding up my purse.

"How did you get it?" I asked, still flustered.

"I found it in on the floor in the hallway. I saw the business cards and was told by the front guard that you were working in this office."

He stepped forward timidly and placed the purse on my desk. I opened it and rifled through the contents taking inventory. Everything was still there—my keys, my wallet, the cash, the credit cards, every-thing. Had I dropped it and not realized it?

"Thank goodness. Nothing's missing," I said. "I can't thank you enough for returning it. Can I give you some kind of reward?"

He shook his head, stepping back slightly.

"Are you sure?"

"I'm sure," he replied.

He looks familiar. Have I seen him in the building before?

Then, I remembered, he was the janitor—the one who had startled me in the ladies room. He wasn't in his uniform this time.

"What's your name?" I asked.

He paused for a beat. "Jim."

"Well, Jim, I wish there were more people in this world like you. It would be a better place."

He looked at me without saying a word, and smiled.

"Are you sure I can't give you a reward?" I asked again.

"No. It was my pleasure. See you around."

"Okay," I said. "Thanks again."

He was gone as abruptly as he had arrived. My heart started to return to its normal beat. Before that man arrived, I was thinking I would have to reach Chris in Valdosta and tell him what happened. I was thinking I would have to change the house locks right away. I was thinking Thomas had taken my keys so he could return to the scene of the crime.

Even with my purse in hand, that didn't change what I knew about Thomas. I grabbed my things and rushed out of the office.

"Joanne, I'm going home," I said. "Please tell Thomas that I can't make our dinner tonight?"

"Okay. Did that fellow have your purse?"

"Yes, I have it now. I just need to go home."

"Are you all right?" Joanne asked.

"Please, just tell Thomas that tonight is off."

With that, I was gone.

Chris

Chris looked at the hotel clock. It was 4:30 p.m. Dinner with Dan and the folks from the hospital was at 7:00 p.m. The duo had managed to save the order but not before they obligated themselves to take the customer to dinner. He picked up the phone and called Atlanta.

"Hello. This is Troy. I can't come to the phone right now so please leave a message."

Chris spoke to Troy's voicemail.

"Hey, Troy. It's Chris. I'm calling to ask a favor. I'm stuck in Valdosta tonight and not coming home until tomorrow. Laura's going out to dinner and I told her that I'd be waiting for her when she got home. I don't want her to come home to a dark, empty house, especially not tonight. It's been six months, you know. So, could you let yourself in and wait for her? Maybe even stay in the guest room tonight if she seems scared. There's beer in the fridge. Help yourself. I'll call y'all later to make sure everything is okay. Thanks, man."

 # Thursday, December 7 early evening

I drove straight home—my nerves were rattled. I tried Vicki's cell phone again but no one answered. I left another message to let her know not to come back to the office.

Once home, I threw my purse down on the coffee table and made a beeline for the bedroom. I knelt under the bed, pulled out my Ruger and popped in the clip. I cocked it once. It was ready to fire. I needed to calm my nerves so I went to the kitchen and poured a glass of white wine.

Not smart. I've got a loaded gun and a glass of wine. I'm jumpy as hell. I'm an accident waiting to happen. Okay, just one glass. I don't need to shoot my husband when he walks through the door tonight.

I sat on the couch, gun in my right hand and wine glass in my left. I replayed the day's events. How had I dropped my purse without noticing? I forgot to ask that man exactly where he found it. Which hallway? Was it the one down from the office or not even on my path of travel?

The more I thought about it, I was convinced I didn't drop it. I would have noticed.

Chris would be home in a few hours and I would tell him everything and see what he thought. He had defended Thomas before. He said I would sooner win the Georgia lottery than actually choose to work with the man who attacked me. The odds were far too remote.

He was right, but what about Thomas' hand-written note?

What about Thomas' middle name?

What about the cologne and the T-shirt?

What about him living close by and knowing so much?

There came a point where the evidence was overwhelming.

I put down the gun and picked up my cell phone. I called Chris, but it immediately went to his voicemail. He was probably on the plane. I needed to talk to him but it would have to wait until he returned home.

I sat on the couch for more than an hour. My feet were propped on the coffee table and I was hunched into a little ball, sipping my wine, holding my gun and reflecting.

Over time, my nerves began to calm, but my brain was still processing all the evidence against Thomas and all the plausible explanations.

I couldn't digest everything in my head. I needed to write it down. I put the empty wine glass and the gun on the coffee table and pulled out my iPad. As it started up, I walked into the kitchen and sat down at the table. I started to type all of my suspicions and each explanation. It was the only way I could make sense of it all and I could show Chris the entire list when he arrived home.

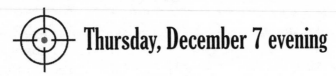 Thursday, December 7 evening

I was sitting at the kitchen table, typing furiously on my iPad. My back was toward the den. I heard a click and looked up. I sat silently to see if I heard it again—nothing.

I waited.

My fingers froze over the keys.

What was that sound?

Slowly, I started to type again, but with jagged pauses so I could listen for any signs of movement. A hesitant step? A creak of the floor? An exhale in the still room?

My hypervigilance was a steady companion—a necessary one. It would keep me safe. But was it tricking me now, creating the eerie sensation that I was being watched?

My sixth sense was triggered and undeniably sharp. The way I felt the night of my attack. The way I felt the night Thomas showed up at my window. And the same way I felt today when startled by the guy returning my purse.

Someone was there—I could feel it.

I looked out the kitchen window—nobody. In my haste to start writing, I had left my gun on the coffee table. I needed to retrieve it. I started to get up when I thought I heard footsteps in the other room. I bolted away from the open doorway pressing my back against the kitchen wall.

I held my breath and listened.

Nothing.

I craned my head to look out the side window, the same one that he pried open six months ago. There was Troy's truck.

Troy was home. Had he come over? But why didn't he call out to me?

"Troy? Is that you?"

Silence.

Then I heard a voice from the other room, singing my name tauntingly. I didn't move, pressing my back harder against the wall.

A black gloved hand extended through the doorway—the index finger dangling a key playfully.

"Laura, look what I copied from your bag today."

That voice. I remembered that eerie, sinister voice.

I glanced at the wall behind me—the alarm panel was mounted directly on the other side. Was the light blinking? I couldn't see it to know. My heart pounded. I breathed in but no air would come.

The hand, then the arm, then one shoulder jutted into the room.

I slid down the side of the wall, looking for any means of a weapon. The one I needed was in the other room.

Standing in front of me was the man who had returned my purse, the janitor. He was wearing the same blue jeans and plaid shirt from earlier in the day. His pupils were wide, almost dilated.

I sensed evil. I saw the look of satisfaction on his face.

But this guy is white?

I thought back to the night of the attack. In the darkness, I never got a good look at him. How had I known he was black? Was it the darkness? Was it my prejudice?

All of this time, I had feared black men. Today, I was sure Thomas was the black man to fear.

Here stood Sam, a white man, in my house grinning at me with a chilling, sickening smile.

Slowly, he started walking toward me. Instinctively, I leapt toward the phone on the wall. He easily blocked me and tackled me to the floor. I tried to scream, but he pressed his thumb into my wind pipe, cutting off the air from my lungs. He began to squeeze my neck as he slammed my head against the stone kitchen floor. I clutched his hands trying to pry his fingers away.

"I've waited a long time for you, girlie. I've been watching you. I've seen you at your office, but you never recognized me, not even today. And I know about your husband. Guess what? He's out of town again. We'll have plenty of time to finish what we started."

I thought of the gun on the coffee table. How could I get to it? When the alarm sounded, I would make a break for it then.

But where is the alarm? Hasn't it been forty seconds?

Suddenly, I realized the alarm wasn't going to sound.

He slammed my head to the floor again. It made a cracking sound like an eggshell against concrete. The throbbing started—first dim and then severe. I needed air. I tried futilely to pry his hands from my neck. His fingers were like a vice squeezing every artery until they burst.

I was going to die today. Chris would come home to my raped, dead body on the kitchen floor, and he and the police would be looking for the black man who did it.

Just then, the alarm blared with an ear-piercing, steady buzz.

"You bitch!" he screamed. "You'll be dead before anyone gets here!"

He pounded my cheek bone with his fist as he continued to clutch my neck with the other hand. I was able to suck in some air. I lay pinned on the floor, gasping and writhing with pain at each blow.

I tried to scream. It had worked before.

Thomas

Outside, Thomas had just pulled up to the curb by Laura's house. When he heard the alarm, he sprinted to the front door, grabbed the knob and tried to open it. The door was locked. He began pounding on the door and calling for Laura.

"Freeze!" a voice ordered. Thomas turned to face the barrel of a gun pointed directly at him. He stopped beating on the door, took a step back and raised his arms.

"Who are you?" demanded Troy.

"I'm Thomas Bennett. I'm a lawyer. I'm a friend of Laura's."

"No friend of Laura's would make the alarm go off! Lay down on the ground. Hands above your head," barked Troy.

"You don't understand," Thomas pleaded as he kneeled to the ground with his arms raised. "The alarm was already going when I drove up. The door is locked. Laura's not answering. We need to see if she's okay."

Troy didn't buy his story and kept the gun pointed at Thomas. He had just played Chris' message and knew otherwise.

"Nice try. Laura's not home. She's gone out to dinner."

"No she hasn't. She was supposed to go to dinner with me, but she cancelled. She's home—the lights are on. We have to see if she's okay."

Just then, they heard a woman's scream from inside the house.

"We've got to get in!" shouted Thomas. "The door is locked!"

Troy reached in his jeans pocket and pulled out Laura's house key—it was never far from his reach. He tried to unlock the door but it wouldn't budge. He took a step back and then slammed his shoulder into the dark wood panel—still no movement.

"The deadbolt," he said. "I'll try around back."

Before Thomas could reply, Troy bounded down the steps in one leap and rounded the corner the house.

Another scream came from inside.

Thomas didn't wait. He grabbed a white wicker rocking chair from the porch and slung it through one of the front windows. Glass shattered. He used the leg of the chair to clear away the jagged edges from the wooden frame. As he climbed through the window, he slit his right arm on a serrated piece.

Once inside, Thomas saw Laura to his right lying on the kitchen floor in a pool of blood. Then he caught a glimpse of someone running down the hall toward the back door. Within seconds, he was in a full sprint tackling the intruder just before the door.

Sam scrambled away from his grip and fought back like a caged animal, throwing wild punches at Thomas, who tried to block them. Sam was ferocious, forcing Thomas back up the hallway toward the den. With each step of Thomas' retreat, Sam jabbed his stomach forcing a guttural exhale. While Thomas was still hunched over, Sam curled his arm with an upper hook into Thomas' jaw, snapping his head to the side. Thomas crashed into the wall with a loud thud. Sam threw another hook, which Thomas managed to block with his forearm, and then pushed Sam off balance. As Sam stumbled backward, Thomas thrust his knee into Sam's side, clearly knocking the wind out of him. Sam recovered quickly and started punching and kicking wildly.

Thomas backed up, allowing more distance between the two men. Sam rushed forward tackling Thomas to the floor next to the fireplace. Before Thomas could get up, Sam was on his feet. He snatched the heavy burgundy vase from the mantle and lifted it above his head, ready to crash it over Thomas' body.

 # Thursday, December 7 evening

I couldn't understand why he left. Did my screams scare him away again?

I put my hand to the back of my head—it was warm and sticky. I tried to sit up. A rush of dizziness knocked me back to the floor.

I heard commotion coming from the den. Without moving my body, I rolled my head in that direction. I saw my gun on the coffee table. I slowly stood up and staggered to the kitchen doorway grasping the door frame. My fingers left a red imprint on the molding. It was then that I saw Sam tackling Thomas.

Thomas?

I stumbled my way to the gun and grabbed it. Thomas was on the floor with his forearms defensively covering his face. Sam was towering above him ready to crash my vase over his head. Mechanically, I aimed for Sam's torso and squeezed the trigger.

B O O M

He jerked forward slightly.

B O O M

I shot to kill.

He dropped to his knees and then fell forward to the floor.

My shoulders heaved up and down, but I kept my arms extended. I held my stance. He could get up and fight again.

Thomas slowly rolled on his side and used the ledge of the fireplace to pull himself up. He had blood dripping from his elbows and down his arm. A few red droplets fell from his fingertips to the floor. Both of his cheekbones were bruised and bloody. He gazed at the lifeless figure next to him.

"That was Sam," I said, dazed. "All this time, I thought he was black."

"You thought he was me," added Thomas.

"How is that possible?" I asked.

How could my brain have played such tricks on me?

We slowly walked toward each other. I lowered the gun and we collapsed into an embrace. His bloody arm encircled me and I rested my bruised cheek on his shoulder. The alarm was still blaring but we barely noticed it.

The sound of additional glass breaking made us look toward the front of the house. Troy was carefully climbing through the broken window. He had been unable to get in the back door and couldn't open the deadbolt that Sam had locked from inside. Troy stared at Sam's lifeless body and then looked up at me.

"What the hell happened here?" he asked.

Thomas replied, "Laura killed Sam."

Troy walked cautiously closer to the body.

"Sam? This guy's white?"

I just nodded.

"Don't touch him," I warned. "We have to call the police."

Ignoring me, Troy knelt next to the still, facedown body and pulled a wallet out of the back pocket. He flipped it open and looked at the driver's license.

"Sam Strickland," he said.

"Strickland," I repeated.

I know that name.

Troy pulled out his phone. "I'm calling 911."

"No, I should," I insisted.

I took his cell phone and made the call.

As we waited for the police, Troy turned off the alarm. The absence of the blaring buzz left an eerie stillness, almost like time was frozen.

"Strickland," I said again to Troy.

Where do I know that name?

The image of a gold nameplate flashed in my mind. My head throbbed as I strained to place where I had seen it.

"Where does he live?" I asked.

Troy read the license. "Lithonia."

Then it hit me.

"Strickland. Linda Strickland. She lives in Lithonia."

"Who?" asked Thomas.

"Linda, Chris' admin. That must be her ex-husband. But why was he coming after me?"

"Did you know him?" asked Thomas.

"I never met the man." I paused. "Well, except today. He brought my purse back."

I thought for a moment.

"Wait. He was at our house before. Chris thought he saw him parked outside but brushed it off."

Thomas prodded further, "Was he angry with Chris?"

"I don't know. Chris said something like the guy had a grudge, but it didn't seem real. All he did was get Linda a divorce lawyer."

"What better way to get even with Chris than to hurt you?" said Thomas. "You take my wife, I'll take yours."

I thought of our wedding photos. He wasn't taking souvenir pictures of me. He was sending a message to my husband.

We heard sirens outside.

The room lost its color. Black and white faded to gray. I collapsed.

Friday, December 7 late evening

Thomas walked up to my hospital bed and took my hand. His eyes were bloodshot and his arm was wrapped in bandages, but they hadn't admitted him. I lay in the bed with my head bound like a mummy and a brace around my neck. I had a concussion that the doctors wanted to monitor overnight, but they felt I should fully recover. Ironically, they had used a CT scanner that Chris had sold the hospital to make my diagnosis. He was on a flight home and should be arriving soon.

"How are you?" Thomas asked.

I tried to nod my head but my neck was immobilized.

"I'm okay," I said. "You?"

"I'll survive."

"How'd you know he would be there?"

"I didn't. Joanne told me about your purse and that you freaked out when you learned my middle name. I realized you suspected me. I was coming over to explain."

"Explain?"

"Yeah, my middle name is Samuel, after my father. He died five days before I was born. I don't like using that name because it reminds me that I grew up without him."

"Oh," I replied, now putting into context Joanne's comment about him not liking to be called Samuel. "But how did you know what he really said to me?"

"What?" Thomas looked confused.

"I saw your notes. You knew what he really said, 'You win for now.' How did you know that?"

"You told the police what he said. It was in the second page of the police report. I couldn't figure out why you changed it for your story and then decided not to use it at all."

"Oh," I replied. "Wait, if that was in the police report, you knew his name all along?"

Thomas nodded.

"Hey, I should let you get some rest," he said, starting to pull away.

Wait. I have more questions.

I blurted out, "Why do you only wear one kind of cologne?"

"What?" he asked.

"What kind of cologne do you wear?"

"Armani."

"But you have others?" I insisted.

Thomas looked puzzled. "Yes, my sisters each gave me a bottle of cologne for Christmas, but I only like the Armani. I'm not following you."

"You have three sisters?" I asked, remembering the three bottles of cologne.

"Yes, I have three—now. I used to have four."

"Four?"

"Anna. My eldest. She died when I was six." Thomas lifted his head to the ceiling as if acknowledging her above. "She's actually the reason I decided to do this story with you."

"How so?"

He looked away for a moment, rubbed his eye and then wiped his hand against his slacks. When he looked back at me I could see he was fighting back tears. It was the first time I had ever seen him emotional.

"Anna was raped and killed in her apartment when she was nineteen. They had a suspect, but the prosecutor wouldn't take it to court. He didn't think there was enough evidence. I think he was just lazy. It's the reason I became a lawyer."

"You once told me you were doing this story for Pinocchio?"

Thomas gave me a strange smile. "Why, yes. When I was a kid, Anna gave me a Pinocchio book and a set of puppets. I used to sit in her lap and act out the story with those dolls while she read to me. And if I ever fibbed to her, she'd call me her little Pinocchio."

"It sounds like you were close."

Thomas nodded. "She was a second mother to me. Well, until we lost her."

"But why help me?" I asked.

"You showed up in my office just after the anniversary of her death. Your story gave the victim a chance at the justice she deserved but never got. It just felt like something she was asking me to do."

 # Monday, December 10

I was released from the hospital Sunday and voluntarily reported to the police station with Chris on Monday morning. Thomas had already given his statement and they wanted to corroborate my version of events.

I learned that Sam had been following and harassing Linda for several months. Though not true, he had accused her of having an affair with my husband and came unglued when Chris got her the divorce lawyer.

Though I believed he was trying to rape me, his ultimate plan was to frame Chris for my murder. The police had found a journal in his car, the same gray car that was in front of our house that day. The journal methodically detailed my whereabouts. Because my appointments with Barbara were always Tuesday afternoon, he knew when to be in the Georgia Building. I was always on edge in that building though I couldn't explain it. Maybe that's why the Chicago trip felt so liberating—my sixth sense could finally rest. Ironically, he did work as a janitor, just not in that building. He was a night shift janitor in a school in Lithonia, which explained his access to the uniform, the chemical smell I remembered from my attack and his ability to stalk me during the day.

Apparently, after aborting his first attempt, he became more determined to have his revenge. The police even found a listening device that he had hidden under Linda's desk. That's how he knew when Chris would be out of town. He also knew about their trip to Chattanooga, though it was an escape for her, not a clandestine lover's weekend.

I wondered how many times he had followed me. Was it him in the stairwell at the Georgia Building? Had Dan actually been telling the truth about seeing someone outside our house that morning? Had he followed us up to Elijay? I suppose we'll never know for sure, though the police were going to subpoena his cell phone records which could place his whereabouts.

I was still perplexed that my memory had failed me. I had been one hundred percent certain that my attacker was African-American. To my surprise, the police told me that seventy-five percent of the wrongful convictions overturned by the Innocence Project and DNA testing involved witness misidentification. I guess I was not alone.

I thought back to Sergeant Stires' remarks about the family's reaction. Would Linda forgive me? Probably so. But what about her two boys? As deranged as he was, he was still their father. I vowed to ensure those boys had a good life.

After a morning of questioning, the police informed me that I was free to go. There would be no jail, no trial, no murder charges. With the evidence they had found and my verification of Thomas' statement, there was no crime. Only self-defense.

 **Three years later**

I looked out the kitchen window to see Troy walking toward my house. His arm was wrapped around the waist of a petite brunette, Bonnie, the girl he had been dating for the last year. Bonnie was carrying a giant brown teddy bear the size of her torso. The bear had big felt eyes and a grin from ear to ear—it was sewn in to be permanently happy. The bear and I both had a lot to smile about.

I had gone back to Barbara and completed my therapy. Well—as much as you can say "completed." I suppose there is always work to be done to grow and improve. Barbara had known about Anna and saw how my obsession was inhibiting my healing and rekindling Thomas' grief—that's why she had "fired" me.

And thanks to Barbara, I can now sleep in total darkness. I can enter our home by myself, day or night, without searching every room. I can pass strangers, both black and white, on the street without fear.

I opened the door for Troy and Bonnie and accepted the giant bear, placing it next to the empty bassinet.

"Come on, Chris," I called. "We're going to be late." I was wearing a sleeveless black pantsuit and heels—dressy-casual for a concert.

Chris walked in the room, cradling our baby boy. He would hold Erick Thomas all day if that were allowed. There was nothing he enjoyed more. Even golf had taken a back seat to this bundle of joy.

Chris passed the baby to Bonnie, who eagerly engulfed him in her arms. He was actually smaller than the bear she had just been carrying. We said goodnight to them and drove downtown. As I sat next to my husband in the passenger seat, he reached over, took my hand and pressed it to his lips. Another reason to smile. Fatherhood had changed him. He was more patient, more mature, even more of the man that I knew he could be.

We entered the parking garage for the Fox theatre and walked hand in hand to the front entrance. The lighted billboard showcased the star attraction in huge letters. Outside, the street was flowing with traffic. Policemen were blowing whistles—directing cars to the parking garage and eager concert goers to the main entrance.

Once inside, the usher escorted us to the front row. I had been to this magnificent theatre many times but never this close to the stage. I tilted back my head to take in the vaulted ceiling with its ultramarine blue night sky. The man made stars sparkled like a million flash bulbs going off over our heads.

The music started. The crowd hushed. I watched the towering burgundy curtains with anticipation. I knew the song. I knew the singer. After a few frames, one of the curtains lifted as if an invisible giant had pinched the edge and pulled it back.

He walked out on stage, just like he had done at Eddie's all those years ago.

Launching into his first number, he turned and looked at me, gave a quick wink, and kept on singing.

Acknowledgements
Special thanks.....

To **Jan Risher,** for your collaboration and good counsel that were just what this book needed, I'm forever grateful to my Goldilocks of an editor—not too much, not too little but just right

To **Patricia Coe,** my best critic turned unsuspecting editor, your amazing insight and intuition took this story to a new level

To **Chelsea Apple,** just when I thought we could do no more, you provided the polish and precision that I would not have found on my own

To **Karen McCarty,** Psychotherapist, for your superb guidance on the character of Dr. Barbara Cole and your selfless, unconditional support from day one

To **Alison Frutoz,** Criminal Defense Attorney, for your expert legal advice and emotional intelligence, and for making the legal portion of this book so much fun to write

To **Brandi Hillewaert,** Civil Attorney, for your wonderful friendship and for the hours of feedback and research in the early days of Thomas' character

To **Richard Spoon,** for your friendship and support and for paving the way with your own book

To **Thomas Barnette,** my college twin and favorite singer, for inspiring the character of Thomas Bennett and for inspiring me to finish this book

To **Joan Diss, Karen Fitzgerald, Dawn Barrs and Bonnie Daneker** for being my first audience

To **Lynn Epstein, Mimi Schroeder, Jill Dible, Nancy Jeanette Long, Erika Childers and Dayl Soll,** the most phenomenal support team I could have ever imagined, I'm in awe of your talent and forever grateful for your collaboration

To **Richard Brakewood**, my rock of support and soft place to land

27881708R00172

Made in the USA
Middletown, DE
22 December 2015